CHOOSE TO MATTER

For my kids,
IZZY AND DECLAN . . .

BECAUSE YOU CAN.

Editorial Director: Wendy Lefkon
Executive Editor: Laura Hopper
Illustrated by DeAnne Williamson
Design by Winnie Ho and Margie Peng

Photographer credits:
Page 23:
Carla Overbeck, Brandi Chastain: Sideline Sports Photography © 2016
Kristine Lilly: Linda Cuttone
Page 24:
Joy Fawcett, Julie Foudy: Sideline Sports Photography © 2016

For information address espnW, 1101 Flower Street, Glendale, California 91201.

ISBN 978-1-368-00338-4
FAC-00858-17076
Library of Congress Control Number on file
First Hardcover Edition, May 2017
1 3 5 7 9 10 8 6 4 2
Printed in the United States of America

SUSTAINABLE FORESTRY INITIATIVE
Certified Sourcing
www.sfiprogram.org
SFI-00993
Logo Applies to Text Stock Only

CHOOSE TO MATTER

BEING COURAGEOUSLY AND FABULOUSLY YOU

BY

JULIE FOUDY

Los Angeles • New York

CHOOSE TO MATTER

CONTENTS

HOW THIS BOOK HAPPENED

I have always thought,
Wouldn't it be fun to write a book?

Not a *let-me-tell-you-about-all-the-things-I-have-overcome* book (from a middle class white kid in suburban Orange County, California . . . *hmmm*).

Definitely not an X's and O's sporty book.

And certainly not a *look-at-just-how-perfect/cute/adorable-I-am* book.

Brrrrp

(I JUST BURPED. . .)

Nope. The book I have always wanted to write is for the teenager starting her journey, or the woman at a critical fork in her journey. It is for every person, wherever you may be on your path, who needs a little nudge. Who needs a little courage. Who needs someone to tell them they can do it. Because you can.

This I know: Life doesn't just happen. You happen to life. You dictate what you want out of life. And good things follow. So many of these life lessons were taught to me by a bunch of amazing, funny, strong women on the U.S. Women's National soccer team. They taught me the value of being courageous, dreaming big, growing daily, and finding joy in all we do. They taught me the value of acting instead of reacting. We all need those types of friends and people in our life. They're the people who push us to feel more, and be more. People who encourage us to take off the label of what you think you should be, and instead just be the person you want to be: label-free. And we need those types of examples in our life so we are inspired to push ourselves forward.

In honor of what I've been preaching to our Julie Foudy Sports Leadership Academy (JFSLA) girls for years:

Don't just dream it; sing it (say it out loud!). . . .

I did. To Disney Publishing (*gulp*).

I said we need a book for teen girls and young women that speaks to them authentically. Not princess-ey, not sparkly, just real—a book about finding your voice, thinking differently, and empowering others. A book that chats with incredible, silly, grounded women with diverse backgrounds who share their journey of growth so that other young women can live courageously as well.

And what do you know? Disney Publishing actually said, "YES." To which I thought, *Oh dear lord.* Then I took a deep breath, smiled, and thought, *Well we might as well rock the heck out of this first one before they change their minds.*

So we summoned a group of amazing women to come chat with me . . . feet up, shoes off. #SockTalks we call them (thankfully, not a scratch-and-sniff book). I spoke with the following women:

Good Morning America cohost
ROBIN ROBERTS.

Soccer superstars
MIA HAMM and
ALEX MORGAN.

Facebook superwoman and
LeanIn.Org founder
SHERYL SANDBERG.

Award-winning Irish scientist,
philanthropist, and teen protégé
SOPHIE HEALY-THOW.

Seventeen-time (*yes, seventeen*)
Paralympic Games medalist
TATYANA MCFADDEN.

Softball star and television trailblazer
JESSICA MENDOZA.

Eleven-time NCAA Softball
championship coaching legend
SUE ENQUIST.

Purveyor of positivity AMY LISS,
who was born with cerebral palsy.

Beautifully inspirational teenager from
Afghanistan, FAHIMA NOORI.

This book is about getting comfortable
when you're uncomfortable, choosing
to matter, and, equally important, being
authentically you. This book is a road map to help you unleash your most
courageous self. There is a method to the madness . . . or at least I like
to pretend there is. I, along with the incredible women involved in this
book, tell stories, share lessons, and pass on some insight and wisdom.
My goal in all of this is to make you laugh, make you think, make you
excited to embrace life and make you eat more donuts. But before we
jump in, here's a little bit on how the book is structured.

HOW THIS BOOK WORKS

When I stopped playing for the U.S. Women's National Team after the 2004 Summer Olympics, I met with a small group of friends to discuss how we could merge some of our biggest passions in life: sports, silliness, and empowering others through leadership. That group, our Fab Five (me, my husband [Ian Sawyers], Kerri McClellan, Edson McClellan, and Todd Smith), came up with the idea that it would be fun to merge all those things into an awesome residential sports camp that also shows girls and young women that

THEY CAN DO AND BE WHATEVER THEY WANT.

And that is how the Julie Foudy Sports Leadership Academy (JFSLA) started in 2006.

For more than ten years, we have watched many young women blossom before our eyes as we mix sports and leadership with healthy craziness. Throughout those years we have also built a curriculum that revolves around these wonderful rings. This book will also revolve around those rings. But I cannot realistically have a book and call them the JFSLA Leadership Rings. (Yes, that is me snoring.) So after much brainstorming and lots of coffee, I unveil to you our new **RINGS**, cue the dramatic music....

JFSLA LEADERSHIP RINGS

LIFE

COMMUNITY

SCHOOL

TEAM

SELF

THE EMPOWER RINGS

Here's how they work.

Each ring will be a different section of this book (color coded page edges match the ring to help you navigate and find what best applies to you in a particular situation). And each section will have corresponding chapters that speak to that section's theme. We start with the core of leadership, your **SELF**, and then advance outward one ring at a time, with each ring representing a larger circle of an empower**RING**, until we get to the last ring: **LIFE**.

At the end of each chapter—or sometimes in the middle (just because I can)—I often have a short, interactive exercise one can engage in that reinforces the chapter's message. We do some writing and reflection in a personal journal at our leadership academies, so I want this book to be yours. To be your thoughts, your guide, your journal to scribble in all you want.

With the crazy pace of life, we seldom take a moment to reflect on who we are and what matters to us. I can prompt you to think about those things, but *writing* allows you to process that in a personal way. No one is grading it. It is not homework, or extra work, but just hopefully something fun and, most important, meaningful. Then, at the end of the book, you will combine all that you have learned about being a leader—for yourself, and those on your team, in your school, in the community—and apply it to the big dance called **LIFE**. (Did someone say *dance*?!)

HERE. WE. GO.

SECTION 1

SELF

"WHHHHHAAAAT?!!!?"

I am fairly certain this was my face the day I discovered one of my favorite quotes of all time.

The quote was:

"Success isn't a matter of chance, but a matter of choice."

—Dr. Colleen Hacker

WHHHHHAAAAAAAT?!

WHY DIDN'T SOMEBODY TELL ME THIS SOONER?
You mean, I control my success? My path? My attitude?

Of course I do. More appropriately, why didn't I think of this sooner?

DING.

It really was a watershed moment . . . suddenly I felt empowered. I did not see this quote until just after college. And as fate would have it, at that time I was surrounded by amazing teammates every day on the U.S. women's soccer team who taught me something perhaps even more powerful: swap out the word *success* with *leadership*.

Leadership

"~~Success~~ isn't a matter of chance, but a matter of choice."

Breakthrough. This concept changed my entire mind-set. All my life, I thought of leadership in the form of power or position. I thought leaders were presidents, CEOs, politicians, celebrities, four-star generals on a horse . . . essentially those in a position to impact lots and lots of people (someone I certainly was not). These incredible women I played alongside showed me the true beauty of leadership and just how broad that definition is.

Leadership isn't just about who yells the loudest (although I was excellent at that), or who wears the captain's armband—or even who scores the most goals. Leadership is so much broader than that. It is also quiet. It is motivating. It is positive. It is celebrating others. It is empowering others. It is standards. It is believing when others don't. It is being calm in the chaos. It is all those things and more. The hardest part is just summoning the courage to *choose* to lead, to raise your hand.

And how do you find that courage, you ask? Great question. Well, let's take a deeper dive and

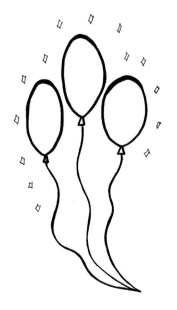

GET THIS PARTY STARTED.

THE EMPOWERRINGS

CHAPTER 1

LEADERSHIP IS
PERSONAL,
NOT POSITIONAL

"The area where we are the greatest is the area in which we inspire, encourage, and connect with another human being."

—Maya Angelou

Start in the heart of the **empower**RING. It's the smallest, yet most mighty ring. Yep, start with your SELF. You know the saying (like my kids started reciting in kindergarten): "You can't love others until you love yourself." Indeed. Now this is not a how-to-self-love book, but it is a **#YouGottaBeComfortableInTheSkinThatYouAreIn** book. Because at the heart of these empowerRINGS, is YOU, in all your glory.

And then ponder this concept: there is no box on your birth certificate that says check here if you are a leader.

 ☑ *LEADER*

Babies don't come out of the womb wearing a cool T-shirt that says, IT IS YOUR LUCKY DAY MOM AND DAD. I WAS BORN A LEADER! or SORRY DUDES, NO LEADER HERE.

Nope. Leadership is in **ALL OF US**. Yes, say it out loud:

Leadership is in all of us.

So forget all your preconceived notions of leadership. It is not a question of IF you will be a leader, but HOW you will lead. Because leadership is personal (most importantly) . . . and diverse (thankfully). It's diverse in its shapes, sizes, and sounds. There is not one mold, one look, one gender. You can be the quiet leader, loud leader, nerdy leader, emotional leader, or thoughtful leader.

The key is being authentically **YOU**: a leader others will want to follow because you are genuine. Leadership is what you make of it. It is *your* style. This was the gift of a lesson given to me by my teammates.

Leadership is Personal, not positional.

So let's start with the personal: What is your style like? What makes you feel most comfortable and real? And just a small reminder—make sure you answer these questions as who you *are*, not who you *wish to be*.

SELF

17

FIND YOUR
Leadership style

In the colored boxes below you will find groups of personality traits. Look at all the choices in each box. Put a number from 1 (most like you) to 4 (least like you) in each box. Then read on to find your leadership style.

I act on a moment's notice.
I consider life a game, here and now.
I need fun, variety, stimulation, and excitement.
I value skill, resourcefulness, and courage.
I am a natural troubleshooter, a performer, a competitor.

I need to feel unique and authentic.
I look for meaning and significance in life.
I need to contribute, to encourage and to care.
I value integrity and unity in relationships.
I am a natural romantic, a poet, a nurturer.

I need to follow rules and respect authority.
I have a strong sense of what is right and wrong in life.
I need to be useful and belong.
I value home, family, and tradition.
I am a natural preserver, a caretaker, a helper.

I seek knowledge and understanding.
I live by my own standards.
I need explanation and answers.
I value intelligence, insight, fairness, and justice.
I am a natural nonconformist, a visionary, a problem solver.

If the pink box is most like you, you are most likely:

Witty, charming, spontaneous, impulsive, generous, impactful, optimistic, eager, bold, physical, immediate, and fraternal.

Your leadership style:

Expects quick action. Works in the here and now. Performance oriented. Flexible approach. Welcomes change. Expects people to "make it fun."

If the turquoise box is most like you, you are most likely:

Enthusiastic, sympathetic, personal, warm, communicative, compassionate, idealistic, spiritual, sincere, peaceful, flexible, and imaginative.

Your leadership style:

Expects others to express views. Assumes "family spirit." Works to develop others' potential Individuals oriented. Democratic, unstructured approach. Encourages change via human potential. Expects people to develop their potential.

If the orange box is most like you, you are most likely:

Loyal, dependable, prepared, thorough, sensible, punctual, faithful, stable, organized, caring, concerned, and concrete.

Your leadership style:

Expects punctuality, order, loyalty. Assumes "the right" way to do things. Seldom questions tradition. Rules oriented. Detailed/thorough approach—threatened by change. Takes a prolonged time to initiate any change. Expects people to "play" their roles.

If the blue box is most like you, you are most likely:

Analytical, global, conceptual, cool, calm, collected, inventive, logical, perfectionist, abstract, hypothetical, and investigative.

Your leadership style:

> Expects intelligence and competence. Assumes task relevancy. Seeks ways to improve systems. Visionary. Analytical. Encourages change for improvement. Constantly "in process" of change. Expects people to follow through.

So which color are you?

Write it here for future reference:

For the record, I am tons of hot pink and a splash of turquoise.

Or . . . here's another personality test. It's short and sweet. At the risk of appearing like a propaganda machine (but a risk I am willing to take), here it is: What Disney ride most resembles you?

(You can have extra donuts if you can guess mine.)

Actually, since I'd rather just eat the donuts already, I'll spare you the suspense: the Disney ride that I think most resembles me is California Screamin' at Disney California Adventure. California Screamin' is a very fast roller coaster that blasts rock music during your ride (if you can hear it over your screamin'). For those who know me, that is not breaking news. For those of you just getting to know me, well, I am from California, I like to sing badly (and loudly), I love when my heart thumps, and I have strong vocal cords. There you go.

And although the personality quizzes are fun, you can't just confine people to a personality color or box (or even a ride). We don't necessarily fit one tidy definition. Life is more complex than that of course. A different day or a different scenario—such as enrolling in a new school or starting a new job—could elicit a different response and color. Nevertheless, they do tell us personal tendencies. They stimulate an awareness about yourself and others.

And what I recall vividly about my first personality quiz, which I took when I was in my early twenties, is how it made me so much more mindful of the *differences* in personality styles. And how important it was to honor those differences. Suddenly I better understood why a teammate acted the way she did or maybe packed her suitcase the way she did. Here's a little-known fact: the way someone packs a suitcase reveals a lot about that person. I had a teammate, for example, who explained to me that she packed her clothes by outfit, in order of the day: So for Monday, I pack these pants, this top, those underwear, these shoes. Under that I place Tuesday's full outfit. And Wednesday's below that. And so on. For the entire vacation. *Don't you do that as well?!*

Ummmm (pause). No.

I remember looking at her strategically and perfectly folded suitcase in complete awe.

NOT MINE

When we better understand how we personally tick, we can collectively thrive as well.

Here's an important reminder: Personality types may influence your style, but they don't *define* your style. Just like bad hairdos (I had none), personalities and leadership styles will evolve and grow. My twelve-year-old personality was surely different from my eighteen-year-old personality—and of course is different now. Experiences shape your personality along that wonderful continuum of growth called life.

Let's get back to the gift of discovering that leadership is personal, not positional.

I remember the relief I felt when I realized I didn't need to be the man on a horse with a tall hat and sword, like those we read about in history books, to be a leader.

And thank goodness for *that*, because I'm not a man, nor do I own a sword. I just need to care enough about something to raise my hand. **To stand up for something. To speak out for someone. Whether I empower one person or the free world. *That* is leadership.**

HORSE AND SWORD NOT REQUIRED. (The hat, however, is mandatory.)

I watched in awe as my former U.S. National Team teammates Carla

SELF

22

Overbeck, Mia Hamm, Kristine Lilly, Brandi Chastain, and Joy Fawcett did their thing on and off the field. They all did it so differently.

CARLA OVERBECK was our "O Captain! My Captain!" (if I may borrow from Walt Whitman) who for many years was the master of motivation and inspiration. Her leadership style was both verbal and quiet, depending on what the situation called for.

MIA HAMM was the face of the team, and yet was the player who wanted the spotlight the *least*. Mia was our ferociously unselfish, shy leader who operated always with a *team-first* mentality.

KRISTINE LILLY was our standard-bearer (I would have loved to clone her). "Lil" was the leader that just got it done . . . consistently great and understated.

BRANDI CHASTAIN was our endless ball of energy and contagious fun. Brandi was the first and last one on the field. Her leadership style oozed passion.

JOY FAWCETT was our fearless mother of three daughters (she had all three while playing BTW.) Bravery and brevity defined Joy. She did not waste words, so when Joy did speak, she *commanded* a room.

LOUDY FOUDY—and then there was this goofball. I have no idea why that "Loudy Foudy" nickname stuck. It may have something to do with the fact that I was blessed with vocal cords that would make a yodeler jealous. (You gotta roll with what life gives you. . . .)

Each of us led with our own style, our own way. Early in my career I learned (and am still consistently amazed by the fact) that we need all leadership types to be effective as a group. Imagine a team with a bunch of talkers, like me. Brandi would have fallen under the "talkers" category as well. As would Abby Wambach. (Full disclosure: we once bought young Abby a T-shirt that said, HELP. I'M TALKING AND I CAN'T SHUT UP. :)) A team chock-full of verbal leaders like the three of us would have meant earmuffs were mandatory; or maybe duct tape. A team full of quiet leaders wouldn't be effective either. And that is the really cool thing about the *breadth* of leadership. All styles are needed and, I would argue, the more diverse the better. But most important, the style you choose for that center of the **empower**RING —SELF—has to be YOUR style and the true YOU.

I cannot be Carla or Mia or Kristine, but I certainly can watch and learn from them. Just as long as I keep coming back to my authentic self.

Which led me to our first two interviewees for the book, Mia Hamm and Alex Morgan. Both are Olympic gold medalists, World Cup champions, and most important, lovers of Lucky Charms cereal. The two biggest faces of soccer in this country, though they represented two different eras on the Women's National Team, both discussed their style of leadership and how it evolved. Feet up. Shoes off. Over socks as promised. #SockTalk.

I, of course, started the interview with the leadership test of all tests:

JULIE: "So there's no easing into this. We're going to start at full throttle because this is really a measurement of your leadership aptitude. Can you laugh without smiling?"

MIA: "*Mmmhohohaha.*"

ALEX: "Ha. *Hahaha. Haaaahhhahah.*"

(Both Mia and Alex nail this on the first try [or not], which leads all of us to burst into big belly laughs.)

MIA: "Didn't you make us do this all the time?"

JULIE: "Yes."

MIA: "This is Stanford education."
(Indeed.)

JULIE: "I make my kids do it all the time, too."

MIA: "*Hohaoha.*"

(That's Mia trying it again.)

JULIE: *"Heghhilaleaaaaaaa."*

You know you want to try it. Go ahead. Laugh without smiling. You will look ridiculous I might add. But that is the beauty of it. Looking ridiculous while sounding ridiculous. They're two things that I have cornered the market on. And truly one of the leadership skills for which I am most proud: letting go of the fear of how I will look, how I will sound, and just being okay with being me . . . a classy nut.

Back to the interview. We moved into personality styles, and although I didn't ask what their favorite ride is, they still shared their tendencies:

ALEX: "When I'm comfortable with people, I'm just all in. I'm very decisive with things. But [when it's] someone who I'm not as comfortable with, I'm not as outgoing . . . I'm a lot more reserved with what I say as well."

JULIE: "Mariel [Mia's real name, by the way]?"

MIA: "I'm quiet, shy, but more introspective. I think more of watching and listening than engaging. My close friends, they know that I like to joke. But I'm just an intense personality. I have so much respect for people that are relaxed and funny all the time, but that's OK. It's helped me get to where I am today."

ALEX: "I feel like I'm a little more reserved now and a little more of a listener, whereas I feel like I was *too much of a talker* when I was in high school and college."

To which Mia then turned to me and Alex and said, "No wonder you two get along so great." Ha. Being from a family often referred to as the "Rowdy Foudys," and the youngest of four, I had to talk to survive. It was Darwinism at its finest. (And if you want to rock the ruffled plaid shirt and feathered hair of this fourth-grader, you *better* be a sweet talker.)

But let me stay on-point. I was wondering if Alex's and Mia's distinct personalities matched their leadership tendencies, so I asked them *how* they lead:

MIA: "I think, ah, I lead just by setting a good example. I think that's the best way I could do it. Just by being responsible and doing the work. You know, I'm not really one that runs in and rallies people vocally. I've tried to do that, but failed miserably."

JULIE: "How'd you know you failed?"

MIA: "Well, because there was no response. The response you usually want to get . . . I had the opposite. It was, like, ignored. I think if they could tell me to stop, they would have [*she laughs*]. I've learned that my leadership style is just by setting a good example, and being fit, being committed, and just being responsible."

What Mia learned is the leadership style that works best for her was the leadership style that most reflected her at that moment in her life. Mia led in a more personal, private way.

Alex also spoke about her leadership tendencies:

ALEX: "I think I'm someone who probably tries, in a leadership role, to build more personal relationships with each teammate. I think for me it's more of gaining trust and respect from each one of my teammates before I feel like I should be vocal. Obviously, there are . . . people who lead by example— that comes naturally for them. But for me to feel like I have the respect of people listening to me, I need to build that relationship for all of my teammates."

THE ONE HOLDING THE UMBRELLA?
THAT IS NOT ME!

Yes, leadership can and will evolve . . . Alex has grown into that bigger leadership role and feels more confident in knowing when to talk, and how much to talk. But I love that Mia and Alex always keep coming back to their style, their personality. That is critical. One of the hardest parts of finding your style is being OK with your style. Not trying to be someone or something that you are not.

Eighteen-year-old SOPHIE HEALY-THOW is an Irish scientist who won Google's top award for teenage scientists (as in top *in the world*), along with her friends Ciara Judge and Emer Hickey. The trio investigated how natural bacteria in plants could be used as a growth aid for crops. And after they did over twenty thousand experiments (yes, I just said twenty thousand), they found out that they could actually increase crop yield by 50 percent with the bacteria. Not to be Captain Obvious here, but *this was a huge discovery.* (And one that EXPERTS told them couldn't happen, wouldn't happen. Yep. More on that later.)

Sophie took time away from studying for her high school finals to discuss science, leadership, and life #SockTalkSkype style.

I first asked Sophie how she best defined her personal leadership style. Her response:

SOPHIE: "I guess the only way I can describe my leadership style is when you see a tour guide, and they're holding the umbrella in the air, and they've got the group following them? I eventually realized that's who I'm NOT. I'm not the person in front of the group with the umbrella telling everybody where to go [*Sophie laughs*].

"I think my leadership style is more of a quiet leader. I like pushing everybody forward. I like making sure that everybody's individual strengths and talents and tools are being seen, and that as a leader I can make everybody else a leader, too."

 I WORE MY LUCK-OF-THE IRISH GREEN HEART FAVIES FOR SOPHIE...

Maybe your style is louder and more verbal. Maybe it is more cerebral. You must think and process before you act. Maybe it is leading by example as Mia talked about. Whatever it is, make it you.

Go find your style. Go find your way. Leadership is many things, and most important, it is YOU.

EXERCISE:

I have a short quiz for you. See if you can answer these three simple questions below. You cannot Google these!:

1. WHO WAS THE MVP OF THE SUPER BOWL LAST SEASON?

2. WHO WON THE ACADEMY AWARD FOR BEST ACTRESS TWO YEARS AGO?

3. WHO WON THE NOBEL PEACE PRIZE LAST YEAR?

HARD to get any of them? Come on. These are FAMOUS people. People in the headlines, in the news. They surely must have impacted your life in a meaningful way. Or maybe not. Now try and answer these three questions:

4. WHAT TEACHER HAS HELPED YOU THE MOST?

5. CAN YOU NAME A FRIEND WHO HAS BEEN THERE FOR YOU WHEN MOST NEEDED?

6. NAME A STRANGER WHO HAS GIVEN YOU HELP WHEN LEAST EXPECTED?

HOW DID YOU DO?

I am guessing the second half of that quiz was easier to do. I have found that most people make the mistake of thinking you need a platform or a microphone (or celebrity status) to impact others in a positive way. This quiz hopefully shows you how flawed that thinking is. Leadership is about empowering others. Helping them strive to be better. And often, the people in our lives most responsible for those moments are not superstars or celebrities but those closest to us. Or those who provide inspiration simply by lending a hand. Lost too often in the discussion of leadership is this most important point:

We ALL have the potential to empower others because leadership is personal, not positional.

So choose to lead.
Because you can.

DON'T JUST
THINK IT, INK IT

+ Use your Noodle and Doodle space. :)

CHAPTER 2

FINDING THE CONFIDENT YOU

"Become so wrapped up in something you forget to be afraid."

—Lady Bird Johnson

So, now to that pesky *choosing* part of the quote "Leadership isn't a matter of chance, but a matter of choice." The part about having the *confidence* to say, *Yes, I can do this* . . . having the confidence to take that step forward even when everything in your body screams DON'T MOVE; and having the confidence to raise your hand when you're not sure you are ready to put yourself out there. We've all been there. And *ahhh*, it is a terrible feeling. Until you recognize you are not alone. You just have to figure out strategies to get through self-doubt. Because once you do, you find out you are not just surviving, but thriving. My personal trick on how to find confidence when it was hiding was to do something totally dorky, because, well, I'm a big dork.

You may not have seen that *Saturday Night Live* skit where the fictional self-help guru Stuart Smalley does his daily affirmations by looking into the mirror and saying aloud to himself,

> "I am good enough, I am smart enough, and gosh darn it, people like me."

(If you haven't seen it, don't worry . . . the only thing you need to know is pour on the cheese.)

Well, I would do that into a mirror (I cannot believe I am confessing this out loud). I'd say it to myself jokingly *of course*, but also nudging myself in a healthy way. Go ahead, try it. Go look into the mirror and say it with great authority, full cheese, with a big grin:

> "I am good enough, I am smart enough, and gosh darn it, people like me."

The point is that finding confidence takes some self-talk. (Actually, that's a lie. It takes *lots* of self-talk.) And talking to yourself is not the most natural or normal thing to many people. But, it's like building a muscle—it takes work and effort. Having doubts about your ability is normal. You are not alone. In fact, everyone at some stage of his or her life—actually, at many stages—feels an overriding sense of, "OH, MY GOODNESS! What the heck am I doing here? I cannot do this." (It's how I felt my first ten years on the National Team.) The issue is, what do you do about it? Do you agree with that doubting voice in your head, or do you figure out ways to turn the negative thoughts into positive ones?

Meet JESSICA MENDOZA, an all-American from Stanford University; she's also a two-time Olympic medalist (gold in 2004, silver in 2008) with the U.S. Softball Women's National Team, and is now an ESPN commentator for baseball (yes, as in Major League Baseball [MLB]). This is so rad: Jessica became the first woman ever to call a playoff game for MLB and now is part of ESPN's top commentating team, which does *Sunday Night Baseball*. That's another first. Oh, and I know her.

I caught Jessica at a softball field and just happened to have a cooler and two chairs. Alas, a #socktalk broke out.

AND YES, THOSE REALLY ARE RAINBOW TOE SOCKS. WELL PLAYED, JESS, WELL PLAYED.

Jessica shared her story about that constant voice of self-doubt in her head and the day it took over.

JESSICA: "It's incredible looking back how insecure I was. I remember in high school, up until the point Stanford called, I was set on going to a junior college because, *No one's gonna call me. I'm not that kind of player.* But that humility, that insecurity helped drive me.

"There's a quote I used when I played: 'Practice like you're the worst player on the field. Play like you're the best.' So when I was at practice, that's when I let the doubt take over. I'm gonna stay after practice and I'm gonna get after it. Because I'm not good enough today. All of a sudden, game day comes; I would stare down that pitcher and be, like, 'Honey you ain't gonna get me today. I'm better than you.'"

And Jessica could do that because she put in the work. She put in the sweat equity. *Until* (well, let her tell you):

"I found myself in a place where my insecurities got the best of me. The Olympic team was to be selected the next month and all I could think about were all the reasons I didn't deserve to be on that team, how I wasn't good enough."

"I remember like it was yesterday. I remember sitting in the bathroom, in tears, in the Dominican Republic during a softball game thinking, *Who am I right now?* This giant cockroach, the size of a cat, came through the bathroom and it hit me, *What am I doing?* My team is out there. Here I am, so caught up in how bad I am and I hate the game that I'm playing. How did I get to this point? And I'm like, *I play for the National Team. I'm representing my country. I'm a month away from possibly making my first Olympic team, and instead of getting pumped about it, the fear has brought me to tears with a cockroach in a bathroom.* No, never again. And I changed."

Jessica spent the next few months finding a way to let her positive voice be heard again. To feel good about herself. To beat down the bad. Jessica talked about her strategy—and the ways she combatted the negative thoughts:

"I had to find a way to look in the mirror and see somebody who was strong and smart and a kick-butt softball player. And I think it helps saying it *out loud*. We're taught to be humble, and it helped me to be able to tell people, 'I'm really good,' and not laugh and say, 'I'm just kidding.' Like, no, I'm really good. I can hit. I can play some mean outfield. You try and hit the ball anywhere near me, I'm gonna catch it. Try saying that and all of a sudden you become what you say you are."

And no, she had never even heard my Stuart Smalley story, *by the way*

Amen, Jessica. Might as well start building that muscle now with this excercise:

Take a sticky note and write down a doubting thought.

Now cross it out and write a positive thought and post it somewhere you'll see it every day.

say it out loud.
Go on.

FLIP IT!

Choose to turn negative to positive (because you can). Here are some of my strategies to finding confidence when it is playing hide-and-go-seek:

• **DO THE WORK:** Putting in the hours of blood, sweat, and tears not only helps your game, it helps your brain. You just **FEEL** more confident in any task when you know you have prepared.

• **TRAIN YOUR BRAIN:** This one is **HUGE**. Find a strategy to replace bad thoughts with good ones.

Our sport psychology specialist on the National Team (and wonderful friend and mentor), DR. COLLEEN HACKER, once told our team, "Your brain can only handle one thought at a time. Just one. So you choose what goes through that [really smart] brain of yours." That was one of the most liberating pieces of information I had ever received. I control the thought. So simple, yet so true. The key, Colleen explained, was recognizing when a negative thought was seeping in and pushing it right back out. I wore a hair band on my wrist during soccer games and would snap it anytime a **GOSH, I AM AWFUL** thought crept in. It was a physical motion meant to **SNAP** me out of that onrushing negative mental jail. Your physical cue can be anything you want: pulling your socks up, adjusting your ponytail, pinching your nose and making a horn sound; whatever. What matters is that it has the wanted effect of keeping you on that confident, positive path. And guess what? It actually works!

You wanna talk about someone who has had to "train her brain" often during hard times? Then I'll introduce you to the incredible ROBIN ROBERTS. Robin is the cohost of ABC's *Good Morning America*, a former ESPN anchor, a best-selling author, cancer survivor, and all-around amazing human being (who can rock the slippers like no one else). We spoke at *Good Morning America*'s studio in New York City for our **#Sock(Slipper)talk**.

She did not hold back. Robin spoke about just how important it was to control the negative thoughts when she found out she had a severe form of breast cancer:

ROBIN: "You got to change the way you think in order to change the way you feel. I found that it was as much mental as physical. The chemo was no joke [*she laughs*]. The chemo, radiation steroids, all that—I'm not gonna sugarcoat it. It was *hard*. I was very good about writing a journal: the first day is OK, but the second day, third day's really bad. I'd write down little things that would bother me, and it was my personal journal on how to go through all these months and weeks of treatment. But I really found the key for me was *positivity*. Optimism is like a muscle that gets stronger with use. You've got to use that muscle."

WE STUCK WITH THE ANIMAL THEMES . . .
SO YOU COULD HEAR US ROAR.

SELF

The key for me was positivity. Robin consistently replaced bad thoughts with good ones. She chose to react to a terrible situation in a positive way, even when things were at their worst. Train your brain.

• **TRAIN THE BUTTERFLIES:** For many, many years on the National Team, I would get very being nervous before games, feeling like I did not belong on the team or maybe nervous about someone in the stands who was there watching me. Or maybe just not feeling up to the task at the moment. I used to dread the butterflies until the same awesome Dr. Hacker said to me, "Butterflies are a great thing. They mean **YOU CARE**. Now just teach them to fly in formation."

One of my strategies on how to channel that energy in a positive way was my hair band again (a quick reminder that nerves are a great thing and to embrace the pressure of that moment). And Billie Jean King. The legendary tennis player and social activist is a friend and has always been a wonderful supporter and adviser to our U.S. Women's National soccer team. I remember telling "The Kinger" (my nickname for her because she is pure royalty) before the 1999 World Cup here in the United States that there was a lot of pressure on the team to do well. To carry the tournament. To fill the stands. To show the world what a women's sporting event should look like. She looked at me with a huge smile, as if to say *of course there is you dummy . . . that is what makes it so great* and said (well, roared in my favorite BJK voice dripping with passion):

"PRESSURE IS A PRIVILEGE FOUDY! You've done the work, now go enjoy it. People would give so much to be where you all are. GO BE GREAT."

I thought, YOU'RE DAMN RIGHT IT IS. It's so true. Embrace that. *Pressure Is a Privilege* became our mantra for the entire '99 World Cup tournament. And wouldn't you know it, from then on, pressure (and butterflies) became something I craved.

• **BREATHE AND BELIEVE:** Take a deep breath. Laugh out loud. Smile. Remember, we all go through these insecure moments. You are not some freak of nature.

Self-doubt, when channeled properly, has defined the best in the world. It is what pushes them to be better, smarter, faster, and fitter.

• **HAVE A STRATEGY:** And not just any strategy. Find a strategy that works for **YOU**. Recognize when these moments of doubt creep in and proactively counter them. This may take time to find, as strategies are personal, as Mia and Alex shared with me. Here is what works for them:

> **MIA:** "For me it is just trying to simplify what I am doing because I think a lot of the times you feel it's this merry-go-round that's going so fast, you're just trying jump on at the right moment. And rather than worrying about everything that's going on, just breaking it down to one . . . simple . . . task . . . at . . . a . . . time."

> **ALEX:** "I do think being able to control *what you can control* at the time is something that you can always rely on, something I always fell back on. There's some things that are just out of your control, but focus on the things you can control: your attitude, your work rate."

FAKE IT 'TIL YOU MAKE IT

Or you can always try this—it's one of my personal favorite strategies, and we perfected it on the National Team: FAKE IT 'TIL YOU MAKE IT (FITYMI). Similar to my looking into the mirror and doing my silly Stuart Smalley impression, it is crazy how well *fake it 'til you make it* works when you try it.

It is part of the "Train your Brain" concept mentioned earlier. If your brain can only process one thought at a time, then dictate what goes in that pretty little head of yours. It only took me about three decades to come to this epiphany, so I am trying to give you a head start. Dictating which thoughts go into your brain is really the trick to unlocking that reservoir of confidence inside you (because that reservoir is indeed there). Dictating is the operative word here. You keep it positive, and you make sure it stays positive. Don't let anyone, anything, or any comment deter that goal. Easier said than done, you may be saying. Perhaps. Or maybe your confidence just needs some convincing . . . even if you have to FAKE IT 'TIL YOU MAKE IT to convince it to come on out. Exhibit A:

The scene: the Rose Bowl on a scorching hot July summer day playing in front of a sold-out crowd of 90,185.

The game: the finals of the 1999 Women's World Cup tournament, and we are tied 0-0 versus China after 120 minutes of regulation and overtime play.

The situation: Penalty kicks are going to decide which country hoists the World Cup trophy.

The reality: *ARGH. Penalty kicks to decide it?!* I say to myself. No soccer player ever wants penalty kicks to determine the outcome of a game, let alone a World Cup final.

The Fake It 'Til You Make It solution: Before the PK's start, you can hear statements like:
"We are fine." "We are so fine." "The Chinese are tired." "Look at them." "They are *exhausted*." (We had no idea if they were tired.)
"Gosh, it is not even that hot. I so wish it was even hotter." (It actually was so hot, it felt like my cleats were melting into the field.)
"We have been practicing penalty kicks tons." (Lie.)
"The Chinese are in trouble." (That one we truly believed.)
"I love penalty kicks. I LOVE PENALTY KICKS!" (No, I don't.)

"Let's do this!" (And we did. We outscored the Chinese 5–4 in those darn PK's and won our second World Cup.)

The outcome: Who knows if anyone really felt what I just cited, but it didn't matter. When we said it aloud, we suddenly believed it. No whining. No complaining. Just optimism. Without a doubt, the ability to stay optimistic, when we could have easily been pessimistic, was a huge key to our success.

And we stayed positive everywhere. In China, though tired of our diet of peanut butter and jelly sandwiches (and warm soda) for the thirtieth straight day, we made up a song about PB and J sandwiches and how much we loved them. Suddenly eating time became enjoyable, full of bad jingles (apologies to the audio listeners of this book for my peanut butter ballad).

Or when we were dealing with another delayed flight that meant five more hours on a cold concrete floor at the airport in some foreign country: *There is no other place I would rather be.* Yes, we said it with mock enthusiasm and sarcasm, but when said enough, suddenly the group was laughing and sharing all the places we would definitely NOT want to be at the moment: on a gorgeous beach in Hawaii? *NOOOOO WAY.* Shopping in Paris? Heck, no. *BOOOOORING.*

Or we'd turn to one of my favorite mantras, which we used to shout out regularly, particularly when a long road trip became a very long road trip. It was:

"LOOKING GOOD. FEELING GOOD. LYING TO MYSELF."

We'd all laugh as we shouted it out. And we would feel better.

In our era before iPads and iPhones, we had to get creative, which sounds so old school, yes. *Buuuuuuuut* . . . it was also an absolute blessing. We had to figure out strategies to deal with adversity. And it often involved humor and shared misery (yes, misery is subjective). And FITYMI honestly worked. Which I shouldn't have doubted. Medical experts have said for years that your brain cannot tell the difference between real and imaginary thoughts. That's right . . . so heap on the imaginary good stuff.

Don't believe the experts? Well believe my ten-year-old daughter, Izzy, then. She told me recently after a nightmare, "Mom, when I wake up from a scary nightmare, I just think about rainbows and unicorns and smiley faces, and then I feel fine." Proof.

I often credit our National Team's FITYMI expertise (and laughter) for getting us through many tough times, where it could have been very easy to lose our confidence and spiral downward. So when you start to feel that aching sense of *OMG*, relax, look in the mirror, snap your wristband, channel the butterflies, turn on your FITYMI switch, and say aloud,

"I am GOOD ENOUGH, i am SMART ENOUGH, and gosh darn it, PRESSURE IS A PRIVILEGE."

QUICK EXERCISE

Try this today: when you are confronted with something you dread doing in the next twenty-four hours, FLIP IT. Actively practice **FAKE IT 'TIL YOU MAKE IT.**
Try it. Go on. What's the downside? You will still dread the dreaded thing if you try nothing. Come up with a silly song, paste a smile on your face, gaze into a mirror lovingly . . . pretend you **JUST LOVE** doing that chore. Include your friends and/or family in this challenge. I find doing things in groups always helps. Or just dance. Poorly.

WHERE THE
MAGIC HAPPENS

What happens if the confident you is *still* hiding?

Fear not. This will happen, and it happens to many.

Sometimes the fastest way to gain confidence is by just *DOING*. Nothing earth-shattering here: by *doing* you find that you can, in fact, do. Also, by *doing*, you'll discover that the world where you are *doing* is new, shiny, and exhilarating. But we all know it is hard to convince your body and mind to do something when it falls outside of your perceived area of comfort. But that's just it. That comfort zone is a perception meant to be shattered.

(You have permission to shatter it to pieces.)

I wish I could tell you the secret sauce to getting out of that comfort zone. There isn't one. And maybe that is why there is magic on the other side. But there are lots of strategies we will discuss to help nudge you out. First off, you gotta gather friends around you that support that first step.

For example, when Sophie and her two friends first started their science experiment on boosting crop production using a natural bacteria found in plants, *experts* told them it was never going to work. Let Sophie tell you firsthand:

SOPHIE: "We did some research, and we asked around some top scientists in the area of barley, wheats, and oats, and some people from the universities here in Ireland. And they basically told us that well, it hadn't been done before. So it's not going to work [*she laughs*]."

JULIE (shocked): "Come on. This is what scientists do, Sophie. They discover a new frontier."

SOPHIE: "Yeah, basically [*followed by a laugh*] I think after hearing that, we were more determined than ever to see if they were right or if we could actually make it work."

Sophie and her friends encouraged each other to keep going. And guess what? They proved the experts wrong. In so doing they also unlocked a key discovery that could help boost crop production by 50 percent. Experts now say their experiment may help alleviate some of our global hunger issues. GOOD LORD.

I find that so amazing because it would have been so easy for them as teenagers to just say to the experts, "Yep, you're right, it cannot be done." But Sophie, Ciara, and Emer kept pushing forward. They were willing to think beyond what others deemed possible. The great unknown can be scary, yes, but that's where you must go to redefine the parameters of possible. As one of my favorite women in history, Eleanor Roosevelt, said,

"Do one thing every day that scares you."

Or if this is more suitable to you, I give you my friend Elly's version of Eleanor's piece of advice:

"Do thirty seconds of courage every day—that's all it takes."

Trying new things is indeed scary. Taking on a new challenge can be uncomfortable. But life is full of uncomfortable. Which is why being "comfortable with uncomfortable" is one of the greatest skill sets in life.

And sometimes life decides that it wants to give you *layer upon layer* of uncomfortable. Robin Roberts was first diagnosed with an aggressive form of breast cancer in 2007. Robin fought the breast cancer. Five years later, life decided *that* was not uncomfortable enough. In 2012, she was diagnosed with Myelodysplastic Syndromes, MDS, a form of leukemia. Her response was awe-inspiring:

ROBIN: *"Ahhh, I will say that there was some anger the second time around."*

JULIE: "Yeah, of course."

ROBIN: "Because I had done all the things. I made my mess my message. You just never know. You just never know. And people have asked, am I looking over my shoulder now? You know, strike two. Am I looking for that third strike? No. Then I will have been defeated, and it will have won. If I live or sit across from you here in fear of this . . . is it gonna come back? Am I gonna have to face it again? I hope not. But I'm not gonna borrow worry. That's the one thing we all do. How many times do we worry about something that never comes to fruition? And how about that wasted time of like, oh, what, what if, what if, what if."

JULIE: "We women are great at that."

ROBIN: "Oh, we are [*she laughs*]. We've mastered it. We have absolutely mastered that."

COURAGEOUS, NOT CRAZY

If you find yourself hesitant to take that jump forward, or even attempt a baby step, Mia and others talked about going back to what is natural, what feels right: being authentically you. We've all tried in our life to be someone that we are not. Ah-ha, I am going to be Just. Like. That. And eventually (*hopefully*) you came to a place where you laughed and thought, What was that stage all about? Staying true to one self can indeed bring confidence.

But EVEN then, raising your hand is scary. It means putting yourself out there to fail. It means risking embarrassment. Well, failure and embarrassment are part of life. One strategy I deploy often when I am worried about embarrassment is to ask myself this: *Self, if I do NOT do this, how much will I regret it?* Because this has been a principle I have always honored: live with no regrets. I do not want to be asking myself a year

SELF

later, a decade later, *Why did I not take that step? What held me back? How could I have said no?!*

What I learned early in my life is that fortune favors the brave.

Proof: In the late 1980s, when we all first got selected to play on the U.S. Women's National soccer team, there was NO Women's World Cup or women's soccer in the Olympics. People told our U.S. team players and officials that we were crazy to dream of having a World Cup for women. We were told soccer was not popular enough. Girls around the world did not play, nor want to play soccer. The Olympic Games would not let women's soccer in. A women's World Cup would never happen. Stop dreaming up such nonsense. Over and over we were essentially told our dream to be Olympians or World Cup champions was CRAZY.

We, as a team, could have easily come to believe that our dream was indeed crazy. But instead, together, we decided we were not the crazy ones. Nope. We were not crazy at all, only courageous. Getting to that point took getting out of our comfort zone, often failing, laughing, and then lifting each other up.

Live. Laugh. Fail. Repeat.

It also took lots of work, self-talk, training of the brain and butterflies, big breaths . . . and, of course, heaps of uncomfortable. But we kept pushing on. We kept believing. Because if you haven't failed, you haven't lived. And guess what? We found the magic. Yep, and you can too.

COME JOIN THE PARTY.

EXERCISE:

Thanks to Eleanor and Elly, I try every day to do something that scares me. And now you will (eventually you will thank me for this). I will ease you into it. At every Julie Foudy Sports Leadership Academy, we kick off the first evening session with a fun game called "I Am Comfortable with Crazy." Try it.

Start first with finding a friend. Turn to your friend and perform one of the following

I AM COMFORTABLE WITH Crazy ACTIVITIES:

1. LAUGH WITHOUT SMILING. (YES, I SAID NO SMILING!)
2. SING YOUR FAVORITE SONG OF ALL TIME, BUT IN YOUR BEST BOOMING OPERA VOICE.
3. AND MY ALL-TIME FAVORITE . . . YOUR BW. YOUR BEST OF YOUR WORST DANCE. THAT'S RIGHT. PERFORM YOUR ABSOLUTE WORST DANCE TO THE BEST OF YOUR ABILITY . . . MEANING THE BADDER THE BETTER. IT DOESN'T HAVE TO BE LONG, IT JUST HAS TO BE BAD. THE BW (BEST WORST) WAS A U.S. NATIONAL TEAM TRADITION BY THE WAY. WE SPENT FAR TOO MANY HOURS IN LOCKER ROOMS AND HOTEL ROOMS DANCING REALLY POORLY. SHOCKINGLY, I AM A NATURAL AT THIS.

Now that you are approaching a comfortable state (though you are still not done), find someone you don't know well. (That is the scary part; it has to be someone you do not know well—or even better, that you don't know at all. Bring a friend with you if you need support.) Do another one of the activities, preferably one you haven't done yet. And repeat.

SELF

Yes, get comfortable in crazy and repeat. It is the repetition (not just of the above three, but all things scary in life) that will help you cross into the magic part. Because suddenly you realize, *hmmm*, I am not only doing this thing I once thought was scary, I am doing it pretty darn well.

You'll find that something really cool happens, regardless of the setting: the next time you deal with something "uncomfortable," you become more likely to take on the task. And before you know it, you will have the entire school, for example, laughing without smiling.

And don't blame me, but without looking, you are there, outside that little circle called your comfort zone. Congratulations. Welcome to the land of putting yourself out there with the confidence that you won't be judged, or even better, you do not care if you are being judged (as we will discuss later). **Welcome to Magicville!** *It's opener there in the wide open air.* *

*From *Oh, the Places You'll Go!* by Dr. Seuss.

SELF

DON'T JUST
THINK IT, INK IT

ROBIN: "I was very good about writing a journal. So I'd write down little things that would bother me, and it was my personal journal on how to go through all these months."

_____
_____
_____
_____
_____
_____
_____
_____
_____
_____
_____
_____
_____
_____
_____
_____
_____
_____
_____
_____
_____
_____
_____
_____
_____
_____
_____
_____
_____
_____

CHAPTER 3

DOUBT WILL
NEVER DEFINE
YOU

*"Be who you are and say what you feel,
because those who mind don't matter and
those who matter don't mind."*

—Dr. Seuss

If there is one thing I have learned over the years regarding that core of our **empower**RINGS—**SELF**—it is BEWARE THE TRAP. And by trap I mean, **resist the comparison trap**. It's so darn tempting:

I wish I could be more like her. I
want to look more like them. I wish
I had her confidence.

We've all done it. Of course we have. We are bombarded with images of how we should look, dress, smile, stand, sit, eat, talk, and even tinkle. And my goodness, it's everywhere—social media, print ads, TV, billboards, the Internet—at seemingly every click. There are messages, overt and subliminal, about what everyone else thinks you should be or look like. On top of that, I've noticed something universal with women: we are far too focused

SELF

on what we don't have. What we *think* we lack. Well, let's start celebrating what we do have. Let's be kinder to ourselves.

Next time I fall into the comparison trap, I am going to remember a person who has every right to make comparisons with others due to her situation, but does just the opposite. Meet TATYANA MCFADDEN, seventeen-time Team USA medalist in the Paralympic Games and sixteen-time marathon winner. Tatyana was born in Russia with spina bifida (meaning her spine was actually outside of her body when she was born). She lived in a Russian orphanage from birth until she was six years old. Paralyzed from the waist down, Tatyana recalls those early years in our #SockTalk at her home in Champaign, Illinois.

 TATYANA: "After I was born [the doctors waited twenty-one day to operate], so it's practically a miracle that I survived and that I lived. Shortly after that, I was put in an orphanage—orphanage number thirteen—and then . . ."

JULIE: "Number thirteen? Just a number?"

TATYANA: "Number thirteen, just a number, yeah, no name. And so from there, there was absolutely no medical treatment, so that means no wheelchairs were available. The orphanage did not have enough money to provide that. And I wanted to be just like the other kids, and so I taught myself how to walk on my hands, using my arms as my legs, just to get around the orphanage. And some people say it's brought strength in sports. But for me, it was just a way to live life. I mean, it was the only way of transportation for me."

Tatyana told me this story with no anger. No *why me*; just in a matter-of-fact manner. *It was practically a miracle that I survived.* She spoke of walking on her hands with her legs dragging behind her, just to move. And then an American who worked with the U.S. government, Debbie McFadden, came to Russia when Tatyana was six years old. Debbie was in Russia doing humanitarian-aid work in orphanages, with no intention of adopting a child. But there was Tatyana, peeking around the corner, with "a huge bow on her head . . . bigger than her head," Debbie said smiling when recalling how they met. Tatyana followed Debbie from room to room that day at the orphanage.

Debbie left Russia but could not get Tatyana out of her mind. She knew there was something very special about her, and when she spoke to doctors about adopting Tatyana, they warned her that Tatyana may not live very long. Undeterred, Debbie returned to Russia, adopted Tatyana, and brought her home to Maryland.

THE WHY NOTTERS

I asked Tatyana's mom, Debbie, what she noticed about Tatyana's personality when she first brought her home.

"Well, [she laughs] this thing—Tatyana always said [in Russian], '**Ya sama**'—and I didn't know what that meant. Literally translated, it is, '**I can do it.**' But it means *I can do it myself.* And every time we would do something, she'd go, '*Ya sama.*' She wanted to do everything in life. I remember I was trying to get her involved in sports, not to be a sports person but to save her life."

When Debbie would take Tatyana to swimming lessons or gymnastic lessons, coaches and teachers told her repeatedly that Tatyana was incapable of participating because of her disability.

"I said, 'Let her just do everything everyone else does.' And they said, 'Well, she can't do everything.' And I said, 'How do you know? We haven't tried it.' And it didn't matter what it was—ice-sled hockey, snowmobiling, whatever . . . she would want to try and do it. And now she tells me she wants to go skydiving. Somebody said why doesn't she do the Iditarod✱?' I said, 'Please don't mention anything else to her. She'll say yes to everything.'

Ya sama. I can do this. You only know if you try. As I always tell my kids, "Imagine if you hadn't tried ice cream for the first time, or chocolate. You wouldn't know that you liked it." To which I get the eye roll. Do not be limited by what other people think you can do. Or what you are told you can do. Or what other people are doing. Resist the comparison trap and celebrate YOU. And equally important, *do not give up on* YOU.

✱*The Iditarod: a famous dogsled race that takes place every year in Alaska. From Wikipedia: The race is over 1,000 miles long and teams generally race through blizzards causing whiteout conditions, subzero temperatures and gale-force winds which can cause the windchill to reach −100 °F. Ummm. NO THANKS.*

Dr. Colleen Hacker often shares this story with our Leadership Academy gals. She would ask if we've noticed that it can take so little for people to give up on something. *Why* is there a tendency to quit something if you are not good at it? She would then say, "Imagine when a toddler is learning to walk. This toddler falls of course with those first steps. And imagine if after falling a couple times, the toddler says, "Well, it is *pretty clear*. I am certainly not cut out for this walking thing. I'm just gonna be a crawler for life."

And as I was remembering this scenario from Dr. Hacker, my mind went to the image of Tatyana crawling on the floor as a disabled child. Tatyana, of all people, had every excuse to be content with crawling. But instead Tatyana and her mom, Debbie, never listened to any of those people saying it wasn't possible. Instead, they approached life with a WHY NOT mentality. My friend Amy Jo Martin, a best-selling author, fabulous entrepreneur, and renegade thinker, calls them *"the why notters"* in her podcast Why Not Now? (Which is beyond excellent by the way.) The why notters. Those courageous souls who say *Why Not* when everyone else is asking *Why*.

Later in our #SockTalk, I asked Tatyana what she thought of the word *disability*:

> TATYANA: "The word *disability* is definitely not in my vocabulary. I never even see the word [prefix] *dis*; I just see the word *ability*. Because I think everyone has the ability to do something, no matter how you do it. It's just finding the ways to do it. I never saw myself as disabled, ever. I'm Tatyana McFadden, and I'm a Paralympic athlete, and a marathoner as well."

And let's add *rock star* to that list.

I want this entire answer from Tatyana hanging on my front door, my kids' doors, neighbors' doors, every schoolroom door . . . OK, I want it hanging on *every* door in the universe. Anyone (and that means all of us) who has ever doubted if they have the training or skills to get IT done needs to read this quote. Everyone has ability. Focus on what you *have*, not what you don't have. Focus on what makes you tick, and don't be confined to that unrealistic quest for perfection.

PERFECT SHMERFECT

Do you know of one person in your life who you think is absolutely perfect? And if you say yes, I would say, *Then you don't know her well enough.*

The only way you learn and grow and get better at life is by taking risks. By falling. By stepping out of your comfort zone. By saying YES, even when you are not sure you can do it. Stop looking for perfect. Perfect is boring and unhealthy—and frankly, impossible. As the great writer Anna Quindlen says so well:

"Nothing important, or meaningful, or beautiful, or interesting, or great ever came out of imitations. The thing that is really hard, and really amazing, is giving up on being perfect and beginning the work of becoming yourself."

One of the greatest strengths we women have is that we often make sure we are overly prepared to take on a task. One of the greatest weaknesses we women have is we often feel we can only do something when we are overly prepared. LET GO of the *I am not good enough, I am not skilled enough, I haven't prepared enough to be ready* mind-set. Resist the tendency to think we lack the proper skill set. Instead . . . raise your hand. Or, said in a different way by a woman who has now inspired a revolution, *LEAN IN.*

That woman is SHERYL SANDBERG, who calls the tendency to question one's ability "the imposter syndrome." Sandberg just happens to be Facebook's chief operating officer (COO—which basically means you run the show), the best-selling author of *Lean In*, and consistently one of *Fortune* magazine's most influential women. (She's No. *7 in the world* on the current list—ahead of, oh, just Oprah, Queen Elizabeth II, and Michelle Obama.). The imposter syndrome, she warns, is the phenomenon of capable people being plagued by self-doubt.

Sheryl and I spoke by telephonic #socktalk about how this self-doubt manifests itself.

 PERFECT.
I HOPE SHE HAS A MATCHING CAPE.

SHERYL: "What I learned when researching *Lean In* is that women feel 'the imposter syndrome' more intensely and more frequently than men. I also learned that with the same level of performance, men will estimate their performance higher and women will estimate their performance lower."

Sheryl goes on to say in *Lean In* (which, for the record, should be mandatory reading for all people of all ages and all genders) that multiple studies in multiple industries show that self-doubt is also more prevalent in women. Take the results of a study of medical students: when asked to evaluate themselves, female students gave themselves lower scores than the male students despite faculty evaluations that showed the women outperformed the men.

Jessica Mendoza also notes that this self-doubt brings hesitation. And hesitation means missed opportunities.

JESSICA: "We, as women, think we need to be perfect. *You don't have to be perfect.* I've been there, where I never wanted to raise my hand or jump into something because I felt I wasn't ready. I didn't feel I was 100 percent ready.

"But if you wait for that day to come, the opportunity will probably be gone, and really, no one is ever absolutely, perfectly ready for any situation. I've raised my hand now when I've been 30 percent ready, 40 percent ready. And I've figured it out."

That is right. *You will figure it out.* Trust that.

JUST GO DO IT DAMN IT!

(The Where the Magic Happens image is flashing not-so-subliminally at you right now.)

Yes. Go on. This reminds me of a great story I heard recently from Hall of Fame golfer **ANNIKA**

SORENSTAM, one of the best to ever play the game. Annika won eighty-nine tournaments on the LPGA tour, with ten of those wins being majors. Annika was so dominant in the early 2000s that she was asked to play in a tournament to take on the men (as in the professional men's golfing tour, the PGA).

Annika accepted the invitation to play in the 2003 Colonial PGA tourney because she knew the experience would challenge her and also make her better. She described the event as both *the most terrifying and the most fulfilling* moment of her career. Annika was so nervous she didn't think she would actually be able to place her golf ball on the tee for her first drive because she was literally shaking. Sorenstam remembered her caddy told her later that when she went to speak to him before her first tee shot, her lips were moving but nothing was coming out.

Now Sorenstam laughs as she recalls these moments. And then says, "For me it was not a mens or womens thing. It wasn't about who was better. It was about being the best me I could be." Annika recounted the real value in that experience: facing that fear and knowing she not only got through it, she grew from it.

Her PGA experience is even more impressive when you understand just how quiet Annika was as a child. Annika was so painfully shy as a young girl that she would purposefully *lose* in the final stretch of a tournament so that she would not have to stand on the podium and give a speech. She was terrified of speaking in public. The only problem? Her parents were onto her. I met up with Annika at the ANA Inspiring Women in Sports Conference. She told me about that moment:

"What happened is my parents called the tournament director for the next tournament and they came up with a plan. They decided the runner-up and the third-place finisher had to say something as well. I didn't know this of course. So we get to [the] next tournament, and I threw the tournament again. But this time when I get on the stage with my little trophy they say Annika, we would like you to say something as well.

"You can imagine my face. And my heart was like one of those cartoon characters with my heart bouncing out of my chest. Somehow, clutching the trophy, I mumbled a 'thank you,' and that is when I realized we all have to overcome our fears one way or another. I wasn't going to let that keep me from doing what I love to do and keep me from playing the very best I could. After that I said, 'OK, fear will not win . . . let's just go for it.'"

Hooray for parents!

SORRY, I DON'T KNOW WHAT GOT INTO ME.

That is right. Just go for it. Because when you do let go of that I AM NOT SURE I CAN DO THIS mind-set, your world opens up.

Doubt is a common emotion, even for someone like Robin Roberts, who has broken every mold for a woman getting into broadcast journalism. The key is not letting doubt define you. I asked Robin if she had those moments of doubt in the past:

ROBIN: "Oh, gosh. Now why do you say that in the *past tense*? Like I, like I don't have doubts now?! [*She then laughs.*] Yeah, especially when you're younger. And I remember being at ESPN.

That's all I ever wanted to do. I had hit the mother lode. In high school, I realized I wasn't gonna be a professional athlete. And I wanted to still have that life, and so that's when I said I'm going to be a sports journalist.

"This is 1979, when I graduated from high school. So I'm looking around. Well there are not many women doing sports on TV. And there sure as heck are not any black women doing sports on television. And I never thought, *Oh, I can't do it.* I was like, *OK. That's what I want to do.*"

I asked her where that courage comes from, and Robin immediately credits her parents for helping her believe that anything was possible. Her dad was a member of the Tuskegee Airmen, the first all-black flying Air Corps in the military. Her mom was very active in the community and the first African American to head Mississippi's Board of Education. "My mother and father were the first this, the first that. And were never on a soapbox telling you about it." Their courage gave Robin the confidence to leap:

ROBIN: "And we always think that if we don't see someone like ourselves doing something, it's a little more challenging. Because it's harder to visualize. But what's the worst thing that can happen? At least go for it, because when you get older, it's not those things you did you regret; it's those things you didn't do, or didn't try."

Ahhh, how I wish I had this nugget of advice from Robin Roberts when I was younger. Because the same thing happened to me. I wanted to be a sports announcer, but when I looked around, I didn't see many people like me doing what I wanted to do. So, I chose a different path. I chose medical school. (That noise you hear is me screaming.) But ultimately I decided that being a doctor was not the right fit for me. Robin, in all her wisdom, reminded me it was only a delay, not a setback:

"But this is the great thing. *You still did it.* You still did it. And that's the beauty of it. I always say **delays are not denials. What we want to do might be delayed, but it doesn't mean we're gonna be denied that opportunity.**"

And ain't that the truth. Delays are not denials. Hard to see this in the moment, but put it up on your mirror on a sticky note if you need to. Write it down:

confidence, though it may be delayed, will not be denied.

So don't wait for your New Year's resolutions to try something new. (Why do we do that by the way??!!). Just like you don't need Valentine's Day to tell someone how much they mean to you, we don't need the start of a new year to start thinking differently. Mend a broken friendship. Try a new thing (or fifty). Fall down. Get up. Fall down again. Get up again . . . and again and again. Sure, you will have scabby knees from falling, but life becomes a heck of a lot more fun. And most important, life starts to be lived from your inner core out, as YOU want to live: confidently you, authentically you, gloriously you.

LOOK OUT WORLD.

CHAPTER 4

THE NON-NEGOTIABLE CHAPTER

"I am convinced that life is 10% what happens to me and 90% how I react to it."

—Charles Swindoll

YEP. That's right. Welcome to the **non-negotiable** chapter. This is a must. So if you are not of the right mind-set *at the moment*, step away and come back to this. Because being the hardest worker on your team is not optional. Being a positive part of team chemistry is not optional. The best leaders I have ever been around set standards and, most important, live up to them.

No one will want to follow a leader who says, "OK everyone, here is what this team stands for! We stand for unity! For hard work! For working harder than anyone out there! For each other! For positive attitudes! For respectful and responsible behavior! For celebrating others! For battling until the very end!" But then, after saying all that, if she undercuts her credibility by sitting in the corner on her phone texting friends, while others get to work, it's meaningless. Or if that leader opts out of fitness and training. Or if that leader quits when things go poorly. Or that leader acts more interested in attaining personal goals and success rather than team success. **_UGHHHHHH_ (and a low growl).**

You all know what I am talking about. You've seen it—and you may have even been it—but no more.

Because here's the best part of this form of leadership. I'm not talking about being the best player on the team, the best passer, the best student in the room, the best artist, the best _____ (fill in the blank).

I am simply talking about being the best **YOU**. I am talking about attitude and effort. The two things YOU control. **ATTITUDE and EFFORT**. Yes, you may have heard this from your parents or from a teacher (and ignored them); but think about it for a second. You wake up every day and get to decide the effort and attitude you bring to everything in your life. To school, to homework, to sports, to work, to whatever group you belong. You decide. That is so dang cool. So why not decide to bring a great attitude and maximum effort.

And here is what I love: Attitude and effort don't know if you are a super-talented person or just a beginner. They don't know if you are the president or the youngest on the job. Even better, they don't care. They only ask that you honor them.

Things you can't control:
parents
teachers
mean girls
the weather
bad hair days

Things you can control:
attitude
effort
confidence

I am thrilled to introduce you to a thought leader in standards and excellence, a legendary coach who won eleven National Softball championships while at UCLA (most by any softball coach), and a life coach who drops wisdom like she's delivering a slot machine jackpot: the great SUE ENQUIST. Sue and I live in the same town in Southern California, so we met at my house over socks and sunglasses of course. #SockTalkSoCalStyle.

IF NOT FOR SUE'S RECENT SHOULDER SURGERY, THIS WOULD HAVE BEEN A #SOGGYSOCKTALK ON A PADDLEBOARD.

Despite the change in venue, Sue was quite willing to share and advise:

SUE: "I think what I'm most proud of in my story is I'm not the girl that did it right all the time. I'm an average kid that lived an extraordinary life. Most important in that is *I was average*. Average body, average skill set, average aptitude. I have so many flaws in who I am, but I was raised by people who said just get better. Just get better. Just get better. And **don't get stuck in your junk**. They didn't allow me to sit in my self-pity or sit in my doubt. Because it just wasn't efficient."

DON'T GET STUCK
IN YOUR JUNK

One of my favorite Sue Enquist sayings, in case you missed it, is, *"Don't get stuck in your junk."* That deserves a bumper sticker or at least a Best Worst* celebratory jig. Such an all-embracing principle for life.

But I digress. Sue went on to say,

> "My dad was an engineer, and a military guy. People would think he expected me to be perfect; but he just expected me to get better every day. And when you do fall, be the first up after failure. And my mother, a nurse, said, *YOU CAN FLY*. Just flap those wings and stay positive. Things will work out."

Sue was taught from an early age that attitude and effort were non-negotiable. They were standards that every Enquist held near and dear. Because here is one thing we all know:

Setbacks (i.e., JUNK) are part of life.

They happen. That is a fact. Life will bring speed bumps . . . guaranteed. You get cut from your team.

SELF

*If you don't remember what a Best Worst jig is, you must reread the exercise at the end of Chapter 2. Because Best Worst *will become* a global sensation. Really.

You do poorly in a class. You are told you are not good enough at work. Where or what doesn't really matter.

But **HOW** you react is the key. When life throws something negative at you (for simplicity's sake, let's use getting dropped from the starting lineup as our example) you have two choices:

1) You can decide to sulk and mope and sigh out loud and feel that life is unfair and ask *WHY ME?* and *What did I do to deserve this?!* You can talk about how crazy the coach is and how hard you have worked and that you CANNOT believe this is even happening to you!

OR

2) You can decide that yes, life sometimes stinks and I didn't want this to happen, but I am going to bust my butt to get back to that starting role. I am going to get fitter, faster, stronger, and smarter. I am going to show my coach and teammates that I want to be in the mix, I want to get back on the field, but that I am going to do this in a positive way. I am not going to ask my coach or boss *WHY ME*, but instead ask what I can do to get better.

GROAN or GROW.

Mope or Motivate. Those are your choices. Choose the latter. Own it and move on. Be the person who chooses to grow rather than groan. Be the one whom teammates turn to and think, WOW, I love that attitude. I love her approach to life and to being challenged. I am not asking you to be content in a "reserve," backup role . . . not at all. Nor am I saying it's easy.

But guess what? You are not the first to lose a starting position, nor the last. And no one else liked it either. So you can decide to be the one on the bench with her head down, bringing the entire team down, or you can be the teammate on the bench cheering and celebrating the collective success (and, equally important, focused on getting back to that starting spot). And remember, you will always have to live with that decision, that either/or, as Sue Enquist explains:

> "When you make poor decisions in the moment, and try to justify them as oh, I was in a bad place, or oh, I'm just supercompetitive, **you can't un-ring that bell**. I'm big on being accountable. Own it. Sit in that and say, 'I will never be able to un-ring that bell.'"

Just don't sit in it for long. The choice is yours and yours only. Groan or grow.

THE POWER OF POSITIVE

And to help you choose wisely, here is one of the best examples of the power of positive attitude: my dear friend AMY LISS, who is a key part of our Julie Foudy Sports Leadership Academy staff. Due to a lack of oxygen to her brain during her premature birth, Amy was born with spastic quadrapeligic cerebral palsy. She needs help with all her daily living skills because she has limited independent functioning of her arms and legs.

I met Amy about ten years ago. Every summer at our Leadership Academy in Chicago, we would do community service at a local Easterseals affiliate. (Easterseals is a wonderful nonprofit that has been helping people with disabilities and special needs for over a hundred years.)

SELF

And every summer, Amy Liss, who is both a client and volunteer there, would greet us at the door and give our JFSLA girls a tour of their amazing facility.

Well, we all fell in love with Amy's positivity and humor. I still kick myself that it took me about five years before I finally had this epiphany: WHY IS AMY LISS NOT WORKING WITH US AT OUR ACADEMY?!! When I asked her if she would come spend a week with us each summer, she responded, "I think you have had heatstroke." Ha. Nope. Since then, Amy and her incredible mom, Kathy, have spent the week with us at our Leadership Academy every year. And it has been the best epiphany I've ever had.

I am thrilled that you, too, now get to meet—as we call her—THE Amy Liss. We sat down at her home in Downers Grove, Illinois, for our **#SockTalk**, where Amy's socks blew away the competition. No surprise there.

> **JULIE**: "Let's start with the most important aspect of this interview. Our socks. What are you rocking today, Amy?"

> **AMY**: "I'm rocking one Nemo and one Dory. They're mismatched, so they're cool."

(NOTE: DO NOT BE FOOLED BY MY SOCKS PRETENDING TO BE SNEAKERS, OR AMY'S PRETENDING TO BE FISH).

My kids would agree. And I, once again, borrowed a pair from Izzy.

JULIE: "Okay, let's go all the way back; Amy, take me back to the day you were born. Who's older, you or Kelly [Amy's twin sister]?"

AMY: "I am by thirty seconds."

JULIE: "*Yessss.* Thirty seconds? I never knew that."

AMY: "Yep. My mom had an emergency C-section because we were born three months early and I weighed one pound, fourteen ounces, was twelve inches long."

JULIE: "One pound, fourteen ounces?"

AMY: "Yep. They called Kelly 'The Big One' because she was two pounds, four ounces, 12 ¼ inches long [Amy smiles]."

Amy has never been able to do the very things we take for granted every day. She can't shower on her own, ride a bike, drink a glass of water, or eat ice cream. A wheelchair helps her get around. She needs assistance to get in and out of bed, to eat, and to do life's basic functions. Yet, despite her seeming lack of independence, Amy always sees the positive.

JULIE: "How frustrating does that get?"

AMY: "I'm used to it. But sometimes I wish I could just do things a little bit quicker; but that's why I'm extremely patient. I'm lucky that my mind works pretty well most of the time. [*She smiles. Amy has an incredible mind and memory.*] And I have good cognition and a voice. A lot of people born with cerebral palsy as severe as me don't have a voice and need a communication device or a special computer to help them talk, so I'm lucky in that respect.

"My voice is my biggest asset, so I like to use it when I can. But the type of cerebral palsy I have affects every muscle in my body, so even my vocal cords sometimes get tired. There's nothing wrong with them, but every muscle inside my body is tight. I had speech therapy from when I was five months old through third grade, but I always tell people once I started talking, I haven't stopped [*another smile*]."

JULIE: "Yet you have every right to complain about a lot of things. And you don't."

AMY: "No, and I get angry at myself when I do complain a little bit because you don't have to look very far to find people that are a lot worse off than me, so I just try and be grateful every day. I mean, I try and be positive 98 percent of the time."

Above Amy's bed, on her ceiling, is a quote that she wakes up to every day. It says,

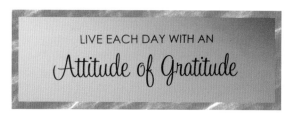

LIVE EACH DAY WITH AN
Attitude of Gratitude

AMY: "That's my motto in life. I look up and I remember those words every day. I try and remember them as I go out and attempt to make a difference in people's lives every day."

Hmmm. Imagine if we all woke up each day with an attitude of gratitude.

Here's another powerful example of how life can either be about what happens to you or about how you react to what life gives you. Meet FAHIMA NOORI, an eighteen-year-old from Farah, Afghanistan. Fahima  has five sisters and a brother. When Fahima was only a year old, something happened to her and her family that would alter their lives forever. Fahima's father worked with the Afghanistan government when the country came under Taliban control. And although I don't often play the role of history professor, I do think it is important to understand some background on the Taliban before I go any further with Fahima's story.

The Taliban are an ultraconservative political and religious faction that emerged in Afghanistan in the mid-1990s after the former Soviet Union withdrew its troops from the country. The Taliban immediately enforced a strict interpretation of Islamic law that wiped out human rights in that country, particularly for women. It has been said by the Physicians for Human Rights (PHR) that "no other regime in the world has methodically and violently forced half of its population (women) into virtual house arrest, prohibiting them from leaving their houses on pain of physical punishment."

Women were forced to stay inside at all times. They

were not allowed to go to school or get an education, and they had to be completely covered (head to toe) if they did go out in public. If you lived in Afghanistan and did not abide by the Taliban's strict Islamic code of law, you could be beaten or killed. So when the Taliban took control of the government (when Fahima was a one-year-old), the Taliban tried to kill Fahima's father, since he was part of the prior Afghan government.

FAHIMA: "At that time, the Taliban tried to throw rockets into people's homes, and one of them was at our home. I was asleep when they threw the rocket into our house while my mom was busy with

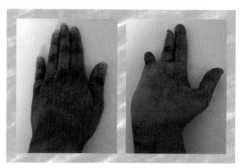

some chores, and my father wasn't home. When the rocket hit, the curtains and other things in the house caught fire. So then they fell on my clothes and my clothes caught fire . . . and my face was burned by the fire, and also my fingers. I lost three of my fingers at that time. And also, my right eye lost its vision. Also, parts of the right side of my body have been damaged a lot."

"At that time, we all escaped to the mountains.

Fahima and her family were forced to live in hiding for months in the mountains of Afghanistan. They eventually moved to nearby Iran "to save ourselves" and get the children back in school. And that is when Fahima started to realize she looked different from others.

"When I started school, day by day I realized that in fact, I was not born this way. I would look around and see my classmates who were very different from me. When I entered the classroom, no one was willing to sit with me. The way they looked at me was very disappointing. They would say, 'What is this? We are scared of her.' After a while, when I grew up, I learned about the accident. The accident happened when I was younger, but I had the scars that stayed with me forever. I have many unpleasant memories from school, from walking on the streets and wherever I went."

Fahima spoke about young children seeing her and crying because they were afraid of her; of how difficult it was to comprehend the emotions toward her at that time. She also spoke about how challenging those times were for her because she knew her scars would not go away.

"It was not something to deal with for a day or even a year. I always thought I would stay like this for the rest of my life. When I would stand in front of the mirror, I would always be thinking, 'How long will this last?'"

And then Fahima experienced a pivotal moment in her life that changed her focus from external to internal: she finished with the best grades in her class in school, and the class started to see how smart she was.

"That is when everyone understood that my talent is not like my appearance, and I'm stronger internally. But even with my success in school at that time, I still thought appearance was important, and never thought a girl like me could do well.

"[That was] until I watched a short documentary about a woman who was a mother and had no hands, and she was also an artist. That is when I looked at myself and said, 'I have everything. I have eyes and I have hands. I can reach my goals if I want.' That is when I started to focus on my internal talent, not my external appearance."

Never underestimate the power of one story, one example in giving others hope.

From that moment on, instead of having a negative reaction to how people treated her, Fahima turned it into a positive:

> "Every time I thought about my bitter experiences, it gave me more energy to work harder and study to get myself out of that situation. Day by day, as I was getting older, I learned that what happened to me was for my benefit. I stand where I am today because of that incident. This was an opportunity for me to show my talent to people."

BRING IT AND SING IT

The power of attitude in life—it really is a beautiful thing. Sometimes it takes people decades to get there, if at all. Fahima learned early the benefits of turning a negative into a positive. And even if you doubt how you are going to get through that moment of crisis, trust that you will indeed get through it. Like Robin Roberts on the day she found out she had breast cancer.

> ROBIN: "I didn't know. I'm like everybody else. I'm as shocked as everybody else. And you just figure it out. I remember when I was not sure how I was gonna find that strength. And, I tell people, it's all in us, we're all a little bit stronger than we think we are. And it's not the way I would have chosen to be tested, but it's the way it was chosen for me. And we all have our tests. And I'm just really grateful that I tapped into it in some kind of way. You just find a way."

Maybe, and hopefully it is not cancer you are fighting, but life has its way of tossing hurdles in front of you. Whether it is something as permanent as cerebral palsy or something that can be as fleeting as self-doubt, how you react is everything. You are not alone, as Alex Morgan points out here while talking about how she bounces back from setbacks in soccer and in life:

> ALEX: "For me it's having that mind-set of being positive or waking up and feeling like you have a fresh start on things. I try to just keep my head moving forward, so much more than looking back."

JULIE: "How do you do that? That's so healthy."

ALEX: "It's always knowing that you have an opportunity to either change or improve who you are, or be the person that you're striving to be. An opportunity to accomplish the goals you've literally written down, year after year, and then going for it. **I count the good things, not the bad.**"

Amazing what you can accomplish when you bring both attitude and effort to the table.

And if bringing both to the table seems about as realistic as understanding $E = MC^2$, then press reset.

Go back to what makes your soul leap. What makes you excited. Find your dream team of supporters. Find your happy place. Seek the joy in things and people. And equally important, **get the "Debbie Downers" out of your life.** (*Debbie Downers*? They're those people [see *Saturday Night Live* for a quick reference] who consistently tell you why you CANNOT do something or whine their way through every activity. Or both.)

And if *YOU* are the Debbie Downer, do something about it. NOW! Because you can.

Attitude and effort. You can't ask it of others if you are not willing to bring it yourself. That's right. That applies to sports and, most important, to LIFE. Friend and fellow JFSLA cofounder, Todd Smith, always says,

"Bring it, don't sing it."

To which I say,

"Bring it AND sing it!"

(Either way, the bringing part is mandatory.)
So say it . . . because you can.

EXERCISE:

How often do we stop the crazy speed of life and take a quiet moment to think: WHO OR WHAT DOES INSPIRE ME? WHAT WILL MAKE ME WANT TO JUMP OUT OF BED EACH DAY AND BE INSPIRED TO GIVE MAXIMUM EFFORT AND A POSITIVE ATTITUDE? WHAT TRULY MAKES ME HAPPY, MOTIVATED, AND EXCITED TO BE A BETTER ATHLETE, A BETTER FRIEND, A BETTER PERSON?

It is such a healthy exercise. And one that seldom happens due to the fast-paced lifestyles we all lead. Do me a favor and try this. It won't take long:

Right now (or else it won't get done), write down three people who make you want to be better. It could be a friend, a parent, a coach, a teacher, or even a random stranger who said or did something that made you want to do/be more. Next to their name, write just a few words about WHY they inspire you.

Now write down three places or things or activities that make your heart race and make you laugh out loud. For example, I love quotes. Quotes make me want to run on the field with my American flag drapped like a cape, belting out our national anthem, Elvis Presley style. I used to read books crammed with quotes before every game.

And finally, write down your go-to karaoke song (always important to know).

The key is to figure out what makes you tick. That may take some time, internal reflection, and quiet moments. Once you figure out the people, places, and things in life that bring out the best YOU, keep those people and things close. And thank them often. We all need inspirational, positive people around us. We all need a support network. We all need our happy place. Make sure you know where it is, and then go there often. Make happy your everyday reality. Because you can.

DON'T JUST
THINK IT, INK IT

"Your attitude, not your aptitude, will determine your altitude."

—Zig Ziglar

SECTION 2

TEAM

Let's venture to the second ring, shall we . . . to TEAM. So now we take all those wonderful skill sets you just learned about regarding your leadership style, work ethic, and positive attitude and we push them to a wider ring. A ring that encompasses your team. That team may be your sports team or chess team, or drama club, or student council or community service team; or it could also be your work team or family, or (well, you get it).

I love this section. Because having a productive, successful team is not about one person or one part of that team. A successful team means everyone contributes. When I look back over my U.S. team career, our most successful teams, which won World Cups and Olympic medals, had one common denominator: we ALL contributed to positive team chemistry. We trusted in each other, and at the end of the day played for each other.

When you can build that unity in any group, it is like harnessing a super power. But harnessing such force is something that does not just happen. You have to actively work on creating that special trust and bond. So coming up are some tips to get you there. And setting your standards and culture is the perfect place to start.

"Let's start at the Very Beginning ... it's a very good place to start."

That beautiful shrieking you hear is me singing.

CHAPTER 5

GOOD
vs. GREAT

"It always seems impossible until it's done."

—Nelson Mandela

There is good and then there is great. Two *very different* things. Yes, there are a lot of very good teams. There are a lot of very good companies. But how many teams or companies are truly *great*? And what makes a good team turn into a great team? Just like there are a ton of good athletes out there. But what makes an athlete not just good, but great?

Consistency. Or, more precisely, being consistently great is key. The great athletes, the great teams, the great companies, regardless of the opponent and the situation, figure out a way to make their standard *consistently great*.

Hmmm, standards. I love them. Yet too often they become a parameter set by others.

We live in a world that wants to outsource standards.

Players look to a coach to define the standards for a team. At work, we look for our boss to do that. And in school, we turn to our teacher. My coach says I need to work harder. My dad says I should run more. My teacher says I have to focus more.

What about you?! Do you know what makes you tick and what makes you timid? If you don't know, start paying attention. Sure, coaches, bosses, and teachers absolutely can help set the tone of a group. They can lay down the goals. But I think a truly successful team, in any forum, has to set its culture and standards from *within*. By within I mean you. YOU have to want it. Not a parent, not a coach, not a teacher, a trainer, or a friend, but you. You have to personally decide that mediocre is not good enough. And not good enough for the team. That you want to be the best that you can be, every single day.

On the U.S. women's soccer team, our very first captain was **APRIL HEINRICHS**. April was the kind of person who would gladly rip your heart out to win a "friendly" game of Pictionary. And I loved it. Because April had standards. She wanted to win and she wanted to win everything, in any forum, now and through eternity. And she didn't apologize for it. Most important, she backed it up with effort and a positive attitude (echo echo echo).

And it became contagious. April's competitive spirit made all those around her better. We'd play a game of Spoons and leave bloody (and hoarse from laughing).

IF YOU HAVE NEVER PLAYED SPOONS, DO NOT SAY THAT OUT LOUD. GO PLAY IT NOW.

TEAM

WHOLESOME DISCONTENT

Before continuing, let me point out a very important matter: there are standards and then there is obsessing over standards. One is healthy, the other is not.

We called our drive to improve on the U.S. team **"wholesome discontent."**

That meant constantly pushing each other to be better in a healthy, positive way. The *wholesome* part is important, as we all have seen the unhealthy side of never thinking you are good enough, smart enough, strong enough, whatever. Our goal was never perfection. Our goal was *growth*. And equally important, helping each other get there.

The unwholesome discontent can come in different forms. I've had friends who go from wanting to eat better/be fitter to an eating disorder. I've had teammates go from a healthy work ethic to an obsessive exercise routine that leads to constant injuries and fatigue. And of course there is the constant search for *perfection*, which can lead to extreme mental stress. Understand the difference and keep it healthy, or have others help you define healthy if you cannot.

Let's make a pact: if a friend seems to be struggling with the *wholesome* part of the equation, as uncomfortable as it may be, ask if you can help that friend. Or alert someone in a position to help. Sometimes it takes a friend pointing out the issue to get a person to wake up to the fact that there may, in fact, be an issue.

We as a team decided early on that we would tap into that wholesome discontent. Our U.S. Women's National Team would always possess something we could control. We would be GRITTY. We would be scrappy. We would be fighters. We knew that if we weren't the most skilled team out there at times, we were always the most committed. If we at least fought, we had a chance. And then, once we added in sophistication, team chemistry, skill, and technique, well, *look the hell out.*

But GRIT was the standard. Grit was mandatory. And guess what? Because we as players set the standards, if we weren't living up to them, we had no coach, no parent, no teacher to blame. We had only each other to look at. And my goodness, you didn't want to let down your teammate. Funny how that whole accountability thing works. Mia Hamm spoke about accountability as it related to our longtime captain, Carla Overbeck:

> **MIA:** "In the end, Carla wasn't asking you to do anything she wouldn't do herself. I know for me personally, I wanted to make her proud when I was out there because you already saw through her play and her organization and her commitment that she was already doing it. So it's like her asking you to track or mark in the box, or, you know, get your head out of your a--! She was already doing it."

And Carla was the first person to help us *get to* that standard as well. She would run with us, encourage us, help us be successful in any way she could . . . whatever it took to ensure we could be our best. But Carla wasn't alone. There were players like Kristine Lilly ("Lil"), who blew through fitness tests like they were a Sunday stroll in the park. Carla's and Lil's abilities to both be accountable and hold others accountable meant there was a sense of pride and respect among teammates. We didn't dare come in unfit or unprepared, because it would be an insult to the player next to us. How dare I complain about running in my outdoor surroundings in sixty-five-degree sunshine in California, especially when I knew Lil was doing it in the snow. That Joy Fawcett was doing it between breast-feeding her children (yes, superhero). Or when I knew teammate Michelle Akers had chronic fatigue and was battling to feel well enough just to be active. We came in ready, prepared, eager to get better, regardless of our role on the team. We were

TEAM

in it *together*. Alex Morgan spoke about this very thing with her longtime teammate, Heather O'Reilly:

ALEX: "That's something special, too, with Heather O'Reilly. When she asks me to grind in and work a little extra hard, I know she would also do it. She's the fittest on our team. She's always up and down the flanks, so I feel like when she tells me to get it together, I'm like, 'I have to do it for HAO [*Heather's nickname*]. I have to do it.'"

I'LL TAKE THE
VW VAN, THANKS

When I look at great teams or great companies, it is clear the two elements they understand so well are standards and culture. And in my opinion, standards and culture are intertwined. Standards are the bar you set. Culture is how you get there, how you treat each other.

Standards are the checkpoints and the end destination on a trip. Culture is the full journey to get there. Standards make sure you get to that end point. Culture dictates *how* you get there. (I'll take the VW van over the Porsche, thank you.)

Both are reliant on the other if you want a happy, successful team. And both are important because when a new player joins the team or enters into the group, there is a foundation they know to respect and build upon. I don't think you can *successfully* have one without the other. With only standards and no positive team culture, the standards become more a chore than a shared dream. They become the long ride in the car with no bathroom stops, no snacks, and no music. All you think about is the end point, rather than how much you love the scenery.

On the flip side, when you just have a positive culture but no standards, the team may be a whole lotta "fun," but complacency becomes acceptable. You may be blasting music, singing gloriously, and eating Cheetos the entire ride, but, oh, wait, you never made it to New York! Because you got lost in Kansas!! When there is a collective belief in the team standards *AND* culture— what this team values, what this team stands for, what this team wants to accomplish, and how this team wants to accomplish that—they work their own magic. **Standards and culture become that beautiful reminder to: a) join the family, or b) go home.** And teammates take great pride in helping the team constantly grow in a positive, healthy way.

When you find a team or entity that values standards and culture, hug it tight. And if you are still seeking that team, help yours get there. Because you can. Getting your standards and culture right reverberates to all points in your life. Your friendships become more meaningful, your family life becomes richer, and your dreams become more tangible.

Amy Liss said it so well:

> "My teammates have allowed me to do things I never thought possible."

On the U.S. women's soccer team, we decided what we wanted our standards and culture to be.

Our standard was simple: To be the best in the world. Not once, not twice, but Every. Single. Day.

We expected to be standing on the top podium. Period. And equally important, to be helping each other get there in a positive, wholesomely discontent way.

For our culture, we valued shared responsibility and humility.

Carla Overbeck would be the first to grab the ball bag. Mia Hamm would carry the water. Joy Fawcett would pick up cones. The veterans would be the first to pick up the equipment bags when traveling. Because when your captain, the superstar of the team, and veterans are humble doers, so is everyone else, or they get reminded pretty quickly. It's what I did to a young player not helping carry the gear: "Who are you? The Queen of England? Pick up some gear please." She promptly did.

Robin Roberts, one of the most gracious and humble women I know, shared something she learned from her mom in regards to the importance of humility and kindness:

> ROBIN: "My mom taught me—when you strut, you stumble. Don't think you're all that. Don't think you're all that and a bag of chips. And I think if everybody was just a bit more humble, especially our leaders, especially those people who are in positions of influence and power, we all would benefit. Just knock it down. Just knock it down a notch, you know? You're not all that. You're not; you're not different."

So true. I have little tolerance for strutters on any team in life. Strutters detract from the team's goal because they make it about the strutter. Hey everyone, check me out. Look at how great I did. Aren't I so dang fabulous? No, no you are not. You are exhausting. And really, if you have to strut, then to me, you might as well just put a flashing sign over your head.

ATTENTION
I AM STRUTTING TO OVERCOMPENSATE FOR THE FACT THAT I HAVE LITTLE REASON TO BE STRUTTING

TEAM

The easy solution is to avoid strutters. And I used to do that. It was much easier to just say, I have no time for you in my life. But what I thankfully learned over the years is how can I blame the strutter without first trying to show her or him a better path. Maybe they have just never been made aware of other options. If you can show the "strutter" the value of doing rather than talking, the value of performing rather than prancing, they can become positive members of your group. Because often the issue comes from a place of insecurity, rather than arrogance. Invest in their growth and their confidence. Now, having said that, if it just comes from a place of arrogance, well then I say **GOOD RIDDANCE**. :)

For our culture . . . we valued family.

And that meant when a young player beame a member of the National Team for the first time, we invited her in. We would go out of our way to welcome her into the group. We valued all staff as being an integral part of that family. And I love to see this has been passed on now by the younger players, like Alex Morgan, who displays this when she talks to me about her leadership style:

ALEX: "For me, leadership is on the field and off the field . . . going to a younger player's room that I usually wouldn't feel comfortable with, but just having a chat with them. And say, 'Hey, what are you doing? You know, what do you need help with? How is the training camp going so far?'

"It's kind of nerve-racking to go to someone's room you don't know or, at dinner, to sit with players that you wouldn't usually strike up a casual conversation with. Even though I'm nervous and I feel like that's a little out of my comfort zone, I go back to *how would they feel?*"

MIA: "They're probably like, '*Holy crap*, Alex Morgan is sitting here.'"

JULIE: "Asking me how I'm doing!"

MIA: "That awkward silence."

ALEX: "Asking me if I need help with my high school homework."

JULIE: "That goes so far, too, because I still have, to this day, players who came in and out of the National Team, who weren't there very long, but will come and say, 'You know, one of my lasting memories is you came up to me, or Mia came up to me, or Carla, or whoever it was and said, *'Hey, how's it going? I'm so glad you're here.'* You know, it doesn't mean you won't kick the Sh*t out of them on the field, but just that moment of . . ."

MIA: "I mean, we're *kind of happy* you're here. What position do you play?" [*followed by laughter*]

And it's so easy to do. What a difference a *few minutes* can make. Literally, a few minutes of just reaching out to make others feel part of the group. What if you just took a few minutes out of every day to reach out to someone new. Or someone on your team. Or someone in a class you're taking. In fact, don't just think about it. Try it. Sit next to someone new on the bus. Eat with someone different. Stop and say hello to someone in the hallway rather than just shuffling along.

Strike up a conversation on the elevator. (Why do heads all go down when you step on an elevator BTW?!) Say hello. Smile. You will be blown away by just how quickly you can make a team or group stronger by making these small efforts (small moments, huge impact). Trust me. Or even better, trust Mia:

MIA: "I think it's stressful, not just for the players that have been there, but obviously the new players stepping in; they don't know if this is their first or their last time in. I think the most important thing is creating that understanding that it is a program and not just a bunch of individuals coming in."

JULIE: "A family."

TEAM

MIA: "Yeah, helping them understand that even though we're competing for certain positions, we're all trying to accomplish the same goal, which is to make this team as good as we possibly can. You know, win world championships and win Olympic gold medals."

And clearly, valuing family does not just apply to winning world championships and Olympic medals. It applies to any team or group that wants to outperform their goals. When people connect emotionally and feel they're a part of something bigger than themselves, they do things bigger than themselves. Just like Paralympian Tatyana McFadden discovered with her collective family:

TATYANA: "Team is so important: my family—that's my parents and my sisters. But also the coaches and the teammates are a huge team as well. They push me and drive me every single day, through my failures and successes, to be a better me. To be a better Tatyana."

And last, but certainly not least, for our culture . . . we valued positivity.

At the end of the day, you can have all the best players in the world on your team, but if they do not bring joy to what you are doing, you will never reach your full potential as a group. This notion of joy and positivity does not get talked about enough in my opinion. We thought a lot about it on our team: regardless of your role, whether you played *a lot* or a little, each and every player affects the energy of the team. Seek those who treasure positivity. Alex Morgan agrees:

ALEX: "It's the people you surround yourself with, that's so important and that's always who I fell back on when I needed confidence. And that doesn't have to be your family always. That could be a teammate. For me, a lot of times that was Abby [Wambach]. Because when you're in high school, at that age, you feel like everything you face is the end of the world. And I still struggle with that sometimes, especially with injuries . . .

just being out and not being able to contribute on the field and help your teammates in the way that you're so used to. You have to figure out another way to be yourself but also how to be a positive part of the team."

Amy Liss knows a lot about the importance of having a positive team around her as well. She depends on that team every single day of her life. Her mom and dad, twin sister, Kelly, and younger sister, Lindsay, form the immediate team. But Amy points out others also are vital:

> AMY: "My team is forever growing, which is really fun. My team is how I get through each day, from my family to therapists to friends to professional athletes who have joined my team that I never thought possible. They just keep me going. They're like a spiritual vitamin."

Hmmm, find your "spiritual vitamin." Value those teammates who affect the team positively. And celebrate them.

And here's a friendly reminder: you, as a member of a team, *regardless of your role*, can impact that positive culture. In fact, you *must* if you want to be not just great, but consistently great. Stop outsourcing those standards and culture. You set the foundation for your team. Yep, you. Go get your team on board.

DEFINE YOUR GOALS, YOUR DREAMS, YOUR WAY.

And here is how you get started . . .

EXERCISE:

TEAM BANNER (name it as you wish . . . maybe you have a slogan or a saying on your team/group/club . . . whatever you name it, DO NOT name it "Team Banner.")

On a large poster board, collectively create what your team banner looks like. Make it with pride. What matters to your group? What words, images, etc do you want to write/draw on this banner. Make it yours.

WITH YOUR ENTIRE TEAM, COME TO A CONSENSUS ON WHAT MATTERS TO THIS GROUP AND WHAT THOSE STANDARDS LOOK LIKE. RUN IT BY YOUR COACH/TEACHER/ADVISER WHEN YOU ARE DONE. GET THEIR APPROVAL AND THOUGHTS. BUT IF THAT PERSON TRIES TO TAKE OVER THIS EXERCISE, YOU HAVE MY PERMISSION TO KICK HIM OR HER OUT OF THE ROOM. :)

OUR MISSION: What do we want to be remembered for?

OUR STANDARDS: What do we want to accomplish? What are our goals?

OUR CULTURE: What does that look like? How do we treat each other? What do we value as a team?

Then have the entire team sign the poster. Put it somewhere you all can see it, or bring it to key events and moments.

TEAM

DON'T JUST
THINK IT, INK IT

CHAPTER 6

LAUGHTER
PERMITTED

"Attitudes are contagious; is yours worth catching?"

—Unknown

People often ask me what was THE most important key to our U.S. National Team's success over the years. After many years of pondering this, I've come to a realization and I think people just about choke when I say the No. 1 reason was . . . (wait for it). . . .

LAUGHTER.

We laughed all the time and everywhere. It is also the thing I miss the most from my playing days. It didn't matter where we were. There was laughter in the halls, on the bus, in the locker room, and on the field. We just had so much darn fun together. There were practical jokes, pranks, and plenty of bad karaoke. (Yes, be thankful Twitter, Instagram, and social media were not around yet.) We enjoyed working hard, playing hard, and giggling just as hard. And because we enjoyed what we were doing so much, we worked incredibly hard at getting better.

TEAM

Complacency was not allowed.

And that is why I am saddened when I see many teams so very serious about what they do. The parents, the coaches, the players . . . everyone and everything just seems so intense. I am not sure when laughter and winning became mutually exclusive concepts in sports (and too often in life). When did happiness and success become opposing forces? Because it sure seems like many teams out there today think to be successful they have to be *very serious*. There's not a lot of smiling going on. Instead, it feels like a whole 'lotta pressure. When did celebration and jubilation mean you were not competitive enough?

UGGGHHH, and yes, I am growling.

My mission is to bring the joy back in sports and to all things pressure-related in life. (How about that for being specific?) Even if it is to one reader at a time. Because the power of laughter and positivity is real.

ENERGY SUCKERS

When happiness and joy become part of the culture of your group, of your team, of your organization, its force will be felt. I love the challenges to building positive team chemistry because:

1) EVERYONE PLAYS A CRITICAL ROLE IN HELPING CREATE POSITIVE TEAM CHEMISTRY.

2) ANYONE CAN BE POSITIVE (IT'S A CHOICE, AS WE DISCUSSED IN THE SELF SECTION).

3) YET, EVERYONE MUST BUY INTO POSITIVE.

Sounds simple enough. But let me be clear here with what I mean by positive. I'm not talking about the oh-my-gosh-everything-is-*sooooooo*-great-and-wonderful-and-always-perfect positive (said with a girlie-girl accent and high-pitched enthusiasm). That positive is just downright *annoying*. Because it's not real. Life is not always perfect (thank goodness; that would be boring). I think I'd rather eat fish heads with eyeballs for breakfast every day than listen to someone talk like that incessantly. I am talking about understanding the power of positive body language, positive mind-sets, and positive decision-making. Because if your team gets this, you are already #winning.

Now to the buy-in part.

We have all been on a team where one person in the group pulls the team's energy down. Whether that person is not doing well, not getting along well with others, or maybe just not feeling well, it doesn't matter. The end result is the same: they become an energy drain. An ENERGY SUCK. And, full disclosure, like strutters, I have little tolerance for energy suckers. Because I consider it a selfish act. I consider it a distraction from the goal. But again I learned that before we blame the energy sucker, we must first show that person a better choice. Invest the time and energy into helping that teammate understand the importance of buying in. We called those moments "*interventions*." :) Most often they work and sometimes they don't, but there's nothing lost, and lots to be gained, by simply trying.

WOULD YOU DATE
YOUR INNER VOICE?

And sure, attitudes come in all shapes and sizes. But in general, it is pretty simple:

You are either helping or you are hurting.

So first figure out where you fall on that seesaw. Am I helping or hurting with my attitude? And if you are not sure, it's time to start thinking about what your attitude does to the rest of the team. Energy suckers have decided that it is more important to complain about the reason they are frustrated—coach, teammate, boss, injury, poor performance, whatever—than to focus on getting better or making things better. It is more important to that individual to visibly (or maybe less visibly but still present) make it known she or he is not happy with the situation.

I do not mean to diminish just how *very hard* it is to NOT be doing well on a team or within a group. It completely stinks. It hurts. Your stomach is in knots and you feel like you want to scream or run or get OUT OF THERE. I've been there and it's a terrible feeling. But how you react in those moments is something I learned to control.

Because that is just it, you either control your attitude or you let your attitude control you.

I am not asking you to suppress that emotion. No, in fact, give yourself a quick moment to let 'er rip (*in your mind*), but then control it, and flip it back to a positive place.

Sue Enquist, told me how she got her players to do just that—to *recalibrate* their negative thoughts. Sue asked them, "WOULD YOU DATE YOUR INNER VOICE?" If not, you need to recalibrate the voice inside your head. Sue noted,

> "You don't have to work on your negative talk track—it comes automatically as a female. You need to learn your positive talk track. You're gonna learn how to say it. You're gonna write it down, because we know when you write things down it activates a different part of the brain."

Now if you are having trouble creating that positive "talk track," here are two quick exercises that Sue used while at UCLA:

1) On one piece of paper, write down the good things you say to yourself and the bad things you say to yourself.

2) With a second piece of paper, sit with your team in a circle, put your name at the top of this sheet, and write "I trust her because:" (with blank lines below it). Then everyone moves her paper to the left. Now whose paper do you have? Say you have Sue's. What do you value about Sue. "I trust Sue because . . . " Keep the papers moving in the circle until yours comes all the way back to you.

Now you have your language. You have your glossary of why the team values you, and what they admire and respect. This is your positive voice. Your *go-to* voice. Play that sound track in your head until the vinyl grooves wear thin (and then replace it with a digital file from your cloud). Fall in love with your inner voice again. And surely, with all these new positive thoughts, your brain has no choice but to smile.

Find your strategy. I learned a new one in yoga recently. Breathe out the negative. I love the visual image of negative things flying out of my body. Snap your hair band. Go to your happy place. Use your positive "talk track." Try thirty seconds of courage. Figure out what works for *you*. (Warning: that may take some trial and error. Also, it changes over time. Life has a fun way of keeping us on our toes.)

A WHALE CAN NEVER
BE A CACTUS

And remember, it's easy when all is going well. Life is good. You are winning, you may even be the star; you are feeling good about what you do. But when you leave that pond and go to a bigger lake, what happens? Or even out to the rough ocean, how do you fare? I quickly figured out that although I may not be the best player in the big ocean, the most important thing I could control is my *attitude and effort* (you will be reciting these words in your sleep before this book is done). And if that can make the group better, then I am winning.

As much as I wanted to be the top goal scorer or best midfielder, I wasn't. Not even close. But that didn't mean I didn't have other gifts to bring to the table. I figured out what those gifts were and focused on helping the group, not moping about where I fell on the ladder. My gift was my positivity, my energy, my engine, my vocal cords, my competitiveness, my humor (yes, admittedly subjective), and my ability to help push the team to be better than we thought we could be.

Instead of focusing on what I didn't have, I focused on

what I could add. Which reminds me of a great quote:

"A whale is unique. As is a cactus. But don't ask a whale to survive Death Valley. We all have special gifts."

—Max De Pree

What are your gifts? Sometimes you may not even realize them, or perhaps they are a hidden talent. Like Amy Liss shared with me:

AMY: "My memory is my hidden talent."

JULIE: "OK, testing your memory. What's my birthday?!"

AMY: "January 23, and you're forty-five. But I'm bad at math, so I don't know the year."

JULIE [*laughing* . . .]: "I'd rather you know the year and not my age."

Amy continues without pause . . . nor prompting:

AMY: "And Ian's birthday is May 2, so start shopping." [*I laugh again because, of course, I have not started shopping and it's a week before my hubby's birthday.*]

JULIE: "What about my kids' birthdays? You know those?"

AMY [*without hesitation*]: "Dec is December 3, and Izzy is January 1."

JULIE: "GET OUTTA HERE. C'MON! *I* can't even remember my kids' birthdays. . . . That's amazing."

Yes, everyone brings gifts to the table. Memory is not one of mine. Figure out what you bring to the group. That is key. I understood my role and, equally important, felt appreciated for my role. This last sentence was a huge one for our most successful teams. Everyone understood their role and felt appreciated for their role. Mia Hamm agreed and added the following:

> MIA: "I look at the teams that were successful . . . everyone felt empowered that their presence on the team was valued. That's so important. Especially if you're not starting. And then that player not starting ends up scoring one of the most important goals because it goes back to that trust and that empowerment. I matter, I'm valued on this team, and, when ready, I'm going to play my best."

WHO STARTED IT?

Here is the part of team chemistry that gets lost so often in the noise: DO NOT FORGET to celebrate and appreciate those who are contributing even in less obvious roles. For example, we played a game called *Who Started It?* We would watch video of a game together, and our goals of course; but most importantly, we wanted to see who started the play that resulted in a goal. Sometimes you had to rewind back to ten passes before you saw it was a toe poke from the left back that started the play. Or maybe it was one little touch that won the throw-in that led to our goal. Or maybe it was a header five minutes prior that changed the direction of the game. WHO STARTED IT?

Sometimes we forget to acknowledge the members of the group who did much of the grunt work. Who made this success possible? Who helped in ways many did not see? Who paid attention to the smallest of details that meant you all were successful?

Make sure you then celebrate them. Life changes for the better when you feel appreciated. This was such a healthy lesson for me. Celebrate others who don't get the headlines or recognition but affect chemistry positively: The person on the end of the bench who cheers. The person who stays late to proofread the school newspaper before it goes to press. The person with five lines in the play, yet practices them over and over. The person who makes you better every single day by simply encouraging or competing with you to be better.

Coach Sue Enquist calls it **unprovoked gratitude**.

SUE: "It's the most powerful kind: When gratitude sneaks up on somebody, it is magnified. We always appreciate being thanked for a gift. 'Thank you for the birthday gift,' 'thank you for the Christmas present.' But when it sneaks up on you, as the recipient of the gratitude, it's memorable. And if you start to set goals on showing unprovoked appreciation, you start paying attention to who's dripping positively on you as well."

THE WE > THE ME

I smile when I think back on the beauty of these moments when you are truly *in it* together. The players who never let a teammate run alone. The players who would jump in and WILL a player to finish a fitness regimen by running alongside her and convincing her that she will make it, and that she will get through this (and then she does). There are also the teammates who never played a minute in a World Cup tourney or the Olympics, although it was a lifetime dream, but yet were the first to cheer for the ones who were on the field playing. Those are the people I wanted around me. Those are the teammates I cherished—**those who cared more about the WE than the ME.**

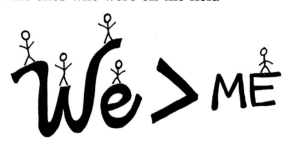

TEAM

I would argue that you should pick *those players* first on your team. Because if you can get that equation right—where everyone understands the power of what they bring to the team, whether it is being the star on your team or a reserve player, the president or intern, the goal scorer or cheerleader—there's a *huge* boost to the entire team, guaranteed. This applies as well in school, at work, and in life.

I asked Alex Morgan what made their recent era of teams so successful. She spoke specifically about winning the World Cup in 2015 and why that team was victorious:

> **ALEX**: "I think a big reason that we all came together through that World Cup is because everyone understood their role . . . and as much as every player on that team wanted to start and felt like they were deserving of starting, they just understood their role and came together and said for this month, *'I need to do it for the team.'* That's not always the case for every player, every time of the year. So that was special."

Special indeed. I often talk to people about Mia Hamm, our biggest superstar while we played, when referencing the power of TEAM. Because Mia operated with one goal in mind: to help the team. Her one and only way of making decisions and doing things was with the team a first priority. And for that, I am forever grateful. Just imagine if the star of our team, the woman who was the face and name of the team, was more interested in what she gained or what attention she would garner. Imagine what type of tone that would have set for the group. Instead, Mia made sure she *first* mentioned how her teammates were the real reason for her success. And genuinely and graciously wanted people to know how grateful she was for those teammates who pushed her to be better every single day.

And it wasn't just teammates, but the entire staff— the coaches, massage therapists, the athletic trainers, the doctors, the parking lot attendant, the mailman who brought her fan mail (OK, I may be exaggerating here but not by much)—she was always thanking others, even ahead of her own brilliance and skills. That's because Mia genuinely believed that those not in the spotlight were just as important to our success as the ones scoring goals.

That team-first mind-set from our superstar created a wonderful, inclusive environment for all involved. And when the WE is more important than the ME, that trust and unity becomes a bond that will last a lifetime. And, no surprise here, if I may go back to what I started this chapter with, when you start with laughter, winning follows.

You actually love being together. Team becomes family. You find yourself wishing moments could last forever (and I happily remind my teammates, like it or not, that they are indeed stuck with me forever). Alas,

LIFE BECOMES A HECK OF A LOT MORE FUN.

EXERCISE:

WRITE A SHORT NOTE, an unprovoked thank you, to three people who make your group better. Maybe they are not the superstars or leaders, but they consistently do what normally might go unnoticed. They work hard, stay positive, and push others to be better. Celebrate those people.

TELL THEM THANK YOU. TELL THEM THEY MATTER AND, MORE IMPORTANTLY, WHY THEY MATTER. TELL THEM HOW THEY MAKE YOU BETTER. IT DOESN'T HAVE TO BE LONG OR SAPPY, BUT THOSE PEOPLE, MORE THAN ANYONE ELSE, NEED TO HEAR IT. THEY NEED TO KNOW WHAT THEY ARE DOING IS APPRECIATED.

AND HANDWRITE THAT NOTE. YES, AS IN PEN AND PAPER. (Is that the sound of shock and horror I hear?)

DON'T JUST
THINK IT, INK IT

CHAPTER 7

TEAM CHEMISTRY
IS A VERB

*"By ourselves we suffer serious limitations.
Together we can be something wonderful."*

—Max De Pree

As I said at the start of this Team Section, one of our greatest strengths on the U.S. Women's National Team was our collective team spirit; it was our chemistry, our faith, and our trust in one another. It was our secret weapon. When we would go down a goal, or have an off game, there was no need to panic. We knew we could gut it out together and lean on each other. Having that sense of UNITY is such a wonderful asset to have with any team, but unfortunately, you cannot just wiggle your nose, snap your fingers, and WHAM, there you have it: *perfect* team chemistry. *Ahh*, if life could be so simple.

As Dr. Colleen Hacker, our sport psychology specialist with the U.S. National Team, used to tell us, "Team chemistry is a VERB, not a noun. You have to work at it. It is not just something that happens." Jessica Mendoza agrees. She thinks the best teams and the best leaders take the time to understand their teammates on a deeper level.

She then adds you can't expect your team to excel by standing up and just yelling, *"Here we go guys! We're gonna beat this team! Rah-rah."* No. Team chemistry must be nurtured, developed, chewed upon, spit out, discussed, nurtured some more, and talked about openly with your team.

It takes time and it takes a conscious effort. Full disclosure: sometimes when I hear *it takes time and it takes a conscious effort*, my natural reaction is, please *do not add* to my already stuffed schedule of work, activities, and stress.

So I am here to tell you not to worry. This time and effort is so much fun. You will want more. And not only is it fun, with a little investment you can reap huge rewards. Because a key to building team chemistry is actually ENJOYING time together. No one wants to sit in a room to ponder and discuss the fifty most important traits to being a better teammate or leader or person (at least I certainly don't). You need to live to learn. You need to be *doing*. Actively engaging with each other to discover how the collective interaction can lead to something even more powerful, and more profound.

BE GREAT IN PLAN B

It is easy to be a great team when you are winning in sports, work, or life. But what happens when adversity hits? What happens when things go wrong? What happens when you have to come up with plan B?

In her most recent book, titled *Option B*, Sheryl Sandberg talks about exactly that: how to wrap your arms around a new, far less desirable, plan. After Sheryl's husband, Dave, died suddenly and unexpectedly, Sheryl was talking to her good friend Phil Deutch about a plan to fill in for Dave at a father-child activity. Sheryl said, "I want

Dave. I want option A." Phil put his arm around Sheryl and said, "Option A is not available. So let's just kick the **sh*t** out of option B."

Sue Enquist refers to adversity as plan B. Whether it is option B or plan B, the challenge is getting through that adversity. Sue discusses here how teams facing challenges can be great in plan B mode:

> SUE: "You have to feel like you can fail. You have to create the conditions, the environment, for the team to be successful in plan B. If not, you'll never win in the cooker. But more importantly, you won't enjoy coming to practice. You won't enjoy being on the team, because you feel so much pressure. You have the talent to win. But you also have the talent to lose—meaning your talent can drive the team into the crapper if you all don't trust each other. I want you to be the best person in plan B, and I want you to be able to tell everybody when you're in the crapper."

Ha. This is beautiful. Yes indeed. We are humans. But how many times have we gone into a practice or meeting or game feeling terrible for whatever reason— sick, injured, tired due to a late night up with school or work—and actually been able to acknowledge the fact that I JUST AM NOT ALL HERE TODAY. I am going to guess that, unfortunately, too few of us can actually admit when we're not ready to play.

But Coach Enquist contends real team chemistry will assuage this dilemma.

> "If I can get you to look at your teammates and go, 'You guys, just so everybody knows, I'm at 30 percent. I don't really know why, but I just *don't want to be here*,' and have other teammates say, '*Dude, I got you today*.' Now I've created the conditions for the environment to be really successful. Because I told everybody we're unique. **We have the humility to know that it's our empathy that's gonna take care of us**, because it can be suffocating when there's no margin for error."

TEAM

The teams that embrace the possibility of failure are rewarded with success. And JOY. It is so much easier to fall off your bike when you know you are landing on grass.

GO FIND YOUR MOJO

Wherever your team or group is along the team chemistry spectrum— doing fabulously well or terribly wrong— doesn't matter. Everyone has to put in the work on team chemistry.

One of the most effective things we did on the U.S. National Team was to be *conscious* of working on team-building. And to buy into the fact that it didn't happen by accident. And similar to establishing your own standards and culture, you can institute fun team-building exercises on your own. In fact, let's do this: let's create a team-building manual that shares ideas, exercises, and strategies that lead to becoming a better group, a happier family. We have done this at our Leadership Academies and it is great fun. For lack of a better name, let's call it our "Finding Your Team Mojo Manual," as our JFSLA students called it one year.

Or even better, just name it the *MOJO MANUAL.*

Whatever you name it, make it your own. Apply it to YOUR special team, group. Integrating themes from this entire Team section, here is the start to our "MOJO MANUAL" that will soon become yours:

SPORTS LEADERSHIP ACADEMY

CHOOSE TO MATTER

MOJO MANUAL

"FINDING YOUR TEAM MOJO" MANUAL

THIS MANUAL HAS BEEN PUT TOGETHER WITH GREAT LOVE AND CARE BY THE RETURNING CAMPERS OF THE JULIE FOUDY SPORTS LEADERSHIP ACADEMY. WE HOPE YOU FIND IT USEFUL IN HELPING YOUR OWN TEAM FIND THEIR TEAM MOJO. PLEASE ADD TO THE MANUAL AS YOUR TEAM SO DESIRES. WE WOULD LOVE FOR THIS TO BE A LIVING DOCUMENT THAT GROWS AND GROWS, HELPING TEAMS EVERYWHERE. MOST IMPORTANT, REMEMBER TEAM CHEMISTRY IS A VERB, NOT A NOUN. LAUGHTER IS PERMITTED.
ENJOY!

> LOVE,
> THE JFSLA ROCK STAR RETURNERS

* Talk to your coach or leader and get on the same page. Any "boss" can help/hurt team chemistry immensely as we all know. (BTW: they should absolutely love that you are taking the lead on this as a team.)

* Appreciate and understand roles on the team and **YOUR INDIVIDUAL ROLE**. Not everyone can be the superstar or starter.

✳ Help others with various roles feel valued. Explain how their positive energy lifts the team. Give examples of how they helped spark the group. (Who Started It, etc . . .)

✳ Have a high energy, positive cheer at the end of every practice/meeting to end on a high note. Make it short and snappy. And sometimes mix it up. For example, after one considerably difficult fitness week with our U.S. soccer team (we were running a whole lot), we changed our cheer to "USA Track and Field!!" with a big huge roar (read: growl) at the end of it. **WE THOUGHT IT WAS QUITE FUNNY. I AM NOT SURE OUR COACHES DID. BUT THEY GOT OVER IT.**

✳ After an intense practice, find ways to reconnect with your friends off the field/outside of work.

✳ Make practices/meetings so much fun no one will want to miss them! (Wink-wink, nudge-nudge to any coach reading this: if you bring in healthy competition, healthy intensity follows.)

✳ Celebrate success with a celebratory jig (offer double points for Best of Your Worst celebratory jigs).

✳ If a teammate is not on board, attack the issue, not the person. Use "WE NEED" statements instead of "YOU NEED to . . ."

✳ Know that teammates are all different, so know the triggers/temperaments of the individual players.

✳ Lead by unselfish examples; be the first to pick up the ball bag, carry gear, carry the water cooler. Remember, **DO NOT BE** the Queen of England.

✳ Show your positive influence by making great decisions on and off the field.

✳ Spend time together in meaningful ways off the field/court/classroom, etc. This leads me to **THE TEAM-BUILDING SECTION OF THE MOJO MANUAL:**

TEAM

FUN TEAM BUILDING EXERCISES:

The last part of this **MOJO MANUAL** is so important. Because it brings in the laughter permitted part of the equation. Better yet: laughter required. This part of the Mojo Manual lists fun, goofy team-building exercises that emphasize the values of unity and strength when the team works together.

Team-building exercises were something we did a lot on the National Team. Dr. Hacker was the master at creating these, but if you don't have a staff member to facilitate them, fear not. You can do many on your own. The beauty of these exercises is you will simultaneously: 1) get out of your comfort zone in a fabulous way, and 2) build trust with each other (clique free!).

Here are some beauties we did with our U.S. team and others shared through our JFSLA students, just to get you started on your list of
FUN TEAM BUILDING EXERCISES:

• **BOWLING BASH:** EACH GROUP PICKS THEIR COSTUME STYLE (SAY A 1970S LOOK OR SOME OTHER CRAZY-THEMED OUTFIT) AND KEEPS IT A SURPRISE UNTIL THE BIG BOWLING DAY. MAKE SURE TO SEPARATE THE DIFFERENT CLIQUES. AN EASY WAY TO DO THIS IS TO DRAW TEAMS RANDOMLY OUT OF A HAT. OR PUT NEW PLAYERS WITH VETERANS. MAKE IT COMPETITIVE (DUH), AND AWARD THE MOST RIDICULOUS OF PRIZES TO THE WINNERS. GO AHEAD AND CLEAN OUT THE BANK FOR THOSE FIVE CENT PLASTIC MEDALS THAT SAY **YOU ARE A WINNER**.

• **PROM DRESS ANYONE?:** THIS IS MY PERSONAL FAVORITE. EACH PERSON ON THE TEAM BRINGS THEIR **WORST, MOST CHEESY** PROM DRESS (OR ANY FABULOUSLY UGLY FORMAL DRESS YOU MAY OWN—UM, YOU KNOW YOU HAVE MANY) AND PUTS THEM IN A BOX IN THE MIDDLE OF A GATHERING. YOU CAN THEN EITHER WEAR YOUR OWN CHEESY DRESS OR PUT ON SOMEONE ELSE'S. YOU MUST PRACTICE/WORK WHILE WEARING THAT DRESS. OH, YES.

• **TEAM MAKEOVERS:** PICK A TEAMMATE AND SWAP MAKEOVERS; EVERYTHING IS ALLOWED SHORT OF HAIR DYE AND A HAIRCUT (UNLESS OF COURSE IT'S WANTED).

• **TRICK OR TREAT:** YEP, DO AN ENTIRE PRACTICE IN YOUR HALLOWEEN COSTUME.

• **CRAZY CLOTHES RELAY:** THE CRAZIER THE CLOTHES, HATS, OUTFITS, AND SHOES THE BETTER.

• **JUMP ROPE SPEED CHALLENGE:** CALLING ALL YOU DOUBLE DUTCHERS. ORGANIZE TEAMS. TIME IT. DO IT IN PAIRS, SINGLE, IN FOURS, WHATEVER YOU CAN HANDLE. GET CREATIVE ON HOW TO SCORE AND MIX IT UP.

• **TEAM SCAVENGER HUNT:** THE GOOFIER THE ITEMS TO FIND THE BETTER OF COURSE. TAKE ON OTHER TEAMS AT YOUR SCHOOL AND/OR AT YOUR WORKPLACE. TAKE ON OTHER CLASSROOMS. THE CATCH WITH TEAM SCAVENGER HUNT IS YOU HAVE TO DO IT ALL TOGETHER. AND MOVE TOGETHER. AND YES STAY TOGETHER. IT'S PART OF THE CHALLENGE. A PICTURE OF ALL TWENTY OF US IN A BATHROOM STALL? NO PROBLEM. OR A PICTURE OF ALL TWENTY OF US, UPSIDE DOWN? EASY.

• **WHO ARE YOU?!:** WITH THE RISK OF SOUNDING LIKE A DISNEY EMPLOYEE (OH, WAIT, I AM), DECIDE WHICH DISNEY CHARACTER IS MOST REPRESENTATIVE OF YOU AND WRITE IT DOWN. EACH TEAM MEMBER PUTS THEIR NAME IN THE HAT. TEAMMATES THEN HAVE TO GUESS WHO IS WHICH CHARACTER. PARTICIPANTS CAN PICK FROM THE CLASSICS TO THE CURRENT— MICKEY MOUSE TO MULAN , NEMO TO OLAF, OR MERIDA TO GOOFY TO BUZZ LIGHTYEAR. I'M STOPPING NOW SO MY DISNEY CHARACTER REVIEW WILL NOT COMPETE WITH YOUR DISNEY CHARACTER REVIEW.

- **COMMUNITY SERVICE (DONE COMMUNALLY):** DO COMMUNITY SERVICE TOGETHER AS A WAY TO GET TO KNOW EACH OTHER. **WITH YOUR TEAM**, CLEAN A FAVORITE PARK/BEACH. PUT ON A SPORTS CLINIC FOR KIDS WITH DISABILITIES. START AN EQUIPMENT DRIVE FOR LESS FORTUNATE CHILDREN. COOK A MEAL FOR THE FAMILIES AT A RONALD MCDONALD HOUSE.

- **DID YOU KNOW . . . :** DRAW NAMES OUT OF A HAT AND LEARN FIVE THINGS ABOUT THAT TEAMMATE. INTRODUCE HER TO THE REST OF THE TEAM.

- **BIG SISTER/LITTLE SISTER:** SET UP A SUPPORT GROUP BETWEEN THE VARSITY AND JUNIOR VARSITY TEAMS. OR OLDER PLAYERS AND YOUNGER PLAYERS. OR VETERANS AT WORK AND NEW MEMBERS ON THE JOB. THE "BIG SISTER" LOOKS AFTER THE YOUNGER SISTER. THEY HAVE LUNCHES, MOVIES, OR EVEN GET A COFFEE TOGETHER. SHE CAN ALSO HELP WITH SCHOOL OR SOMETHING THAT HAS BEEN HARD FOR THEIR "LITTLE SISTER" TO COPE WITH. ESSENTIALLY, IT'S GETTING AN OLDER TEAMMATE TO "TURN AND PULL" (REACH BACK AND HELP A YOUNGER TEAMMATE).

- **CHEW AND CHAT:** SIT WITH SOMEONE DIFFERENT AT A MEAL OR ON THE BUS (SOMEONE YOU DON'T KNOW WELL OR WANT TO GET TO KNOW BETTER). OUR VETERANS ON THE U.S. TEAM WOULD SEEK OUT NEW PLAYERS IN THESE SITUATIONS.

- **I SEE YOU:** SUPPORT THE INTERESTS OF OTHER TEAMMATES. GO WATCH THEM PLAY LACROSSE, PERFORM IN THE BAND, NEARLY ANYTHING THAT'S ANOTHER PURSUIT.

- **SCHEDULE A NOT-YOUR-NORMAL DINNER PARTY:** DO GAMES WHERE TEAMMATES HAVE TO INTERACT WITH OTHERS OUTSIDE OF THEIR COMFORT ZONE AND OUTSIDE OF THEIR NORMAL CIRCLE OF FRIENDS. PLAY SOME OF THE FUN TEAM-BUILDING EXERCISES JUST LISTED. OR SPOONS ANYONE?! WHATEVER, MAKE IT DIFFERENT AND INCLUSIVE.

- **OUT OF THE BOX:** AND SINCE THE IDEA IS TO THINK OUTSIDE THE BOX, THE ULTIMATE EXPERIENCE I WISH I HAD THOUGHT OF WHILE STILL IN HIGH SCHOOL AND COLLEGE IS HAVE A DJ COME TO PRACTICE. BECAUSE **WHY NOT**.

MAKE THESE FUN EXERCISES COMPETITIVE WHEN YOU CAN. ADD ELEMENTS OF PRESSURE. KEEP SCORE. CALL OUT THE GOLD, WHITE GOLD, AND BRONZE MEDALISTS. OK, YOU'RE PROBABLY WONDERING WHAT THAT SECOND CATEGORY IS. LET ME EXPLAIN:

WE LOST TO NORWAY IN THE GOLD MEDAL MATCH OF THE 2000 OLYMPICS IN OVERTIME. THE THOUGHT STILL BRINGS COLD SWEATS BECAUSE WE PLAYED ARGUABLY THE BEST FINAL WE HAVE EVER PLAYED, AND IN MY HUMBLE OPINION, WE WERE THE BETTER TEAM ON THAT DAY. BUT AS IS THE CASE IN SOCCER AND LIFE, THE BEST TEAM DOES NOT ALWAYS WIN. SO IN HONOR OF HOW WELL WE PLAYED (AND HOW MAD I STILL AM), I DON'T SAY WE WON THE SILVER MEDAL, I SAY WE WON WHITE GOLD.

BUT I DIGRESS. THE MOST IMPORTANT THING YOU DO, AS A GROUP, IS TALK ABOUT WHAT YOU'VE LEARNED AFTER THE EXERCISE. WHAT WORKED, WHAT DIDN'T WORK. TAKE FIFTEEN TO THIRTY MINUTES TO DEBRIEF AND REVIEW WHAT YOU JUST DID TOGETHER. TALK ABOUT HOW THE LESSONS LEARNED DURING TEAM BUILDING CAN APPLY TO BEING BETTER INDIVIDUALLY AND COLLECTIVELY. YES, TEAM BUILDING IS SILLY AND FUN, BUT EFFECTIVE TEAM BUILDING MAKES SURE ALL THIS SILLINESS HAS A PURPOSE. #THEBESTKIND

GO MAKE THIS MOJO MANUAL YOUR OWN:

1) GO THROUGH THE MANUAL AND ADD WHERE NEEDED. CHANGE THE NAME. CHANGE THE LAYOUT. REMEMBER: THIS DOESN'T JUST APPLY TO SPORTS TEAMS. ADJUST FOR WHATEVER YOUR TEAM IS. MAYBE THERE IS AN ISSUE YOUR TEAM IS DEALING WITH THAT YOU WANT TO BRING INTO THE MANUAL. OR AN IMPORTANT ELEMENT MISSING THAT HAS WORKED WITH YOUR TEAM. TAKE THE NEXT STEP.

2) ADD SOMETHING TO THE RUNNING LIST OF FUN, GOOFY TEAM-BUILDING EXERCISES ABOVE AND SHARE IT WITH US. I WILL KEEP THE MASTER MOJO MANUAL TEAM-BUILDING-EXERCISE LIST, SO TWEET, INSTAGRAM, OR FACEBOOK ME YOUR IDEAS (YES, I'M ON ONLY THREE SOCIAL MEDIA SITES AND AM INDEED A SLACKER). TAG IT #MOJOMANUAL SO I KNOW IT IS FOR OUR TRUSTED MANUAL.

TEAM

DON'T JUST
THINK IT, INK IT

CHAPTER 8

THERE IS NO *I* IN TEAM, BUT THERE IS A *ME*

"The strength of the team is each individual member. The strength of each member is the team."

—NBA coach Phil Jackson

You know the old saying,

"There is no I in TEAM."

We would laugh and add,

"But there is a ME!"

And we weren't joking. You have to also be focused on the ME for a team to be successful. HUH? You may be scratching your head given all my talk about team bonding, celebrating others, and the WE before ME. Yes, the WE is absolutely important, but you can never forget the ME. For the *ME* is what makes the *WE* tick. Let me explain.

Sometimes people think being a great teammate and a competitive individual is an either/or concept. Meaning you cannot be a total TEAM player and at the same time be focused on winning a starting spot, wanting to do well personally, and striving for personal achievements. They argue that the two concepts are polar opposites by nature. Not true. Unless you care about getting better *personally*, the group does not reap the benefits of that competitive spirit.

Yes, the best teams have individuals who continually strive for growth and success. And equally important, keep it in perspective. Which, I'm sure we can all agree, is sometimes not easy. Because of course we all want to be the one scoring, getting the assists, closing the deal, getting the recognition for our positive performance. THAT is a healthy mind-set because it means you are driven to get better. But what happens when you don't score, don't close the deal, and don't perform well? Do you pretend it doesn't matter just to be a good teammate? I don't think that is healthy either.

The emotion of being mad or upset is not a bad thing. It means it matters. Of course it matters. But the next step is how you then deal with that emotion. How do you handle those conversations with teammates, with your coach, with your adviser? Because most of us have seen the destructive side of taking that emotion and turning it on teammates—or the teacher or parents.

Make sure you handle that emotion with measured perspective, as we talked about in Chapter 6. Do not get stuck in your junk. Because feeling driven to do more is a gift. Embrace that healthy emotion and then give it a healthy outlet: work harder, recommit to fitness, and review what is working (and what is not working) with your training or approach to work.

Don't blame someone else, but instead accept the challenge. I am not a starter . . . *yet*. I am not a core member of this team . . . *yet*. I am not finding success . . . *yet*.

TEAM

The really cool thing is you get to write your story. Or as one of our JFSLA campers, Lucy, termed it just this past summer: *your passion, your story, your glory.* I am still adding to my story; and I hope I am adding to my story at 115 years old. Because we all get to dictate how our personal story unfolds. But as tempting as it may be to turn to the last page of the book, sometimes it is best to just stay focused on being the best you in that moment. As Sue Enquist says,

SUE: "You don't have to be the best. You just have to be improving every single day. And that gives you peace of mind because you're only focusing on what you need to do to get better. Next, learn to listen to the conversation in your head."

Because when you pay attention, you start to identify who is the loudest talker in your head. Meaning which voice, the good or the bad, is winning. Sue advises,

"Start listening to it. What does the conversation sound like in your head? Write it down. On good days, what do you say; on bad days what do you say? Good, now you've built your awareness. Now you can hear it. Then start adding positive words and phrases to your talk track. And make sure that strong voice is going to get the last word."

Because when you know the language, you will be able to write your story. And control your story. And get better with your story every single day.

But what happens if the Debbie Downer voice is winning because you are not finding success? Of course we all want to do well. It is that competitiveness that drives us to be better. Try shifting your focus to the journey of *today*. Just today.

TEAM

And a funny thing happens when you worry less about the outcome. You find that success. When you focus on the process and enjoying the heck out of that process (without your even knowing it), the rest will come.

The legendary women's basketball coach Pat Summitt once wrote a letter to one of her freshman players at the University of Tennessee before her first game. That player, Sheila Collins, still has the letter thirty-five years later. Sally Jenkins, a fabulous writer with the *Washington Post*, shared the letter in an article she wrote when Coach Summitt passed away. The letter is dated Nov. 22, 1982:

> DEAR SHEILA,
> THIS IS YOUR FIRST GAME. I HOPE YOU WIN FOR YOUR SAKE, NOT MINE. BECAUSE WINNING'S NICE. IT'S A GOOD FEELING. LIKE THE WORLD IS YOURS. BUT IT PASSES, THIS FEELING. AND WHAT LASTS IS WHAT YOU LEARNED. . . .

Coach Summitt goes on to say the journey of life, in all its forms—the miseries, the joy, the heartbreak—is played out in a game. And you may be the hero. Or you may be absolutely nothing. And here is what you will do with this game, this life:

> YOU TAKE WHAT COMES AND YOU RUN WITH IT.
> WINNING IS FUN . . . SURE.
> BUT WINNING IS NOT THE POINT.
> WANTING TO WIN IS THE POINT.
> NOT GIVING UP IS THE POINT.
> NEVER LETTING UP IS THE POINT.
> THE GAME DOESN'T END WHEN YOU COME OFF THE COURT.
> THE SECRET OF THE GAME IS IN DOING YOUR BEST. TO PERSIST AND ENDURE, "TO STRIVE, TO SEEK, TO FIND, AND NOT TO YIELD."
>
> I'M PROUD TO BE YOUR COACH,
> PAT SUMMITT

TEAM

That makes me want to run through a steel-fortified, double-thick damn brick wall.

SO A MAN, AN OLD MULE, AND A FARMER WALK INTO . . .

And here's the beauty of "the ME" excelling . . . "the WE" reaps the reward. With one small snag. The ME must believe in the bigger goal, the bigger dream. Because at the end of the day, the mission of any team in any industry is to be successful as a group. As Sheryl Sandberg knows all too well.

> SHERYL: "Facebook is so team centric. It is in the water here. At work we succeed as teams. We really do. No single individual salesperson goes in and sells a great ad campaign to a client. That's because the engineering group built a great app, the marketing team gave them great material, and so on. I cannot think of an individual that succeeds alone."

When you can find the balance of competition and healthy unity, the return is exponential. This reminded me of one of my favorite stories on the power of ME + WE:

A man was lost while driving through the country and accidentally drove into a muddy ditch. The man walked to a nearby farm to ask for help. "Warwick can get you out of that ditch," said the farmer, pointing to an old mule standing in a field. The man looked at the decrepit old mule and looked at the farmer who just stood there repeating, "Yep, old Warwick can do the job."

The man figured he had nothing to lose. The two men and the mule made their way back to the ditch. The farmer hitched the mule to the car. With a snap of the reins, he shouted, "PULL, FRED! PULL, JACK! PULL, TED! PULL, WARWICK!"

And the old mule pulled that car right out of the ditch. The man was amazed. He thanked the farmer, patted the mule, and asked, "Why did you call out all of those names before you called Warwick?" The farmer grinned and said, "Old Warwick is just about blind. As long as he believes he's part of a team, he doesn't mind pulling."

(EXCERPT FROM *CHANGE IS GOOD, YOU GO FIRST...* BY TOM FELTENSTEIN REPRINTED BY PERMISSION OF SIMPLE TRUTHS © 2012)

And when you harness that individual and collective power of believing in the mission,

WELL THAT TEAM CAN MOVE MOUNTAINS. (OR CARS.)

EXERCISE:

We did a fun exercise with Dr. Colleen Hacker on the U.S. National Team to create a positive road map for the **ME + WE**. It will help you stay focused on how you can personally help the team be successful.

It's an exercise I like to call
TOSSING THE TRASH.

Here is how it works:

FIRST, SIT DOWN WITH YOUR TEAM AND DECIDE WHAT YOUR COLLECTIVE GOAL IS FOR THAT SEASON, EVENT, OR BIG GAME. FOR EXAMPLE, AT THE START OF AN OLYMPIC YEAR, WE WOULD SAY, "OK, OUR GOAL IS TO WIN THE OLYMPICS. GOLD MEDAL. PERIOD." WE WOULD THEN EACH HAVE OUR OWN BLANK PIECE OF PAPER AND DRAW A LINE STRAIGHT DOWN THE MIDDLE, FROM TOP TO BOTTOM, SPLITTING THE PAPER INTO TWO VERTICAL COLUMNS. IN THE LEFT COLUMN, EACH PLAYER WOULD INDIVIDUALLY LIST ALL THE THINGS THAT SHE COULD PERSONALLY DO THAT WOULD **HELP THE TEAM** ACHIEVE OUR GOAL OF WINNING THE OLYMPICS. IN THE RIGHT COLUMN, EACH PLAYER WOULD LIST ALL THE ITEMS THAT COULD **NEGATIVELY DISTRACT (HURT)** HER FROM HELPING THE TEAM WIN THE OLYMPICS.

TEAM GOAL: _____

HELP TEAM	HURT TEAM

I love this exercise because it is so simple, yet it makes you stop and reflect personally on what in your life is helping you and what in your life is distracting you from being the best team player you can be.

Now, mind you, that right HURT column cannot list an item like "homework is such a distraction," "school really gets in the way," or "doing the dishes at night is hurting my mental preparation" no matter how much you really believe this. You get my point. Distraction items could be things like this: "I am overextended in too many areas," "I need to stop wasting energy on a friend's drama," or "the negative voice in my head is getting too loud." Such items take you *away* from your team goal.

The left side of the column, meanwhile, are things that HELP. They allow you to stay focused on what matters (then define what matters): have better sleeping habits, recommit mentally and physically to fitness, spend more time off the field with teammates, turn up the positive voice in my head. These are the things that help the team achieve your ultimate goal.

Here is the most important part: When you are done making your list, tear or cut the paper right down the middle between the two columns. Take the right side, the "HURT THE TEAM" column, and crumple it up into a ball. Toss it into the trash! Yep. Anything on the right side, we would throw away. Literally. Each player would rip the paper in half and toss the negative in a

big trash can in the middle of the circle. Everyone would cheer, do a celebratory jig because those negative items were "gone" (it is quite therapeutic actually); then tape the other "help" column up on the bathroom mirror.

And full disclosure, it was the crumpling and the tossing part that I loved. It gave me permission to be the best me I could be. A physical gesture to mentally remind me to focus on the positive. Audible *ahh*. So now go celebrate the new, focused, driven, happier you. And tape that left side of the paper somewhere you can see it often. Like to your forehead.

DON'T JUST
THINK IT, INK IT

Think about all the teams you have played on over the years. Which one sticks out as the best? What were the reasons? Write about the qualities the team had that made it stand out from the others. What traits can you take from that team and implement to help your current team get better?

SECTION 3

SCHOOL

ONWARD AND OUTWARD.

Now to the third ring in our **empower**RINGS: **SCHOOL**.

It's a bit of a bigger pond than your team of course, but it's not the ocean yet. Full of plenty of drama, but hopefully not big sharks. This section is all about how to be a leader at your school, in the hallways, in the classroom, and—vitally important—how to communicate through all of it.

We will talk a lot about **communication**, being a **verbal leader**, **dealing with negative peer pressure**, and, *of course*, how to make sure you are **positively navigating the maze of awkwardness** that is a mandatory rite of passage for anyone in school.

SO LET'S START RIGHT THERE.

CHAPTER 9

AWKWARD
IS AWESOME

"Awkward interests me. At least when you are feeling awkward you are always thinking. When you are feeling fabulous, for example, rare occurrence that it may be, you stop thinking altogether. Which gets you into all kinds of trouble. Hence, you are better off feeling awkward."

—Elizabeth Brundage, author

Yes, awkward is indeed awesome. And here is the good news. Awkwardness is nondiscriminatory. It's the biggest common denominator in everyone's elementary, middle school, and high school experience. (And who am I kidding? Add college to the mix as well.) Everyone goes through it. FACT . . . even the seemingly coolest kids feel it.

The best news? You will survive. And laugh about it later. Or like me, learn that *awkward is awesome*. At some point in my life, though I'm not sure when, maybe my mid-twenties, I came to the realization that I just needed to embrace awkward. I also came to the realization that wouldn't it have been great to realize this earlier! Because when we **EMBRACE AWKWARD**, life becomes so much easier. We stop worrying about nonsense. We stop worrying about those things in life that set us apart, and instead celebrate those very things that set us apart.

That is when I had my lightbulb moment and started thinking about what nuggets from life, sports, friends, enemies, and school would have been great to know actually *while I was going*  through the awkwardness of those teenage middle school/high school years. Because let's be honest: Those awkward years are not easy. They are downright painful at times. We so badly want to be anything *but* what we are. Yet there we are, in all our glory. What I called the good, the bad, and the ugly phase. It's as if the Awkward Angel is smiling down saying, "Ha, how else can we break her awkward meter?"

Well, grace and smoothness were never part of my DNA in middle and high school (OK, ever), so my awkward meter was full throttle.

Plus, it never helps when your brothers' friends call you Jimmy.

So to compensate and show the world I was indeed NOT a boy, I would wear big earrings (and big pearl necklaces apparently).

I would still get called a young boy at the grocery store or around town, because being an athlete meant I was often in sweats. I didn't want to give up my athletic attire, nor my short hair, as I thought my short hair would grow UP, not out. (The high school picture proves my theory.) So the simple solution was this: wear even larger earrings more often. Like the size of hubcaps.

JIMMY'S TOP 11

Back to that lightbulb moment: What if had actually known that I was not alone and that the awkwardness would go away. *AHHHH*, the thought. So here is my attempt to help you get to the point of maybe not loving awkward, but at least accepting awkward. Which is my-not-so-subtle way of telling you these are not easy steps (the perfect setup for my favorite movie line: "If it were easy, everyone would do it. It's the hard that makes it great." Name the movie and I will give you extra donuts. Oh, I caught you peeking. It's *A League of Their Own*. I just ate your donut).

Without further ado, my **TOP 11 THINGS** I wish I had known as a pimple-faced, short-haired tomboy who my brothers' friends called Jimmy are:

1) Be **PROUD OF YOU.** Lose the idea of perfect. There is no such thing. Even with my padded bras and big earrings and crazy hair, I learned to love my quirks.

2) **DON'T WASTE YOUR TIME OR ENERGY** on mean girls (or boys). Surround yourself with happy people who treat everyone nicely.

3) **LAUGH MORE.** And laugh at *yourself* more. School brings enough pressure. Take time to find the humor in things. Even when you have a big ol' zit on your nose. Or are half-chimp, like I was (thank goodness for Nair hair removal). Or have friends who bring drama. Laughter helps it go away. Find like-minded friends who can laugh with you, not at you.

4) **FEAR DOES NOT MEAN YOU ARE FAILING.** Fear simply means you are living and growing. Show me one person who is fearless and I will show you a robot. Accept the feeling, and then move forward with courage.

5) **TEAMS THAT ACCEPT FRESHMEN**, rather than haze freshmen, are usually the most successful. Although, I am a big fan of practical jokes on freshman. (That's a lie. I am a big fan of practical jokes on those of all ages.)

6) The "popular" kid who drinks a lot, parties a lot, and maybe even does drugs becomes the kid who never left the area and never went on to college. That cool kid is no longer cool. **DO NOT BE THAT KID.**

7) Which reminds me: "Cool" is subjective. Who defines it by the way? Don't let others define it. And certainly do not let pictures on social media define it. *You* define it. Define it by being consistently kind and seeking nothing in return. **KIND IS COOL.**

8) **OPEN UP YOUR WORLD.** I am convinced life is relationships and connecting with others (actually face-to-face contact). Take a moment each day to introduce yourself to someone new, someone outside of your "circle" of friends. Lift your head up from your cell phone and show someone you care to say hello. It is amazing how empowering it is just to feel recognized.

9) **PLAY SPORTS.** And if you don't play sports, just move. Be active. If you burn out on one activity, find a new one. Create a new one. Sports gave me discipline, strength, and confidence . . . and a million more gems: healthy = happy.

10) **TREAT THE WORLD WITH RESPECT AND THEN ATTACK IT WITH RELENTLESS PASSION**—whether you are five or fifty or a hundred years old.

Oh, and last, but certainly not least, here's lucky, fabulous, marvelous No. 11:

11) **WEAR BIG EARRINGS.** They solve the world's problems. **OR JUST EAT BIG DONUTS.** They are good for the soul.

THE GIFT THAT
KEEPS ON GIVING

And because this list is the gift that keeps on giving, I asked others what they would add, starting with Robin Roberts:

ROBIN: "I would really tell myself what other people think of you is none of your business. Stop, stop caring what people are saying or thinking. Why do you care? Why do you care so much?

We get so caught up in what our reputation is. It's nothing more than what other people think. It's all about character. So I would honestly tell myself, I would tell myself, slow your roll."

JULIE (smiling): "Slow your roll."

ROBIN: "Don't be in such a hurry. Why are you in such a hurry? It goes by in a blink of an eye. And I would tell myself to slow down, and don't concern yourself with what people are saying and doing."

It is so hard in the moment to slow your roll and enjoy the moment. Mia Hamm agreed:

MIA: "What would I tell my younger self? Just to relax and enjoy it. I would always focus more on what could go wrong rather than what was going right. Don't be so quick to get through it rather than just really enjoying that moment."

It really does go in a snap. Everyone tells you that, and you say yeah, yeah, but it's so darn true. Sometimes you have to slow down to find the good in experiences, relationships, memories, and moments. In college I remember a habit I developed that I now look back on with a big grin. When I recognized a neat moment or sunset or experience, I would stop and shout out loud, ***"MOMENT! I am having a moment."*** Then we all would stop, enjoy the beauty of the moment, smile, laugh, and carry on. Be the person in your group who sees moments. And calls them out. Appreciating life for its little moments is a healthy habit for life.

I also of course asked Sophie Healy-Thow, who is just finishing her high school years, the same thing.

SOPHIE: "Oh. That's a hard question. What would I tell my younger self? You have your own opinions, your own thought process, your own ideas, beliefs, individual goals. You have your own talents, and you are your own self. So don't listen to what that person is telling you; don't try and be like them, because you will never be like them. You came here with what you got, and you can grow on what you've got. Just embrace it and don't listen to anybody else."

I think I literally tried to hug Sophie through the computer screen. So damn great. And such a healthy perspective for an eighteen-year-old.

Sheryl Sandberg spoke of the comparison trap—and not succumbing to it:

SHERYL: "Of course we all do it in high school. In lots of ways. *I want to be more athletic, I want to be more confident.* But what we really want to be is ourselves. Focus on that. And don't hold yourself back based on stereotypes. Because you can be anything."

Alex Morgan also shared her perspective on what she wishes she had known in high school:

ALEX: "So many things . . . it's so hard to pinpoint one," [*laughing*]. "Confidence was a big thing when I was younger; just knowing the right people to look for, to turn to when I wasn't feeling confident. But I also feel like it did form who I am. Probably because I didn't know a lot of things I wish I would have known, I went through a lot of learning experiences that have made me better."

What a wonderful outlook. In other words, she grew *because* she stumbled. And far more mature than I would have ever been at that age. I would have still been complaining about my hair that defied gravity.

I asked Tatyana McFadden to offer her perspective on this as well.

TATYANA: "I think the advice I would give to anybody, not just a person in a wheelchair, not just a person with a physical disability, is just about *living life* . . . with what you have. It's not what you don't have, but it's what *you have.* And really just getting out there and enjoying it no matter what."

FYI, *getting out there* and enjoying life does not mean through a video game or screen.

INSTAGRAM IS NOT
REALITY (NOR IS REALITY TV)

When my son, Declan, was five years old and we told him we were signing him up for snowboarding lessons, he asked, "But why are you signing me up for lessons Mom? I don't need lessons, I already know how to snowboard."
Me: "Oh, really. How do you know how to snowboard, Declan? You have never been on a snowboard before buddy."
Declan: "MOM [*said like DUH, MOM*], I snowboard on the video game. I am great at that." He was completely serious and convinced that he could snowboard for real.

I actually had to explain that snowboarding on a video game and snowboarding on snow were two very different things. I recall him looking at me and grunting.

Yes, the draw of social media and video games is everywhere. And it is enticing. But you need to decide just how much you want a screen to define you. Seeing a pretty picture is not the same as hiking through a pretty scene. Seeing a pretty sunset is not the same as smelling the salty air from your paddleboard as the sun sets over the ocean. Feeling connected is a powerful emotion (as discussed in No. 8 on my list of eleven things earlier).

But feeling like you need to be connected to the Internet or social media at all times is draining and unhealthy. How you balance it is never an easy task. Because think about it for a second. Your generation of middle schoolers and high schoolers—and even those of you who are in college right now—have grown up with photos, videos, and an Internet that makes everything immediately accessible. As a result, videos get shot and downloaded right away; selfies are shared instantaneously, and devices are always in use that *constantly* link you to friends all over the world. Add in the pressure of making your world and your life look absolutely riveting . . . every single day.

Robin Roberts spoke of that false reality we portray online:

> "Who's gonna post something bad about themselves? It looks like everybody's life is perfect. But nobody's life is perfect."

Yet, the pressure to *appear* perfect is real. The pictures scream, "*Yoohoooooo.* Look at me! I am smiling, I am happy. My life *oozes* fun. *My life is great.*" But guess what? There's clearly more to that life than what you see on a screen. Maybe the parents are going through a divorce, or life at home is not so great, or dad drinks too much. Or you are not doing well in school. No one posts THAT stuff.

A decade ago, you *may* have found out afterward your three other friends went to a movie and dinner without you. Now you see them smiling and saying, "Yep, we are having *so much fun* without you." You may already know this, but it is worth this reminder: using Instagram or Snapchat, or any social media platform, as the barometer for someone's happiness is not only silly, it's false and misleading.

Don't get caught comparing yourself to a false form of reality. Put that phone away, look up, and be present. As hard as that may be. Seek balance. Sophie Healy-Thow agrees while admitting it is terribly difficult to find that balance:

> SOPHIE: "We don't want to miss out. And even though we say that we're not interested in anybody else's lives, we're on social media to find out about other people. And although that sounds incredibly nosy, it's just natural, and we're just humans

at the end of the day. You can get sucked in so easily. I think it's so important to know that although you may have these brilliant relationships online, off-line you can have even more rewarding friendships and relationships, plus stories to tell. The goal is to not be stuck in your little world, head down, not knowing who's sitting beside you half the time. We have a beautiful world, and to not take advantage of its blessings is just a shame."

And remember, if the bad starts to outweigh the good on social media, it is time to reassess your balance. It is perfectly fine to not respond, to not leave a comment, to un-follow, to leave or delete a conversation. The hardest thing is stepping away. Yet the most rewarding thing is stepping away. Whatever you do, DO NOT, I repeat, DO NOT engage in social media when emotional. STEP AWAY. Take a breath. Call that person on the phone or meet in person. Nothing positive ever comes from engaging in fights on a screen.

And last, but not least, Sue Enquist leaves us with her closing piece of wisdom for something she wished she had known in high school:

"Take in all the advice above. And then live as if you have no clothes on. Go back to your anchors, and be great in plan B."

Ha. All this is great advice for dealing with awkward situations, and yet I keep finding myself going back to Alex Morgan's statement:

"You need to go through those awkward moments to learn. To grow."

Perhaps adhering to the list I presented earlier will never take away *awkward* because awkward, if not completely *awesome*, is at least *necessary*. May the list I offered simply help you navigate it all, keep you from falling apart, and have you smiling (the clenched teeth grin counts as smiling).

EXERCISE:

In honor of **EMBRACING AWKWARD,** list all the things you are awesomely awkward at and why they make you so dang cool. We rarely take the time to think about our awesomely awkward, so take a moment.

For example: I have always wanted to perform on Broadway in a musical. Never mind two small details: I cannot sing or dance. But I tell people, my energy makes it **SPECIAL**. And so when people call my dancing "special," I take that as a sign:

BROADWAY, HERE I COME!

There really is something incredibly liberating to accepting your inner awkward and letting it fly free. Go ahead.

I AM AWESOMELY AWKWARD AT:

-
-
-
-
-
-
-

DON'T JUST
THINK IT, INK IT

CHAPTER 10

DANCING IN THE RAIN

"Life isn't about waiting for the storm to pass, it's about learning to dance in the rain."

—Unknown

OK, now that we have accepted that awkward is a part of life and nothing to fear, let's move on to another area that can cause discomfort in school and in life: conflict. Whether it's with a dear friend, a stranger, a teacher, a classmate, a parent, or a situation . . . conflict, like *awkward*, is part of life. And most often, not a pleasant part of life.

People will get upset at petty things and large things alike. They will get upset at things you don't understand and things you think you understand.

My advice is to stop worrying about the why and start acting on how to best get to the end result—**conflict resolution**. The best leaders make sure conflict does not fester and address it. Yes, that's easier said than done.

I have always believed that addressing conflict means working and practicing to *find your voice*. Speaking up takes practice. Solving conflicts means being careful about what we say—the right words at the right time, delivered the right way. But there is one form of conflict that can be seriously disruptive, and we must speak up when we see it happen to others and when it happens to us. Yes, facing down a bully is truly a huge challenge.

HEY, HATER

So let's start there with bullying. Conflict resolution often proves to be the hardest to find if you are a victim of bullying. And understandably so. The bully wishes to cause you embarrassment, make you feel inferior, and get a reaction out of you. If you do not have the confidence to calmly tell a bully to stop, do not give the bully the satisfaction of knowing they have gotten under your skin. Walk away, show no reaction. And most important, seek help from an adult.

The biggest mistake for people being bullied is not reaching out for help. It is critical that you find someone you trust to confide in. Do not try and handle bullying alone. Sophie Healy-Thow was the victim of bullying in high school and now is an ambassador helping others facing similar situations. She talked openly about her experience and how she dealt with it:

SOPHIE: "It really took me back a few steps, because you never think that you could be bullied and you could be that victim. You never think that it can happen to you. You never think that you're gonna be called those names, or something's

SCHOOL

gonna be said behind your back. It really ripped me apart inside for a while, and I didn't know how to react to it at all."

Sophie did not reach out for help immediately and the bullying continued. She recalled not knowing how to best deal with it, as if frozen, inert.

"The bullying continued until I had the courage to say something about it. Until I had the courage to turn to my mom, actually, and say, I'm not happy with what this person has done. I'm not happy with what has been said to me. And can you help me? And I think that's such a huge lesson to learn, to not be afraid to ask for help, **to turn to somebody you trust.**"

Eventually, Sophie also tried to confront the girls who had been bullying her. That helped for a while Sophie said, but in the end she decided the healthiest path to conflict resolution was to move to another school.

Carolyn Conforti Browse, codirector of Leadership Development at JFSLA, and Dean of Campus Life at Blair Academy, in Blairstown, New Jersey (we call her #DeanofEverything), plus Prep School Coach of the Year in softball (oh, only *eleven* times), teacher, and leadership rock star, recommends that any confrontation with a bully be in a safe public place, and that it's best to include a silent, supportive witness, a friend.

Browse advocates the message always needs to be, "You may not understand that your behavior bothers me and is wrong. I want you to know that if it does not stop I will discuss this with our teacher/coach/principal. This is YOUR choice, but I mean what I say. Please stop this; if you don't, I will have no choice." Carolyn also suggests that it should be practiced out loud ahead of time, preferably with an adult that you trust. Sometimes this works, sometimes it doesn't, but it will increase your confidence to find your voice.

Sophie completely removed herself from the situation and found new friends in a new environment.

One of the challenges of bullying is the scars it can leave behind. Bullying can take a real toll on your confidence. It is why young and old alike should take bullying seriously and not just brush it off. And as Sophie points out, the good news is you will get through it and find the right friends when you do in fact deal with the situation.

> "There are genuine, sincere, friendly, loving, caring people out there that you will just click with, and then it kind of washes away. And you know it's happened to you, but it has made you stronger. What really disheartens me about it is that some people never get away from that situation."

Sophie went on to talk about how her biggest concern is when kids actually start to believe what the bully says. The most important thing is to not blame yourself but instead find pride in who you are, as Sophie discusses:

> "You can't let them get inside your head. And these bullies, they have some sort of weird power to make that happen. You just can't listen to it.

> **"You've just got to embrace all your uniqueness and your weirdness and your nerdiness, or your sportiness or your artiness. You've just got to embrace it, because that's who you are.** And I think when you realize that and you open yourself up to the world and open yourself up to people, that's when they accept you for who you are. And I think that's the life lesson that everybody should at some point in their lives learn, just to be yourself. Don't listen to anybody else."

YES. YES. And another YES. Your nerdiness, your weirdness, your awesomeness . . . whatever it is, embrace YOU. Yep, you. Bullies sometimes seek out people who differ from the mainstream; yet being different should be celebrated, not bullied into submission. Imagine if we all looked the same, talked the same, dressed the same. **YUCK**.

Brrrrp

THE ART TO COMMUNICATING
(maybe Not with a Mean Jerk, But still . . .)

Fortunately, many of us will not be victimized by a mean jerk. But we will have people in our lives who misunderstand, or are mean to others, or cause problems, whether they intend to or not. There is an art to communicating while dealing with any type of conflict resolution at school, at work, on your team, and even at home. The great news is we can learn how to get better. And at any age or phase in your life. Here are some tips we give the girls at our Leadership Academy, developed by Carolyn Conforti Browse.

1) FIRST AND FOREMOST, TO DEAL WITH CONFLICT, WE MUST COMMUNICATE. (GASP!)

Yes, it's that thing that we so often avoid at all costs. GO AND TALK TO THE PERSON. Not in the heat of the moment. Not when you are angry or feeling hurt. Not through texts or social media. Get some separation and then, when the timing is right, calmly ask that person if you can talk about the issue. And then consider these things while communicating:

2) TRY TO SEE IT FROM THEIR SIDE

As hard as this can be, put yourself in their shoes. Try to step back from the situation and understand what the other person may be going through. Why would she/he say this to me? Why would she/he choose to do drugs or smoke? Why would she/he lie to the coach? Or ask me to lie? What is going on in her life?

Also, what you **think** may be motivating an individual's actions, may not really exist at all. Sometimes we interpret actions to mean one thing and we are completely wrong. (For example, an e-mail/text often can be misunderstood because the tone is nearly impossible to convey.)

3) BE BRAVE ENOUGH TO DISAGREE

This is not easy. I repeat: this is not easy. But disagreeing, done respectfully, is healthy, especially when you feel strongly that you or the group are being led in the wrong direction. For example: "I know you think it's no big deal, but I see it differently. I can't lie to our teacher. I can't. . . ." Sometimes the right decisions are not the most popular. Seek respect, rather than popularity, when summoning the courage to disagree with someone. And as Sophie points out,

> "What I found really helpful was to not think of the person you're going up to as having more knowledge than you, or being better than you. I think that's a big barrier when you're introducing yourself to somebody new, or if you're trying to fix a situation that has occurred."

4) CONFRONT THE PROBLEM NOT THE PERSON

This is critical because you are essentially saying this is an issue WE must address, rather than it being the other person's fault. Resist the urge to blame others. When a person feels they are personally being attacked, as we all have felt before, defensive measures kick in. It is much more productive to not attack the person and instead focus on what the greater mission is.

5) GROUP VS. PRIVATE

It's critical to know what to say when you're in a group vs. what to say in private. Sometimes personal differences should be just that, addressed personally. For example, in a group setting try this: "Our team can do so much better if we all agree not to talk behind each other's backs and support each other."

In a private setting, try this: "Jen, I know you are frustrated with Melissa, but we agreed not to talk badly about our teammates. I'm uncomfortable/sad/bothered/ when you say stuff like that about her."

6) START WITH A POSITIVE AND/OR ASSUME A POSITIVE OUTCOME

You know the sandwich rule: positive first, followed by constructive feedback, followed by a positive. Essentially, the criticism sandwiched between two positives: "You worked so hard in practice today. We need that from you every day! You have the ability to help the team by bringing that energy consistently."

Or, "We need you with us, mentally and physically. We need your positive energy to lift us up. So now is the time to get rid of that negative attitude. You control that. We are better with you. Here we go!"

Or bury a criticism in the positive: "Where are those lightning feet I know live down there? We need them now!" Or, "Where is that monster engine I so love in you? Let's rev it up!"

Or exaggerate the negative until it is humorous, and then

get out of Dodge. That was a strategy I deployed often. If I didn't want to do something negative and there was peer pressure, I countered with sarcasm: "Hey, it's not my turn to be 'Losers of the Month Club' president. I'm good. Thank you, but NO THANK YOU." And I'd walk away with a smile (even if I was in a complete panic).

AND HERE ARE SOME TIPS ON HOW TO DEAL WITH SPECIFIC SITUATIONS:

<u>If your captain or leader is not being a positive influence on the team:</u>
Tell her how much you need her guidance, advice, and leadership. Note how important she is to the team. How some of her decisions lately have affected the team in a negative way. How you need her to bring the team together with positive actions, as teams are stronger when they are together, when they are unified. If that doesn't work, try, "Hey, I have some great ideas I heard recently that might help our team. Do you want to try something different?" (Then show her the **Team Mojo Manual!**) And if none of that works, well, you tried. Most important: do not let her negative energy affect the team, as hard as that may be when coming from a leadership position.

<u>If your coach or leader seems to be missing the big picture:</u>
"Coach, I am worried about some stuff going on with the team. Can we talk some time?" Suggest ways to make the team better. Hint: add competition, fun, celebration, and joy into the equation. (But be prepared that your coach or boss may or may not want your opinion. Either way, keep a positive attitude.)

Here's, an important reminder: I think the best leaders never speak or tolerate public trash talking of their coach from their teammates—even if you agree with them. Confront bad attitudes early, as negative energy does **nothing** to help the team win. I promise you. Instead, deal with it by addressing it privately: "I understand your disappointment, but it doesn't help the team for you to be talking that way." And if something negative is said in front of the team, address the issue without again attacking the person: "That will not help us get back to winning ways. What will help us is for us to stick together, to work harder and support each other."

<u>To a troubled classmate or teammate:</u>
"You are amazingly talented, but you can't be your best until you get your head straight off the field and outside the classroom. What's happening with your boyfriend/family/poor grades/eating/etc.? How can I help? Why don't I talk to the school counselor with you? We need to call in some help and Ms. M is a good person to talk to."

MY CAT IS CHOKING ON HAIR BALLS PLAN

AND LASTLY, IN NEGATIVE PEER PRESSURE SITUATIONS, HAVE A PLAN: If you are struggling to summon the courage to say NO, do not worry. Go to your plan (read: create a plan). I had a friend who smoked occasionally when we were young. I tried it once and felt like I had a hole in my lungs the next day at soccer. So the next time she asked me to join her for a smoke, I had a strategy. My go-to plan was, "Hey, no thanks, I don't want to smoke because I don't want to let my teammates down. We have some big games coming up." I then smiled and walked away.

So the next time you get asked to (drink/party/stay up late/_____ [fill in the blank for whatever negative thing you are getting pressured to do]), use my excuse: **I don't want to let my teammates down. We have some big games coming up.** Or if you are not on a sports team, I don't want to let my group down. We have a big performance/rehearsal/weekend of work coming up. Then smile and walk away. Don't even give them the chance to respond. Friends who want you to be successful accept this and understand. And for those "friends" who don't, well, that is a friend you do not want in your life.

Or maybe your plan is to summon friends to help you. One year a JFSLA camper shared her plan for negative peer pressure. She told us this: **My friends knew that their job was to help me get out of a situation when I used a certain buzzword or phrase. They knew this buzzword meant a call to action. So if I said, "Hey, my mom just called, and oh dear, my cat seems to be choking on hair balls," that meant help get me out of that situation. ASAP. And it worked! My friends moved in and took over.**

That was the actual buzz phrase BTW. **Hair balls.**

Ha. Brilliant. **Now those are friends.**

Regardless of the outcome in a tense situation, stay focused on the team goals and your individual goals. Don't give up the very thing you all dream of accomplishing because one person—or a few—may not buy in. Remind your group about your standard, your culture to get them back on course. And make sure you are also living up to those very same standards. There is nothing worse than a person urging others to work harder or be more focused when they are the worst in the group at that very thing. And realize that conflict and confrontations are inevitable. Learning how to positively deal with them is a skill set that will serve you well in life. The hardest part is just starting the conversation. You can do it. Go through the steps above, take a breath, smile, stay calm, and find that voice and/or hair ball plan.

Soooooooo, to get your voice sufficiently warmed up and confident enough to actually have the courage to speak up when needed, I will introduce you to one of my favorite exercises that we do at our Leadership Academies. It is called Tag Team Storytelling. And it's brought to you by our wonder woman, Carolyn Conforti Browse. Impromptu speaking is actually great training for dealing with negative peer pressure. In real life, you will not have time to develop a full response and will need to think quickly. Do not fall prey to the wrong answer (or not talk) and give into peer pressure because you couldn't find your voice or your plan!

EXERCISE:

TAG TEAM STORYTELLING

This may surprise you but a poll taken by the *Washington Post* once reported that of all the fears people have— snakes, heights, losing a loved one, death, etc.—one topped everyone's list: the fear of public speaking. So let's take away the fear by doing it in a group setting and laughing our tails off. Try this with a group of friends, classmates, complete strangers, family, or your team.

INSTRUCTIONS:

Form teams of three or four people.

ROUND 1:

Bring one team up to the front of the room to start it off. Group members will stand shoulder to shoulder, facing all the others. To begin, do a one-minute speech. Someone in the audience chooses a topic from the upcoming list and hollers to the team at the front:

"Ready?! Please start your riveting story of the day by telling us about (topic chosen). Start now!"

Start the timer. Immediately, the person on the left starts the story by saying the first three words of their very compelling story. Immediately after she stops, the person to her right will continue the story by saying the next three words of the story. Immediately following, the next person will say the next three words of the story, and so on.

After the last person speaks, the first person goes

again and continues the story. And so on until one minute passes. It is important to have each person go immediately so the story moves and that person not only has to listen, but improvise quickly! Ensure that no one speaks more than three words at a time. This will continue until the story on said "riveting topic" is told. When the minute is almost complete, the timekeeper will say, "five seconds left," and the next person talking has to cleverly end the story. Everyone will applaud the group (of course). Bravo! :)

Here we go. Please start your riveting story of the day by telling us about (pick a possible topic):

* Why crunchy peanut butter is better than creamy peanut butter.

* Why country music is better than rap music.

* Why squatting over a toilet is better than using those paper toilet seat covers in public bathrooms.

* Why Minnie Mouse is so much cooler than Mickey Mouse.

* Why green vegetables are better than candy.

* Why curly hair is better than straight hair.

* Why chocolate ice cream is better than vanilla.

* Why playing in the rain is more fun than playing on a perfectly sunny day.

* Why braces are better than retainers.

* Why physics class is fun.

* Why gas station bathrooms are so much better than restaurant bathrooms.

* Why math teachers are a little bit nutty.

* Why riding the bus is better than driving to school.

* Why the principal is always smiling.

* Why pencils are better than pens.

* Why chocolate chip pancakes make a wonderful dinner.

* Why you would rather eat worms than lick the bottom of your shoe.

* Any topic of your choice.

Now for your chance to GROW! After all the teams have completed round one, we shall add in a little more of a challenge.

ROUND 2:
Stay with the same teams or switch people to another squad; it is up to you. Now, however, when your team goes up, find a different spot in the line. The person on the left will start again, but each person has to talk longer. Instead of just speaking three words, each person has to talk for ten to twenty seconds each,

listening and continuing the story as before (though these stories will last a minute and a half). The next person will know when it is her turn to go when her teammate turns to her.

SOME THINGS TO THINK ABOUT
TO HELP YOU WITH COMMUNICATION AND CONFLICT RESOLUTION:

• **WORDS ARE ONLY PART OF YOUR COMMUNICATION AND PRESENTATION.** If you come in with a negative tone and body language, your message gets lost before it even gets delivered. Sometimes it is more about HOW you say it and less about what you say. Sure, I care about what you say, but I am much more likely to listen to what you say if I like the way you are saying it.

• **THE IMPORTANCE OF POSITIVE BODY LANGUAGE:** I cannot say enough about this when dealing with any type of communication, conflict, or just good ol' chitchat. Be conscious of looking people in the eye (not crossing arms, not looking down). People often respond to the visual cues (smiles, nods, positive body language) unconsciously. If you are smiling, open, and friendly, people will respond in kind. This happens in sports all the time as well. What is your body language saying on the field/court when under pressure? Frustrated? Confident? Calm? Panicked? What about in life? Are you screaming, sulking, crossing your arms in frustration? Be aware of what signals you are sending out and focus on making them positive ones. Also point out to a friend when she is exhibiting negative body language.

- **RESIST THE URGE TO PANIC!** We will talk about this more in Chapter 12, but how do you handle the stress of having to talk without any time to plan!? Do you beat yourself up, do you work on staying positive? Train your brain to choose the positive and not to panic. Do you panic on the field when the team is not doing well? Or at work if something goes wrong? Or you make a mistake? All these exercises apply to how you react to stress in pressure situations.

- **DEAD AIR (COMPLETE SILENCE) IS YOUR FRIEND:** PAUSE rather than say, "Ummm, you know." If you don't know what to say, don't panic, just take a big pause, act like you mean it, and say nothing. Pauses are very dramatic and will get the listener to pay even more attention. Sometimes I do this at speeches or on TV when I have lost my way. I take a deep breath, pause, gather my thoughts, even if it takes a couple seconds, and then carry on.

CHAPTER 11

EARMUFFS

"You must do the thing you think you cannot do."

—Eleanor Roosevelt

The question so often asked in a group or in class is:
Where are my good communicators?
(The answer is "NOT HERE" if the entire group is
wearing earmuffs and it is eighty degrees outside. Ha.)

And the comment we often hear when a group trends
toward the quieter side is: we need more vocal leaders.

Becoming a vocal leader is the biggest leadership
challenge for people at any age. Leading by *example* may
come naturally to many people, but when asked to be a
more vocal leader, people often think, "Nooooo, that is
not me." And then the next thought probably is, "OMG,
what will my teammates/classmates/colleagues think
if I start giving directions and talking on the field or in
the classroom? What if I sound silly? What if I say the
wrong thing? What if they do not like when I speak up?"
Stop with the *what ifs* and start channeling the *why nots*.

Being a vocal leader is indeed a challenge, but when done
right, your friends will actually love it. Because I would
bet most teams, if not all, are desperate for leaders who
speak up. And equally important, those who have the
ability to confidently convey positive leadership when
dealing with a negative issue make the group stronger.

How many times in life have you said to a friend, "Wow, that was a great idea, why didn't you say something earlier?" Do not be the person who is full of great ideas, yet fails to say them out loud. Yes, let those ideas run free.

There are four keys to keep in mind when learning to be a more vocal leader (and the bonus is they apply to all scenarios, all teams, all of life, for eternity):

• **LET IT OUT:**
First, you have to summon the courage to let that voice OUT. We all know it is there inside you (your parents will back me up on that one I am certain); now just let 'er rip. Once you fight through that initial awkwardness, you will find you are quite comfortable (and good) at talking in a group setting. Taking that first step is the hardest part. Strong vocal cords are not even required. Go ahead, try it. Get out of that comfort zone. You may find your vocal cords were always waiting and willing.

• **BE CONSCIOUS OF WHAT YOU ARE SAYING:**
Now with your newfound ability to chirp, be conscious of WHAT you are saying. Be concise. Be positive. Be strong when you need to be. (For example, "Julie, great hustle, but I need you back on defense more"—believe me, I heard that one lots.) Also be informative. In soccer we say things like, *step to the ball, slide to the right, drop, force her left, mark goal side!*

Think about how the inflection in your voice makes all the difference. For example, you wouldn't say, "Hey Brandi, it would be *sooooo* great if you could maybe think about defending and *um,* I don't know, perhaps put some pressure on the ball, if you feel like it." No, you would forcefully say with inflection, "YES, BRANDI, STEP TO THE BALL, STEP UP. GO NOW. *YEEEESSSS!*" Brandi knows with the concise urgency (yet not panic) in my voice, that she needs to get moving and *pronto.* Actually, I use the name Brandi as an example there, but my real teammate, BRANDI CHASTAIN, was indeed fabulous at giving this information on the field. She had this booming voice that would give clear directions, and it was so helpful. I cannot tell you how many times at camp I watch girls and young woman struggle with giving concise, urgent directions in a loud tone. Maybe they think it is being bossy when in actuality, it is just being competitive.

That is how teammates help each other. By talking to each other and with command. And, no secret here, you must have that communication if you want to be on a winning team or part of a successful group.

• **BE CONSCIOUS OF HOW MUCH YOU ARE TALKING:** This is for the talkers and non-talkers alike. We have all had those people in class or on a team who answer everything. Who talk all the time and have a difficult time actually *not talking* and instead listening. So much about positive leadership is being a great listener as well. If you are the type that talks more than listens, reverse that ratio. Your friends will thank you (and me).

> "Because if you can be a great listener, you can be a great server of your teammates."—Sue Enquist

If you are the person who listens but then is afraid to talk, reverse that ratio as well.

Summon the courage to get your opinion out there. Your voice matters and can help the group. Plus, you will feel so much better for helping the team with your voice. I remember when JOY FAWCETT, our rock star mom of three girls (she had all three girls while she played on the U.S. team BTW!), finally summoned the courage to talk to the whole team. Mind you, it took her a good ten years, but when she spoke, she offered up complete gems of advice. She always had such great insights and was a fabulous problem solver on and off the field. I'm pretty sure I looked at her and screamed, "WHY HAVE

YOU NOT BEEN TALKING WHEN WHAT YOU SAY IS SO INCREDIBLY HELPFUL!" To which she probably replied with her Joy giggle, "Because I can't get a word in with you." Yes, I worked on (and am still working on) reversing my ratio and becoming a better listener.

- **PAY EXTRA ATTENTION TO THE TONE IN WHICH YOU ARE SAYING THINGS:**

This is huge. How many of you have a teammate who is indeed vocal and verbal, but oh, my goodness, you just want her to STOP TALKING.

Every time she talks there's just something: maybe the tone is too loud, too panicked, too negative, too much. Whatever it is, all you can think is, please, someone, anyone, get me earmuffs. *Don't fall into that vocal leader trap: the coach asked for a more verbal leader and coach, so I am being more vocal!*

But the tone in which you are being vocal can vary greatly.

As Dr. Colleen Hacker always pointed out, "Come on you guys!" in a very whiney, what-the-heck-is-wrong-with-us tone is very different than, "Come on you guys!" in a strong, confident, we-got-this tone. Be the voice of calm, but talk with purpose. Be steady. Be confident, even if you don't feel it ("Fake It 'Til You Make It" as we talked about in Chapter 2). The critical aspect with tone is recognizing when the team needs a pump-me-up with a positive, stronger tone and when you need to be the calming force.

It's also important to understand the differences in personalities with your teammates, because then you can tailor your tone to specific teammates. For this, Sue Enquist notes,

SUE: "You could put your son and daughter in the same drip, drip, drip [*her phrase for positive influencers dripping on you*]. And one could still come out seeing things differently. It's important to understand that people's DNA is different: Do you innately see the world half full? And if not, it's OK. We just speak to you with a different language.

"For example, how I speak to my brother and my father differs from how I speak to others. They don't see the world half full. They're engineers. That means that they measure gaps in everything. Or, do you see the world full of bridges? I do. When they see a gap, I see a bridge. And that is OK. We just need to get comfortable speaking their gap language.

"So, I had a player, the greatest athlete ever, honor student. And when I say, 'Oh my goodness, you went nine for ten in hits today, that's so awesome,' she doesn't respond. But if I go, 'You got one wrong. Let's see if tomorrow you can get zero wrong,' she gets it. You'll notice I didn't say you could get 100 percent right. Speak gap language to them."

That also means paying attention to how people in your group process things. I had a teammate who could not handle any type of direct feedback while on the field, unless the person offering it was very calm and positive. I would sometimes forget, holler (read *scream*) at her to defend more and promptly lose her mentally for the rest of the game, because she was upset. Then with others I could be very direct and animated, and that tone got them fired up.

Know what makes others tick and what makes them timid. As I mentioned earlier in the book, the longtime captain of the U.S. National Team, CARLA OVERBECK, was the *master of which tone was needed at what time*. She was our center back, and she would direct when needed, light a fire under your butt (without tearing you down—a wonderful skill set) when needed. But she would also provide a calming, steady voice when the game called for it. Her favorite phrase when all chaos had broken out, and we were in a complete panic, would be, very calmly but loudly (and almost smiling), "We're fine. YES . . . WE. ARE. FINE." Or when needing a spark, "*Julie, we NEEEEEED you.*" Carla always seemed to strike the right chord at the right time, and we were so much better because of her communication acumen. That is what a positive vocal leader can do—lead, inspire, and rally a group together like no other.

JUST BE YOU

Lastly, a gentle reminder that not everyone needs to be a verbal leader. And that is OK as well. JUST BE YOU. Mia told me about a moment when she realized that maybe being the most verbal leader was not going to be her style.

> "I remember in college my senior year at UNC [University of North Carolina] it was like, OK, I was voted captain and all of sudden I thought I had to be different. That I had to be this VOCAL LEADER."

Mia goes on to say that head coach Anson Dorrance asked her, as a captain, to lead the team in a simple postgame cooldown, but that it didn't go so well.

> "I can't tell you how many eye rolls I got. They were doing their own pace. I'm like, 'No, that's too fast. That's not what we're supposed to be doing.' They didn't respond."

And then another time in a pregame huddle, Mia was trying to rally the team and give them the "pump up" talk. After the game UNC assistant coach Bill Palladino pulled her gently to the side. Mia recalls the conversation:

> "Bill said, 'You know, you can't do it every game. You just

gotta pick your times. In the end that's not your strength. Your strength is how hard you work in training. Your strength is scoring goals in game. Your strength is running down balls defensively. That is your leadership style and embrace that.'

"It goes down to that authenticity. It's who you are. And so after that conversation, outside of the ten minutes I was balling uncontrollably, thinking no one likes me, everyone wants me to shut up, that's when I decided what my leadership style was. And being comfortable with that."

And that is not to say you will not evolve into a different style of leadership or become more verbal, as with Sophie, who shares her story of being labeled the "shy" kid in school. Becoming a verbal leader may require time and growth.

"For years and years, people saw me as the shy one, as the shy girl in the classroom. And I really took that to heart because I knew I wasn't shy, I was just quiet. And I think there's a big difference, and that gets mixed up a lot, I think, between shy and quiet.

"I think that brought me down for a while, and I think I then became the shy person that everybody thought I was, and I didn't think I was a good leader. And when we were doing group work in the classroom, I would always let somebody else take charge because oh, no, I couldn't do that. No, I'm the shy one, you know? It definitely messed up my own perception of whether or not I could become a leader."

What, you wonder, was the key for Sophie to bust out of her shy bubble? Well, a school science project of course. Sophie needed answers and the only way to get them was to go out and ask questions:

SOPHIE: "I was forced, I was pushed out into the open. I was a bit like a rabbit in headlights; I didn't know what to do. But I had to figure out fast because that was the only way that I could get my end results in my projects [*she laughs*]. And I found that I actually liked conversing with people [*laugh*].

JULIE: "*How about that?!* You get out of your comfort zone and you find you actually like it out there."

SOPHIE: "Yes. Exactly. I just love when that happens. **Then you realize that your comfort zone wasn't your comfort zone at all. That, that whole world that was outside your comfort zone was where you belong** [*laughs*]."

Audible *AHHHH*. It is a beautiful thing indeed when you discover the whole world outside your comfort zone is really where you belong.

And while you are there, go find your voice, find your tone, find your timing (ratio), and

GO FIND THAT WORLD.

Your teammates and classmates will thank you for it . . . unless, of course, they have earmuffs on.

GO BE THAT LEADER.

EXERCISE:

This is an exercise we do at our Leadership Academies that was started by one of our fabulous staff members, Sarah Strickland. Sarah is the head women's soccer coach at Appalachian State University and joins the road show every summer. This exercise is about standing up and speaking out. We call this exercise **STAR MOMENT**.

After every practice, when the girls are all sitting together (or you can do this in smaller groups with your team), a captain or leader of the team calls on a girl to stand up, say their name (if don't know each other yet), own the moment (speak loud and clear), and tell us about one star moment they had personally and then one they noticed in someone else today. It could be on the field, off the field, something they said, or something they did. You get it. The captain or appointed leader then repeats the process with another girl in the group. And so on.

We use this for our academy of course, but this can be used for any team, in any environment. We love Star Moment for many reasons. But here are just three:

1) IT GETS THE QUIETER GIRLS TO PRACTICE USING THEIR VOICE, AND THEY DISCOVER THEY CAN INDEED TALK IN FRONT OF A GROUP.

2) IT GIVES GIRLS AN OPPORTUNITY TO POINT OUT FIRST THEIR OWN STRENGTH AND THEN ACKNOWLEDGE SOMEONE ELSE'S AWESOME MOMENT.

3) BY CELEBRATING YOURSELF AND OTHERS, YOU START TO PAY MORE ATTENTION TO YOURS AND THE BEHAVIOR OF OTHERS ON THE TEAM OR IN THE GROUP.

DON'T JUST
THINK IT, INK IT

CHAPTER 12

DO NOT
USE PANIC

"In the raining of the roads, do not use panic."

—Actual roadside sign I saw in China, written in English

We were on one of our many trips to China in the early to mid-1990s with the U.S. Women's National Team when we saw a sign quoted above, on the side of the road in Beijing. We all laughed so hard that it became a team saying (or at least my saying). Whenever something crazy would happen, or things got a bit hectic, we would yell to each other, "DO NOT USE PANIC!" and then laugh out loud. Because whether we like to admit it or not, we have all had that moment where we totally lose our stack.

And for sure, we all have that friend (or maybe it is you!) who, in times of craziness and chaos, *always freaks out*. Her face, body language, tone, breathing, bug eyes, you name it . . . screams panic. It pretty much looks like this.

SCHOOL

One of the most treasured skill sets I have come to admire in people has to deal with how people contend with adversity. How people react in times of chaos. We all can be happy and calm and confident when life is good. When all is going well. But what happens when life shoots arrows at you and they are *coming in hot*? What do you do? And as we know, school can bring far too many of these moments. Whether it is starting a new school, a new class, doing poorly on a test, or just the anxiety around exams, friends, *whatever*, school can be full of drama. Yet, as Martin Luther King once said, "The ultimate measure of a person is not where one stands in moments of comfort and convenience, but where one stands at times of challenge and controversy."

And Martin Luther King then followed up that great line with, "So do not use panic." (*Orrrrrr*, maybe not.) But essentially, it is the same thought . . . the best leaders react with calm and confidence, even if they are feeling anything but calm and confident.

Which reminds me of something my kids now do in the car when we are driving and they see a police car. They scream out loud in a mock panicked voice, "Police! Act normal! ACT. VERY. NORMAL."

That really is the key. Act very normal in moments of crisis (or perceived crisis). The best leaders know how to do just that.

MAKE LIKE A DUCK

Yet, acting normal when your heart is beating out of your chest is not such a simple task. Adversity, the moment it hits, is not pleasant, as we all know. Often, self-doubt follows. But I actually think adversity is one of the great gifts in life. Because crisis can bring growth. Note the word "can." Staying with China, did you know the Chinese symbol for crisis has two characters: one for danger and one for opportunity? I love this as you decide which way you will go. When you learn to turn adversity into a growing experience and opportunity, you, my geniuses, have just solved one of the riddles of the world. And if you have a hard time remaining calm during chaos, I have the perfect solution for you: **MAKE LIKE A DUCK.**

Yes, I said *duck*.
Let me explain:

When you see a duck on the pond, it is most often chillin' in the sun, calm as can be, sunning away, whisking the water off its back . . . cool as a duck can be. That is what you see. But what if there was an underwater camera and that underwater camera was dropped into the pond and placed to look up from below? It would tell a different story. You would see two webbed feet pumping away, peddling like crazy in the water, chaos in motion. But thankfully life doesn't have an underwater cam, so all we see is the calm, confident, smiling duck. Yes, I think ducks smile.

So in times of turmoil, make like the duck. In fact, **BE THE DUCK.** No one knows what your insides are saying and doing. They don't see that sinking feeling in your gut. They don't see your internal butterflies bouncing into each other. All they see is the confident, calm you . . . unruffled by the current situation. And guess what? Those around you will respond the same way. Instead of panicking, they too will derive confidence from how calm you are. So whisk that water off your back, soak in the sunlight, and most important, grow from the little bumps in the road that life places on your path. **REMEMBER, QUACK, DON'T CRACK.**

Mia Hamm reminded me of a huge moment when our U.S. team quacked rather than cracked. It was the 1996 Summer Olympics semifinal game versus Norway. It was halftime and we were losing 1–0. The backstory is we had lost to Norway 1–0 the year before in the semifinal of the Women's World Cup. And *ahhh*, that one hurt. It's the kind of loss that still sends chills down my spine. One year later we were staring at the same thing.

> MIA: "We were down 1–0, but we walked into halftime and no one panicked. There was an absolute calm. And sure we were nervous because of the scars of the prior summer, but everyone instead oozed confidence. The conversations at halftime were focused on how we would go forward, score goals, and beat Norway. We walked out and did just that."

We stayed calm, and confidence followed.

I DON'T LIKE YOU

It also helps that we repeated over and over to ourselves during the preceeding twelve months that we *would not* let panic and doubt take over as it did in the World Cup loss the previous year.

Keeping this perspective is a must. Sometimes you can control the universe's plans for you, but sometimes you cannot. What you can ALWAYS control is how you react to that not-so-pleasant feeling.

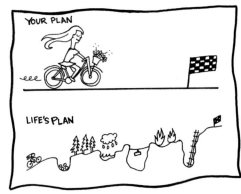

Tatyana McFadden had lots of legitimate reasons to walk away from a new challenge when she was repeatedly bumping into adversity. But for Tatyana, paralyzed from spina bifida since birth, quitting on something wasn't in her DNA. Tatyana tells her story about wanting to compete in a new sport (cross-country skiing) to qualify for the 2014 Sochi Paralympics in Russia. Russia was her birthplace, and her lifelong dream was to compete in front of both her Russian and U.S. families.

> TATYANA: "Well, it was probably one of the hardest things I've ever done, *in my entire life.* I put away the racing chair. I left my track coach, Adam. I left my teammates. And I moved to Colorado to start with a new coach, a new team, and a new sport. And I got into cross-country skis."

This is what I love about the *why notters.* They try things. They are bold. Mind you, Tatyana had *never been on* skis before. Never. Most people would start with this premise: Well, since I've never done that sport and the Sochi Paralympic Games are just around the corner, I don't have the time to learn a new sport. That dream is just too crazy. Too uncomfortable. Too difficult. Not realistic (whatever the excuse—and there are plenty). No one would have faulted her for saying, "Hey, I don't have enough time or I gave it my best shot, and it is just not working." But not Tatyana. She instead starts with the thought *WHY NOT.*

> "I was thinking, oh, I'm superstrong, like I have the endurance, I have the strength. I just need to pick up the style and the, the art of cross-country skiing. I just need to know technique. Well, technique was the hardest thing to pick up. And I noticed that I really was *terrible at the technique.* I was falling into last place at every single competition. You had to *turn the page* to see my results."

She said this still quite horrified. Tatyana was not familiar with turning the page to find her results because in track and field, her results were always first page, top of the page.

And it was very emotional. There were times where I'd call my mom and I'd say, maybe this is just too ridiculous and too wild. I'm dreaming too big right now. You know, maybe I should just go home and not pursue cross-country skiing. And my mom's like, 'Tatyana, you've gone through too much and gone too far to let that dream go. You're so close, you're right there.'"

→ EXACTLY WHY WE ♡ MOMS :)

Tatyana fought through those moments. And here's how she did it:

"I had to change my attitude. And I had to let go of that negativity. It was really tough hearing from other people that I was not good. And that I should go back to wheelchair racing. But I think that's what made me switch my mind and say no, *I am here. I am allowed to be here just like anyone else.* And I am doing this because I have the dream of being with my adoptive family and my birth family."

She chose to fight through it, to flip her focus to the positive. Tatyana failed in the first two cross-country qualifying races. But in the the *last possible race* before the U.S. team went to Sochi, Tatyana qualified for the U.S. Paralympic Ski Team.

So Tatyana, winner of ten Summer Paralympics medals at that time, was off to Sochi, Russia, for her very first Winter Paralympics. And while many people would just be happy getting to Sochi, Tatyana went over and won a silver medal in front of both her Russian and U.S. family members. Of course she did. Check that one off the bucket list. *dream* ☑

Tatyana's ability to stay calm and positive in the face of adversity is remarkable.

This reminded me of a story Robin Roberts shared in her book, *From the Heart*. Robin tells a story about her first day as a TV sports anchor in Nashville, Tennessee. She gets a phone call at her desk and it's a guy on the other end with a gruff voice saying, "I don't like you." (Yes, that is actually what he said: "I. Don't. Like. You.") He then goes on to tell her she doesn't belong in sports, no woman does. Robin lets the guy say his piece and calmly responds, "Give me six months. Watch my reports. Then call me back."

Here Robin is starting a new job and she's already got a detractor, yet she doesn't lose her composure or back down. She holds on to her self-belief. Sure enough, three months later that same person was back on the phone: "Is this Robin Roberts?" She thought uh-oh, I know that voice. Robin replied "Yes," waiting for a tirade. He says, "Aw, I guess you're all right."

CALMNESS
↓
CONFIDENCE
↓
OXYGEN
↓
HOPE

But let's get back to *why* I value the ability to stay calm in chaos. First, it is incredibly hard to do when those all around you are in panic mode. It shows an internal strength that I greatly admire, and most important, it gives oxygen to a group; it delivers hope. Imagine throughout history, in moments of crisis, if Winston Churchill had instead been screaming in absolute panic about Nazi Germany's intimidating strength at that early stage in World War II. Or President John F. Kennedy publicly fretting about how we could handle the Cold War and our Russian adversary. Or if Rosa Parks had jumped up and down, shouting in defiance on the bus. By staying calm, Parks ignited a spark. Historians credit her quiet strength and calm act of disobedience with launching the civil rights movement. By showing self-control, you instill confidence. By staying confident, you can overcome adversity.

And independent of what is happening around you, the best leaders remain constant. Regardless of the environment—it could be total chaos, complete calm, absolute bliss, full sorrow—this person is not guided by the conditions, but instead by her core.

Sue Enquist was very close to another UCLA coaching legend, John Wooden. Wooden coached the UCLA men's basketball team to ten national titles in twelve years, including a record seven in a row, during the 1960s and the mid-1970s. But that wasn't Wooden's legacy. Ask any person old enough to know Wooden, the "Wizard of Westwood," and the first things they will mention are his character and his leadership. Sue calls Coach Wooden "Papa" and says he was her single greatest influence. She shares a story about the day Papa changed her leadership thinking:

SUE: "One day Papa told me, 'You're a conditional leader, Sue.' I said, 'conditional leader?' I had never heard that term before. Now, remember at this point in my coaching career, we're sitting on a lot of championships. So I'm feeling pretty good about my understanding of the language of being a leader. Papa went on, 'You fall in love with the team when they're winning, and Sue, I don't know if you notice, but **you talk WE when you're winning, and you talk THEM when you're losing.**'

"When Papa said that, a man of so few words, that stopped me in my tracks. That was a huge thing for me to learn. **I learned to be an unconditional leader. To love them when you hate them.**"

Ha. And to love them when things are good. Love them when it's crazy time. Love them when it's ugly, beautiful, and everything in between. What kind of leader are you? Are you only helping when times are good? Are you only calm when all is going well? Are you only confident when your team is winning? Love them when you hate them. Give that love at all times, under all conditions.

And finally, remember when the pressure escalates, when your body starts to panic. Remind yourself to smile, look others in the eye, breathe, stand tall, and focus on calmly guiding the group to its core. Even if you have to quack to get there.

In the raining of the roads,

DO NOT USE PANIC.

EXERCISE:

OSMOSIS: So much of good leadership is body language in moments of panic, as we have discussed. And especially as the pressure heats up, the importance of passing on positivity ramps up. Remember, the world cannot see your butterflies, the world cannot see your feet paddling like crazy under water. What they can see is your calm, confident reaction. And just to give you an idea of the power of your positive body language and how it affects others (hence the exercise is named Osmosis), go try this. I do this all the time while out jogging and it is fascinating:

* GO TAKE A WALK OR JOG AT A BUSY PARK. OR ON A BUSY TRAIL. TAKE A FRIEND OR FAMILY MEMBER WITH YOU. AS YOU WALK PAST PEOPLE, LOOK THEM IN THE EYE AND SMILE. OBSERVE THE REACTION FROM A SIMPLE SMILE AND EYE CONTACT. MAKE SURE YOU LOOK THEM IN THE EYE.

* THEN AFTER A WHILE, CONTINUE TO SMILE AT PEOPLE AND MAKE EYE CONTACT, BUT NOW SAY "HELLO." OR "GOOD AFTERNOON." OR, "WHAT A GREAT DAY TO BE OUTSIDE!" ANYTHING POSITIVE. WATCH THE REACTION. WHEN YOU PUT OUT POSITIVE ENERGY, POSITIVE ENERGY COMES BACK TO YOU.

There is an older man named Chuck whom I often see walking with his cane on the beach trail near my house. Every time I see Chuck it literally makes my entire day. Because Chuck will make a positive comment and/or give a smile to almost every person who passes him going the other way. Sometimes he will yell "OORAH!" (must do like the Marines) to a fast runner who excitedly OORAH's him back. Immediately a serious or gloomy face lights up.

Very stressed-looking people suddenly smile back. As people run by, he cheers them on. Many stop to talk and say hello. I am constantly blown away by how much joy he passes on in such a simple and organic way. The power of positivity in personal interactions is telling. **GO TRY IT. YOU CAN SEE IT FOR YOURSELF.**

SECTION 4

COMMUNITY

This book started with how you, yourself, can be a leader. We then busted a move out to the next ring, your team. Next, we went even broader: how to lead in your *school* and among your peers. And now we take those lessons from *self*, *team*, and *school* and apply them to, yes, a larger ring of empowerment, your **COMMUNITY**.

Because to me, the ultimate goal of leadership is to make those around you better. Leadership is about elevating others, getting them to maximize their potential, and ultimately helping them achieve their dreams. So I ask you, **"How can we each pay it forward? How can we impact the people around us so that we are a catalyst for helping others?"** Well, you can start by helping a friend. And suddenly, you are helping a few friends. Next, you are helping a community. And before you know it, you may just be inspiring the world.

#babystepsbaby. So, WHY NOT take that first step forward and

CHOOSE TO MATTER.

CHAPTER 13

CHOOSE
TO MATTER

"Sometimes it is the people who no one imagines anything of, who do the things that no one can imagine."

—Alan Turing (as played by Benedict Cumberbatch) in *The Imitation Game*

It's easy to feel that the world—and even your local community—is a great big machine plunging ahead, and that you can't make a difference. This is especially pronounced when you're younger of course. But that feeling can happen at all ages. You have to trust that you can indeed make a difference by going out and doing something. And if you don't believe me (yet), I will show you some amazing examples of young leaders who did. The ability to lift someone up is in ALL of us.

Forget the misconception that you have to be a movie star or celebrity to really help a cause or a community. In fact, the best work is often done by people you have never heard of. They simply cared enough to be moved into action. Action that matters:

COMMUNITY

"What will matter is not what you bought,
but what you built,
Not what you got, but what you gave.
What will matter is not your success,
but your significance.
What will matter is not what you learned,
but what you taught.
What will matter is every act of integrity, compassion,
courage or sacrifice that enriched, empowered or
encouraged others to emulate your example.
What will matter is not your competence,
but your character,
Not how many people you knew, but how many will
feel a lasting loss when you're gone.
What will matter is not your memories,
but the memories of those who loved you.
What will matter is how long you will be remembered,
by whom and for what.
Living a life that matters doesn't happen by accident.
It's not a matter of circumstance but of choice.
Choose to live a life that matters."

—William Josephson

Because. You. Can.

One of the most rewarding aspects to actually choosing
to matter, to giving, is you spill some on yourself.
You give and it comes back to you. You gain so much
emotionally by giving. Just like the saying, "You
can't spread sunshine without sprinkling a little bit
on yourself." When you give, you grow. It really is an
emotion that has no equivalent in my opinion. Because
what you do matters. What you give matters. How you
help matters. The person you are helping benefits, and
your own life blossoms as well.

And a healthy (read: *loud*) reminder: it is not about how much money you raise or how many people you help. Don't let figures define your capacity to give. Or even worse, impede your capacity to give. Many people think they must emulate the seemingly astronomical accomplishments they read about from celebrity fundraisers: Emma Watson raised $700 million in two minutes for this cause. Taylor Swift raised $2 billion in five seconds for that cause. (I am making this up of course, but we've all seen the headlines.) Yes, this is all fabulous, but that is not the only way to help others of course.

GIVING COMES IN MANY SHAPES AND SIZES . . . at our Leadership Academy we call them the three T's of giving: Time, Talent, and/or Treasure. Do you know how many organizations need volunteers to give of their **time**? Lots. Do you know how many organizations need people to give of their **talent** (whether your talent is putting on a soccer clinic for kids who have never been exposed to sports, or teaching art to young kids, or maybe reading to the elderly at a senior center because they can't see well)? Lots. Do not think you must only raise money (**treasure**) to make a difference. And don't make the mistake of thinking you have to shift the world's axis in one day. (We will give you a week.) It could be as simple as a passing on kindness, extending a hand to help someone in need. Imagine the sum of many small gestures played out by millions and millions of people. Simply by acting. Simply by doing. Anthropologist Margaret Mead said it best:

> "Never doubt that a small group of thoughtful citizens can change the world. Indeed, it is the only thing that ever has."

I don't know if you all have noticed this, but we have a lot of talkers in life. People who talk a great game about all that they want to give and do, but too often fail to follow through with action. People who do community service so they can put it on their college application. So they can check that box. That is why this Gapingvoid cartoon made me smile (but then again, they always make me smile). Well, now imagine a world

where people DO, not because they think they *have* to DO, but because they *are excited* to DO.

THE NEW LAND OF DOers

Life lesson No. 578: The world needs fewer talkers and more DOers.

So in honor of all doers or soon-to-be doers, let's in fact DO. Right now. Yes, now. Let's set a goal for how you can help others in your community. We are going to create a leadership project that you will carry out in your very own community. We shall call it the "CHOOSE TO MATTER" LEADERSHIP PROJECT. If that sounds daunting, fear not. We will take this in baby steps remember. And we will grow and grow and grow until we are indeed Leaders of Action. *Soooooooo....*

WELCOME to the new land of doers! An important distinction in this land of DOers however: WE DON'T JUST DO TO DO, WE DO TO EMPOWER. Here is an exercise to help us start building our Leader of Action muscle:

EXERCISE:

To be a doer, the most important first step is to find out what makes your soul leap; what makes your heart thump. And it can be for both good and bad reasons. Maybe your heart thumps because you can no longer tolerate some of the mean things said to people on social media. Or, on the positive side, maybe you love the feeling of helping children with disabilities. Take some time to think about what makes you feel intensely. What stirs your curiosity?

PASSIONS	ISSUES
• the laughter of my kids	• I want girls to believe they can do whatever they want to do.
• the beach	
• empowering others	• I want people to unlock their confidence if it is hiding.
• sunshine	
• coffee	
• donuts (duh)	
• sweating	• Passing on kindness.
• hiking	
• giggling with friends	
• exploring	

(Mine would look like this.)

1) TAKE A PIECE OF PAPER AND DRAW A LINE DOWN THE MIDDLE FROM THE TOP TO THE BOTTOM. ON THE LEFT, LIST YOUR PASSIONS. THESE ARE THINGS YOU CARE DEEPLY ABOUT, AS WE DISCUSSED PREVIOUSLY. ANYTHING THAT MAKES YOU FEEL INTENSELY. ON THE RIGHT, LIST ISSUES YOU WOULD LIKE TO CHANGE IN YOUR COMMUNITY. IF YOU COULD WAVE A MAGIC WAND, WHAT WOULD YOU CHANGE?

2) NOW, MERGE YOUR PASSIONS ON THE LEFT WITH ISSUES ON THE RIGHT THAT YOU WOULD LIKE TO ADDRESS. YOU CAN EVEN DRAW LINES LINKING THE TWO SIDES. WE HAVE FOUND THAT WHEN YOU LINK PASSIONS WITH ISSUES, YOUR LEADERSHIP PROJECT STARTS TO COME TO LIFE, AND EQUALLY IMPORTANT, IS MUCH MORE LIKELY TO BE COMPLETED.

Maybe your magic wand wants to tackle school issues: bullying, peer pressure, or stress. Or team issues: getting your team to care more/bond more/enjoy more/work more. Or maybe it's global issues that you would like to change: the homeless who are cold in the winter, kids who lack equipment/fields, and/or have no safe place to play. Or maybe health and environmental issues are on your radar screen: cancer, the beach that is dirty and polluted, our school, which does not have a proper recycling program.

Whatever they are, write them down. Think outside the box. Challenge yourself to think beyond the obvious. And most important, think about what makes you excited about change and what your community needs.

As your leadership-project idea comes to life, here are some important things to consider:

• **THE PROJECT DOES NOT NEED TO RAISE MONEY.** It could be volunteering your time, putting on a clinic for young kids, doing an equipment drive, organizing an anti-bullying meeting or club at your school.

• **MAKE IT DOABLE:** You may have heard the phrase, "Think globally, act locally." If cleaning the oceans is your passion (awesome!), start first with your local bay or lake. If helping all kids with disabilities is your passion, find a local group that needs volunteers. Or suggest that you can volunteer and run sports clinics, art classes, science experiments (share your talent!). :)

• **MAKE IT FUN:** What makes the most sense to you with your schedule? How many times per month or in a year would you want to volunteer. Or do a park cleanup. Maybe it's once a year. Maybe if volunteering it is once per month. The idea is not to change the world in a day, but to start . . . even if that means one person at a time.

• **START THINKING ABOUT YOUR DREAM TEAM OF SUPPORTERS:** Who can help you? Who can give advice? Who has expertise in this area that I can reach out to? Who could serve as mentors?

Now that you have put some thought into it, let's jot those ideas down on paper (don't just think it, ink it).

WHAT IS YOUR PROJECT IDEA?

WHAT COULD YOUR PROJECT DO?

WHOM DOES THIS PROJECT SERVE?

WHO IS ON YOUR DREAM TEAM?

1.

2.

3.

4.

5.

Remember, less is more! And this is still just the brainstorming part of the process. We will put more meat on the bone soon. For now, finding your areas of passion and thinking about how you can mold that into an idea for change is the most important first step.

CHAPTER 14

YOUR
MAGIC WAND:
ACTION

"I hear and I forget. I see and I remember. I do and I understand."

—Confucius

You have probably heard the old saying, "Give a man a fish and you feed him for a day; teach a man to fish and you feed him for a lifetime." It speaks to the quote above: "I do and I understand."

Carolyn Conforti Browse recently reminded me of an important principle to being leaders of action: the Triangle. More specifically, the three prongs to **Action**: Feel. Think. Act. We of course need to spend time "FEELING" what our "Choose to Matter" Leadership Project could be. We also need to spend time thinking about how we can make that project successful. But eventually, we need to act. You can feel it, think about it, but ultimately, each individual has to commit to taking the step forward. To action.

Or as Robin Roberts says,

"The secret of getting ahead is just getting started."

And much of being moved into action is caring so deeply about something that you must raise your hand. Tatyana McFadden talks about that moment in high school when she knew she needed to step up:

TATYANA: "That was probably one of the hardest things I've ever had to do. I had to fight for equality for physically disabled people to be able to participate in high school sports. So in 2004, I came off being a Paralympic silver and bronze medalist, and the only thing I wanted to do was to join high school sports. And so I showed up and I was doing everything that I was supposed to do. And at the end of track practice, I got in line with all the other girls, and I was next to get my uniform. And when it was my turn to get the uniform, the coach told me, 'oh, you're not gonna be competing this weekend. You don't get your uniform.' And I looked really puzzled, and I said, 'Well, I don't understand. I did everything I'm supposed to do. Why am I not competing? Why am I being excluded?'"

Tatyana went home and told her mom about this. Her mother told Tatyana there must be a huge mistake. It is illegal for them not to give you a uniform to compete. After conversations with the high school, the school finally gave Tatyana her uniform but would not let her race alongside the other runners.

TATYANA: "Going to that first track meet was absolutely also one of the hardest things I've ever done. I was the only female wheelchair racer. And so they stopped the entire track meet. And then let me go around *by myself*."

JULIE: "Oh, no."

TATYANA: "Yes. And then they continued the track meet. So I feel like it was the wrong perception. I think people didn't really see me as an athlete. They saw me as oh, poor little girl, we're stopping the entire track meet for her. And letting her go around. **This is something that I did not want to ever happen again.** And I didn't want anyone else in the future to deal with this . . .

especially my sister, Hanna McFadden. She's an amputee. And she's also a wheelchair racer. So I asked my mom, 'Well, what can we do?' And she said, 'You know, we can file a lawsuit. We can file a lawsuit for no damages, just for the right for physically disabled people to participate in high school sports.' And so we did, and we won. We won in Howard County, and then we won in the state of Maryland. And now, it's federal law."

And now it is federal law. This started as one person not wanting others to go through the same humiliation she did. This started as one person caring enough to raise her hand. This started with the wish for all people with disabilities to have access and opportunity. And Tatyana built her team to support her fight for equality. Her mom, the Women's Sports Foundation, and a desire to enact positive change mean physically disabled people all over the country now have the right to participate in high school sports.

So pull that magic wand back out. Let's put that wand into action with our "Choose to Matter" Leadership Project. In the previous chapter, you listed some topics that made you passionate about change. That made you eager for transformation. How can you help make that positive change? How can you put that idea into play? I don't know about you, but for me, when I look at the BIG picture, it can seem completely overwhelming. And when I get that way, my mind just closes the shades. I sweep it under the rug hoping it will go away. As we know, that solves nothing. So, as I have gotten wiser and more mature (cough), I have found that when I am overwhelmed by a topic or a thought, if I break it down into more palatable steps, the anxiety starts to melt away. *Ahhhh.* Baby steps, baby. Plus, I eventually discovered that it's just a good habit for life: writing down measurable, realistic goals and action plans that go with the goal.

BE S.M.A.R.T.

Start first with a goal that is realistic. A goal that you can complete. THIS IS SO IMPORTANT (yes, that is me talking really loud with all caps). Because if your goal is too large or too broad, it will become a source of angst rather than action. And clearly, that is not the desired outcome. I cannot emphasize this enough. Imagine if millions of people, one project at a time, started doing small deeds that led to bigger actions. And unless you start small, that deed often never gets started. Better to help one person smile than get stuck in paralysis.

With that in mind, to help you simplify things, make sure your project goal is a **SMART** goal. SMART is an acronym for:

Specific
Measurable
Attainable
Relevant
Timely

Instead of your project goal being "I will clean all parks all over the world" (which is fabulous, yet hardly attainable), have your SMART goal be, "I will clean my local park three times a year, recruiting at least twenty friends and family to help me each time (followed by donuts and coffee, which always helps attract friends)."

Or another example.

PROJECT GOAL:
"I will raise money to help fight breast cancer."

Although admirable, be more specific.

SMART PROJECT GOAL: "I will raise $500 for breast cancer research in the next four months by doing a used equipment sale of old uniforms, shoes, and gear collected from various teams in the area."

You get it. Make sure that SMART goal is Specific, can be Measured, is Attainable, is Relevant to what you are passionate about, and is Timely. Unless you put a time limit on these, life happens and you forget. Make the timeline realistic but not so far along that you will never start it. If in doubt, err on the side of putting your goal time for completion earlier rather than later. We have found with our JFSLA students that the further away you get from an idea, the harder it is to take that first step.

If you are having a hard time figuring out what you want to do, I find that I am most inspired to do things when I know I have friends or teammates that rely on me to get things done. So, if you are also like that, maybe think about grabbing a friend, or five, and seeing if they want to do a project with you. Plus, it becomes a great excuse to hang out, laugh together, and do good . . . *all at the same time.* **#lifegoal**

OK, doers. Enough babbling from me. Now let's do. So, here is your simple guide to help you get there in a **SMART** way.

CHOOSE to MATTER
LEADERSHIP ACTION PLAN

PASSION:
I will . . .

MY S-M-A-R-T PROJECT GOAL :
I will . . .

SPECIFIC	MEASURABLE
What **SPECIFIC** problem do you want to solve? (Think about why you want to do this. What is it that drives your interest toward this cause?)	How will you **MEASURE** this goal? (How will this change the problem? Simple is good!) My 3-5 step **ACTION PLAN**: 1. 2. 3. 4. 5.

ATTAINABLE	RELEVANT	TIMELY
Whose support will you need to make the goal **ATTAINABLE**? Don't be afraid to ask for help.	How is this project **RELEVANT** to you? Why do you care deeply about it? What outcome will make you happy at the project's completion?	It is so important to give yourself a **TIMELINE** to accomplish this project. We are all busy, so set up a calendar to help you get this done.
I need help from:		
I need the following supplies/equipment:		
Those will cost me:		

If you are stuck for ideas, or just want to see how the template could look, here is a sample project idea.

MY SMART PROJECT GOAL: I will help the environment by organizing a neighborhood park pickup day in November and getting at least fifty people to come join me.

SPECIFIC	MEASURABLE
What **SPECIFIC** problem do you want to solve? (Think about why you want to do this. What is it that drives your interest toward this cause?)	How will you **MEASURE** this goal? (How will this change the problem? Simple is good!) My 3-5 step **ACTION PLAN:**
I want to clean up the trash in my neighborhood park so that people from the community will use it more often.	1) Contact Parks and Rec 2) Set a date with them 3) Organize a plan to get the word out— soccer clubs, teammates, local churches, community paper, flyers, etc. 4) Organize volunteers 5) Clean park!

ATTAINABLE	RELEVANT	TIMELY
Whose support will you need to make the goal **ATTAINABLE**? Don't be afraid to ask for help.	How is this project **RELEVANT** to you? Why do you care deeply about it? What outcome will make you happy at the project's completion?	It is so important to give yourself a **TIMELINE** to accomplish this project. We are all busy, so set up a calendar to help you get this done.
I need help from:		
my mom, dad, parks and recreation dept., and the community to help me spread the word	1) The park will look clean	August: initial meeting with parks and rec to set date
	2) People will play in the park	September: get the word out—how do I do that?
I need the following supplies/equipment:	3) It is fun gathering the community for a great cause	October: confirm volunteers
- trash bags for pickup - flyers to get word out - donuts, bagels, coffee for volunteers	4) I will have CHOSEN TO MATTER!	November: "Park Pickup" day!
Those will cost me:		
- trash bags= $25 - flyers= $25 - bagels, coffee= $50		
TOTAL COST= $100		

BY DOING, YOU DISCOVER YOU CAN, IN FACT, DO

You may be still asking WHY . . . WHY SHOULD I DO THIS? And if you are, I'm fairly certain that this is what your brain is processing:

The reason you should do this is that, by doing, you grow and blossom and realize how incredibly gratifying it is to take on a project that serves others. I can *tell* you about how gratifying it is . . . I can *tell* you about how much you will learn about yourself in the process . . . I can *tell* you about blossoming; but *unless* you do, you will not fully understand. You must live it. And life is full of choices. So why not choose to matter? Scale it to what is possible, to what is doable. Take a deep breath. Smile. Remember, less is more.

If you feel you do not have the time to organize a project, give by simply passing on kindness. Yes, that may sound cheesy, but think about it for a moment. What if you made it your "Choose to Matter" project goal to pass on a smile every day to one person in need? No extra time needed. No pre-plotted planning necessary.

COMMUNITY

Just write it down on your action plan above (writing it down makes you accountable). Or again, if you're overwhelmed by the idea of taking on a larger project, maybe your SMART goal is to simply write a quick note—it could be two sentences—every week to a friend or stranger who did something nice that you noticed. You can thank them in a handwritten note. That's right, write it down. Don't just think it, INK IT.

Or, as Sue Enquist recommends:

> "You just start paying attention to somebody who looks like she needs help. What does that look like? Maybe she's sad, maybe she's crying, maybe she's alone at lunch. Be the one that just sneaks up on her and gives her a little love. If you are an athlete, start there. When was the last time you put your hand on the shoulder of the nonstarter? I always tell starters, you get the gift every game day of seeing your name on the lineup card. Can you go give her a gift?"

***And if you still think you cannot*, I give you these Julie Foudy Sports Leadership Academy students who thought they couldn't—and then did.**

EMMA BLACK

Meet JFSLAer EMMA BLACK from Clarks Summit, Pennsylvania. Emma did one of my favorite project ideas, called Goals that Matter, and she got her entire team involved. She first started this project when she was fourteen years old.

"I did a project that I called "Goals that Matter." It was a fundraiser for the Special Olympics. After working with Special Olympians at the Julie Foudy Sports Leadership Academy, I realized how I had always taken my own athletic abilities and opportunities for granted. I asked teammates, friends, and anyone who was willing to make a pledge for each goal that my soccer team scored in our fall travel season. Pledges ranged from 50 cents a goal to $1.50 for each goal. This fundraising turned out to be successful, so I continued it throughout the next year. After two fall seasons of travel soccer, I ended up donating $1,400 to a local branch (in northeastern Pennsylvania) of the Special Olympics. It motivated my team, and I knew that every goal we scored was meaningful whether we won or lost the game. *By doing*, I realized how helping others makes me want to do more. I will continue to do more and give back. That is why today I am coaching a travel soccer team. I hope I can teach the girls life lessons and service while giving them an opportunity to fall in love with the game that gave me so much."

Now imagine getting your team to do the same, with each teammate getting pledges per goal, per basket, per point . . . whatever makes sense for your sport. For whatever cause you all choose to support. I love it.

KATE DIAZ

Meet JFSLAer **KATE DIAZ**, from Chicago, who merged her passion for music with a cause. . . .

"The first year of my 'Choose to Matter' project I was twelve, and I played music every Saturday at a restaurant near my house. During the holidays, I made my weekly shows into fundraisers and donated all iTunes and CD sales of my original song "Christmas Smiles" to children's cancer. I ran the project each December for five years and sold copies of the song for a dollar, raising about $2,000 and increasing awareness for children's cancer in my local community.

I chose children's cancer because it was on my mind that year, as my dog had died of cancer, as well as two of my grandparents, and also someone I knew a year younger than me, which made me realize children's cancer is horribly unfair.

By doing my project, I learned that fundraising is not easy. Through trial and error, each year I tried different ideas to try to raise as much money as possible, and I saw what worked and what didn't. Most rewarding was that through my project I met so many generous people who not only donated by getting my song, but also went out of their way to spread the word, many with personal stories about children's cancer. . . . The JFSLA 'Choose to Matter' mantra has stayed with me ever since attending the camps, and I have since written other songs for other causes."

Kate is now studying, writing lyrics, and playing music in college. Recently she Skyped into our New Jersey Leadership Academy to talk to her fellow JFSLAers about life, school, and leadership. She also sang some of her new songs for the students . . . for which we all gave her a standing ovation. She is a rock star and we call her family (so by the transitive property, I am a rock star as well). Go check her out. She is amazing.

CASEY STEWART

Meet JFSLAer **CASEY STEWART** from Philadelphia. Casey not only went to our first four JFSLA summer sessions until she aged out, she now is part of our staff. (She is stuck with us for life whether

she wants to be or not. :)) As a senior in high school, Casey launched this project:

"I'd grown up not just in the soccer world, but in the running world as well. My dad was an avid marathoner and my sports family extended to a group of intelligent, compassionate running enthusiasts. One man, Rich, had traveled to Ethiopia at the invitation of some elite runners he had met along the way. Rich saw the need for lifesaving medical care in some of the athletes' communities when they invited him into their homes. He started an organization called the Entoto Foundation that raised money through charitable races and partnered with world-class doctors to provide essential medical care for Ethiopian children.

"With the help of my soccer teammates and with the support of my community, I held a track meet on my school's track to raise money for the Entoto Foundation. We organized several mile runs, kids' runs, and a relay race. We raised money through donations from the community, entry fees, and a raffle held at the end. We raised over $1,000, which was later matched by one of Entoto's board members.

"My teammates helped me with setup and fundraising, and they ran the races with me. This project was incredibly challenging. *By doing*, I was forced out of my comfort zone. I had to learn to speak, not just for myself, but for a cause I was passionate about. And the project was incredibly rewarding. We learned later that the money raised went to help a man, Girma, who e-mailed me after his heart surgery. He was healthy thanks to the help of my teammates and my community and the hard work of my running family at Entoto. By doing, I was more confident running community service projects in college, and now I work for Up2Us Sports to continue my passion for helping empower others through sports, a passion sparked by the JFSLA."

JILLIAN MARK

Meet JFSLAer JILLIAN MARK from Odenton, Maryland. Jillian chose to support cancer research

with her "Choose to Matter" project, as the disease is one her family and many others have had to fight. And Jillian is a wonderful example of how one project can bring a community together. The most recent event was their fourth cancer walk in the last five years.

"I have attended the JFSLA camp in New Jersey for the past four years, and I am now a senior in high school. For my 'Choose to Matter' project, I hosted a walk in 2012, 2013, 2015, and 2016 called Care to the Core, with a group of friends, for the research of cancer. Cancer is a topic close to our family, in addition to many others. It takes loved ones too soon, and makes others realize how precious life is. I watch the pain cancer has inflicted on my stepmom and hear about the cancer that eventually took the life of her mother, Gramma Cashie. She died before I met her. I also lost my auntie Gretch to cancer in April 2015. She lived her last months celebrating and smiling, teaching me to do the same. I made that a lesson of my walk. . . . To enjoy the time we do have, rather than worry about what we have left. Our goal each year has been to spread awareness and remind people to enjoy life. We have had four walks supported by family, friends, and neighbors. We have raised over $6,500 to donate to cancer research institutions. The success of our Web site (www.care2thecore.weebly.com) tracks our progress through the years. We have faced a few challenges, such as being denied donations by companies, as well as not having enough advertising out to the public, which left us short of our goal that year. However, we have been lucky enough to have many companies donate to us, parents to assist us to make this possible, and support from all over. *By doing*, I have learned that stumbling is OK. I kept getting distracted by ideas and ideals, but I am always reminding myself to come back to the major goals: enjoy life and donate money to the children's hospital. I've learned that if you can find something you are passionate about, you will be excited to work to achieve it. . . . It won't seem like a chore, but a challenge you want to work toward. I knew this project would change me, but I didn't realize by how much. My advice to future 'Choose to Matter' project participants is to find something you are passionate about and stay committed."

GULAFSHA ANSARI

Meet JFSLAer GULAFSHA ANSARI from Mumbai, India. Gulafsha came to our Leadership Academy along with ten other girls from India thanks to a wonderful nonprofit called Magic Bus*.

Well, not surprisingly, the Magic Bus girls become an immediate hit with the American girls at the camp. They share stories, tell us about their country and their villages, and leave the American girls with something so valuable: perspective and gratitude. Thanks to a grant from the U.S. state department this past year, we launched an exchange where JFSLA alumnae also go visit Magic Bus in India to share in their culture and leadership

* For the last six years, we have brought girls who participate in the Magic Bus India program to our leadership academies. We try to bring in six to ten Magic Bus girls each year. These girls come from the slums of various cities in India. Most have never left their slum. None have ever been on an airplane. So you can imagine the courage it must take to fly all the way across the world to join us. They land in America and jump right into our week-long residential camp. They are immediately faced with a different culture, different language, different food, different time zone, different smells, different everything. And then, they are asked to play soccer with American girls, learn about leadership, and get out of their comfort zone (I'd guess there is a check next to the jump-out-of-your-comfort-zone box!).

development programs. Ten of our JFSLA alumnae traveled to India for two weeks, and then ten of the Magic Bus Girls came to America for our Leadership Academy. The phrase I heard from every single JFSLA alumna that went to India this past summer? **Life changing.**

At our leadership academies, we also ask the Magic Bus girls from India to wave their magic wands and think about what they would like to change in their communities. Here is Gulafsha describing her service project:

"I wanted the girls from my community in Mahim, Mumbai, to come out and play, as they are always confined to the four walls of their houses and mostly the kitchens! There are deep-rooted prejudices in my community about the mobility of young girls.

"My vision was to empower these young girls from our community, so I started approaching their parents to grant them permission to play at least once a week. Initially I faced a lot of opposition from the elders in my community. I got my mother to accompany me when I would make visits to the homes of these young girls.

"I planned to have my first session, and ten girls ranging in age from nine to twenty-three turned up. With no resources and with the help of my older brother, I conducted my first session doing minor activities for the girls to get comfortable in the new environment and also with each other.

"I held my second session the next week. At this session I now had twenty participants. The girls named their group 'GIRLS SPIRIT.'"

Every Sunday over the course of five years, Gulafsha (in the yellow shirt) conducted a clinic for girls in her community. But it wasn't always easy.

"Despite my best efforts, it was difficult to retain girls after they turned eighteen. Most of them were married off. To sustain my project, I started targeting girls ages eight to sixteen. But even then, there were challenges.

"There was an eleven-year-old girl who was very interested in joining the group, but couldn't because her family is very conservative and her grandmother and father wouldn't allow her to play. I managed to convince her father, who gave permission for his daughter to play, but she was still facing opposition from her grandmother. This eleven-year-old girl only came to the sessions when her grandmother was not around."

For five straight years, Gulafsha trained girls in her community to play soccer, be strong, and be confident. Every Sunday, Gulafsha became a voice of hope and encouragement for these young girls. But sadly, in August of 2016, with thirty girls as part of "Girls Spirit," her project had to come to an end. The community that she worked in was undergoing redevelopment, and the girls all moved away. Just before the end of her project, Gulafsha gave every girl a soccer ball so that they could start playing the sport with other girls in their new communities. These girls now gather on Sundays to play with other girls in their various communities, teaching more girls to "Choose to Matter."

MORGAN FOWLER

Meet fourteen-year-old JFSLAer MORGAN FOWLER from Shaker Heights, Ohio.

"I decided that for my 'Choose to Matter' project, I wanted to donate canned goods to the Cleveland Food Bank for local people who need it. I had set a goal of collecting one hundred pounds of canned goods for the Cleveland Food Bank by December 2016 for the project. Fortunately, I was able to partner with my church, and in celebration of one hundred years of Fairmount Presbyterian Church, together we collected over FOUR HUNDRED POUNDS by mid-September. I spearheaded the campaign. There were also monetary donations of $620 from family, friends, and parishioners. The food bank's Web site states that for every $1 donated, it provides four meals, so that $620 is just under 2,500 meals! My mom and I even went to the warehouse to deliver the food. This was so neat, as I saw how many people, just like me, are trying to end hunger one step at a time. I hope to get my friends, youth group, and community members to help me volunteer at the food bank as well. *By doing*, I discovered that it felt so good to see how generous people can be when asked. By doing, I learned how much you can achieve by working together with people who share a common goal."

Morgan started this as one girl with a goal. And now her church, friends, and community are all helping as well. Never underestimate the power of one person and one idea.

MIA NIETO

Meet fifteen-year-old JFSLAer **MIA NIETO** from Moraga, California, who turned a fun talent and hobby into her "Choose to Matter" service project.

"For my Julie Foudy Sports Leadership Academy community service project, my friend Jessalyn Simon-Parker and I decided to make duct-tape bracelets and wallets. We had been making them for fun and were getting pretty good at it. We realized that if we sold them, we could make some money to donate to charity. We made tons of duct-tape stuff and put it online on Etsy. We wanted to pick a charity that we knew a lot about, so we decided to donate to Upward Roots. [Upward Roots is an awesome nonprofit in Northern California that aims to empower underserved youth through youth-driven community service . . . cofounded, btw, by two JFSLA staff members, Lindsay Jones and Heather Dittmer.] We were able to buy the duct tape with a grant from the Julie Foudy Leadership Foundation. We made about $150 in all. We sold them around our neighborhood and online. By doing, I learned that there is nothing like that feeling you get when you help others. I learned that even the smallest gesture goes a long way. Generosity becomes a cycle. If I help someone, they feel great because I cared about them. Then, that person wants to give to others because they realize how great it is to receive help. And then, if everyone is doing this, it automatically makes the world a better place. *By doing*, kids will realize how *they* want to live their life and how *they* want to make a difference."

ELIZABETH OVERBERG

Meet thirteen-year-old JFSLAer ELIZABETH OVERBERG from Ankeny, Iowa. Elizabeth did her first project at all of nine years old when she and her mom, Katie, entered a JFSLA contest we had calling all moms and daughters to "Choose to Matter." Elizabeth tells her story:

"My best friend Ryann has cerebral palsy, and we've been friends since kindergarten. Ryann can't eat by herself, talk, or control her body very well. An accessible playground and baseball league for kids with disabilities was going to be built in our community, but the project needed funding. I was drawn to this idea, but I needed to ask one person about it first— [so] I asked Ryann if she would like to play any sports, and she said yes. "I wrote a script and went door-to-door and asked people if they would like to donate. I was nine years old then and pretty nervous at first about asking people for money and answering their questions, but after a while it was fun. I ended up raising over $800. After I delivered the money to the city for the park, there was a YouTube video of me and Ryann, which helped raise another few thousand dollars. There is a plaque of donors at the park and they listed 'Elizabeth Overberg,' but it was really a lot of people. The best part is, I've had playdates with Ryann at the new playground, and I love watching her play on the baseball field."

In 2016, Elizabeth did another project with JSFLA.

"After going to JFSLA for my first time (I was finally old enough), I decided to do my community service project for PEOPLE PE, which is a gym class for kids with disabilities.

"I decided to make T-shirts to raise money for junior high and high school PEOPLE PE classes. The T-shirts had a picture of Ryann and me holding hands at opening day at Miracle League, an accessible playground and baseball field. The words on the shirts said, 'Hands are made for helping.' I received a grant from the Julie Foudy Leadership Foundation and also got donations from some local companies. I sold those T-shirts at school and at sporting events for $10. I ended up raising over $1,800, giving each school $600 to spend on their PEOPLE PE classes. By doing, I really learned how much I could accomplish. Just some simple actions by me created a chain reaction, and soon my projects were touching and helping more people than I could have ever imagined."

KARLI JONASEN

Meet JFSLAer KARLI JONASEN from West Allis, Wisconsin. Karli was interested in climate change and the global water crisis because of her high school science class. She tapped into that passion for her project.

"I organized a fundraiser in 2009 for Global Water, an international environmental organization. I put together a bake sale for a week and sold treats during the different lunch periods. I also designed and sold T-shirts that spread awareness about the global clean water crisis. Thanks to the help from my high school (West Allis Central High School) for allowing me to hold my fundraiser there, and friends, family, and teachers who donated desserts for the bake

sale, we raised a total of $1,000. That money went to Global Water, which helped build a water well in a village in Honduras.

"By doing, I found my confidence. I was quiet in high school, and the project helped me find my voice because it encouraged me to advocate and educate on something I cared about, the clean water crisis. The project also helped lead me onto a career path. I went to college to study the environment and the international relations/politics that goes along with it. The project gave me a chance at a young age to realize what it is in this world that I care deeply about. And it helped me prove to myself that I can do anything I set my mind to."

CAMMI TIRICO

Meet JFSLAer **CAMMI TIRICO** from Ann Arbor, Michigan. At thirteen years old, Cammi organized a "Choose to Matter" project to channel her passion for helping kids with disabilities and promote inclusion with other kids in her community.

"I love my friends, basketball, soccer, and lacrosse. I also LOVE helping people!!

"When we were asked at the JFSLA to craft a project to help the community, I knew exactly what I was going to do. I was going to start a Project Unify team at my school. Project Unify is a program made by the Special Olympics (Olympics for athletes who have mental disabilities) to promote inclusion with other kids. Project Unify is also a strong advocate of removing the R-word (retard) from everyday language. My teacher, Ms. Bert, was amazing, and there was a great team of classmates working on this project.

"The hardest part was getting started, but once a few kids agreed, it spread like wildfire. Right now we have fifteen general ed kids and eight cognitively impaired students and counting. We have had an assembly to teach our school about how the R-word is offensive. We also had a 5K run and have our first competition in late May!

"This whole experience has been life changing. By doing, twenty-three kids have new experiences and memories that will last a lifetime, and I know that I can make a difference in my school and community."

MCKENNA ALEKSIVICH

Meet JFSLAer **MCKENNA ALEKSIVICH** from Geneva, Illinois. Over her years at our academy, McKenna has organized three different projects and still does the Goals for a Cause project today.

"1) Four friends and I volunteered twice a week at the after-school program at the autism school for just about the whole school year. We participated in their educational and recreational activities and helped the students work on their social skills.

"2) I organized a soccer gear collection drive through Peace Passers to collect over 840 pieces of soccer gear (jerseys, cleats, shin guards, balls) that were then sent to Uganda. I worked in my hometown and reached out to area clubs and schools as well.

"3) I started a 'Goals for a Cause' project with my high school team my junior year where we asked people to pledge a donation per goal we scored during the year, and we raised money for charity. I'm currently doing it for the fourth time, and the second time with my college team. Over the past three years, we raised $11,662 for different charities."

I love that McKenna has hit on all three T's: volunteering her Time, using her Talent, and raising Treasure through her Time and Talent.

SAFIYA O'BRIEN

Meet thirteen-year-old JFSLAer SAFIYA O'BRIEN from Berkeley, California, who put together gift bags for an orphanage in East Africa. Safiya wanted her project to focus on the kids of her mother's hometown in Chang'ombe, Tanzania. She put together and delivered fifty-five backpacks filled with toys and soccer balls and coloring books to the children at an orphanage there.

"My mom moved to the USA when she was ten years old, and this was her first trip back home. She always told me about the poverty in the city she lived in. I decided this was where I wanted to do my service project. I wanted to do more than just travel there. We arrived at the orphanage in Chang'ombe to find it was just a tiny house with a muddy front.

"We brought some bean seeds to plant with the kids. We all went inside after all the beans were in the ground. The head of the orphanage, whom they call *Mama*, called all the kids to get their bags. After I handed out the bags, I played some games with the kids. *By doing*, I learned that I am more than capable of doing the things that I dream of if I put my heart into it. By doing, I grew and now have a more positive mind-set . . . I want to make a difference in the world."

SYDNEY SMITH

Meet twenty-year-old JFSLAer **SYDNEY SMITH** from Geneva, Illinois. Sydney is the perfect example of what is possible. What started as a small equipment drive with her JFSLA leadership project seven years ago has now grown into

her own foundation, the One Goal Foundation. Sydney tells the story:

"One Goal Foundation began seven years ago with a gesture of kindness and a sad story. I was approached by a new coach, Doco Wesseh, after a tough practice. He asked if he could show me some moves and ways that smaller girls could protect themselves and keep or even steal the ball from the bigger girls. While we were playing, he told me that children from his country, Liberia, didn't have many soccer balls, so they filled bags with trash so they could play. I made that my JFSLA 'Choose to Matter' project. I went home and walked to all of my neighbors' houses, asking if they had any new or used sports equipment that they would like to donate. And that's how it all started. Initially, my service project was to collect new and used soccer equipment so all 1,000+ children in

[Liberia's] Monrovia area could have cleats, their own soccer balls, and maybe a few uniforms for game days. After I met that goal, we began raising funds and equipment to build a school for the over four hundred children who can't go to public schools. We have the exterior and roof completed and are now working on the plumbing and electrical. Lastly, we wanted to contribute to the city. So, after receiving one acre of land from the mayor of Monrovia, we built a competition-quality soccer field. We will begin construction of the One Goal Sydney N. Smith Team Center in January, which will have a locker room for the home and away teams, bathrooms for each team, and a central shelter for the referees and spectators in times of heavy heat or rains.

"We did most of our fundraising through training clinics. We hold foot skills or shooting clinics all year long and let players know that all fees will be used for One Goal Foundation needs. We typically have between fifty and ninety players show up, paying anywhere from $35/day to $125/week for three-hour training clinics. All fields and coaching fees are waived, so it's total profit to the foundation. Many colleges have also been hugely supportive, like the University of Chicago and Aurora University, which donate uniforms, balls, and equipment.

"*By doing*, I became a part of something much greater that sparked a need for change and compassion within me. I gained confidence in myself and learned to believe that although I was just one young girl from the suburbs of Chicago, I still had the power to make a difference in others' lives. I learned that no matter how small I seemed, I could still make a change and help those less fortunate all over the world. Today I see a completely different person in myself than when I first started my project five years ago. I am more vocal and determined now, I feel more comfortable in my own skin, and I am proud of what I have accomplished so far. I gained compassion and a drive to continue to help those around me, no matter how impossible it seems in the beginning. By choosing to make a small difference in your community, you have the ability to change the world—and after seeing myself accomplish all that I thought was impossible, I truly believe now in what's *possible*."

We overflow with pride at what these courageous girls have done. Over the eleven-plus years we have now been doing the leadership academies, we have watched hundreds and hundreds of girls do similar life-changing projects. Most thought they did not have the time. Most said they didn't have the skill set. Most thought they could not do it. UNTIL SOMEONE TOLD THEM THEY COULD.

I will leave you with this last story of courage . . .
It has to do with child marriage, which is still a common occurrence in many traditional communities in India. While at various leadership academies, many of the Indian girls from Magic Bus have talked of wanting to end the practice of child marriages for girls in their villages (child marriage for girls under eighteen years old was outlawed in 1929 under Indian law, but the ban is still not enforced in some areas). They spoke of how some girls as young as eleven, twelve, and thirteen were forced into marriages by their families and communities. One summer, a Magic Bus camper returned to her village in India and stood up at a community town hall session. All the elders in the town—men and women—were meeting. A Magic Bus staff member, Rahul Brahmbhatt, told me the emotional story. He said that when she stood up, she spoke about her "Choose to Matter" Leadership Project. She spoke of how she wanted to end child marriage in her village. She spoke of why she thought forcing girls into marriage at such a young age was not healthy for the girls or for the community. She spoke of why girls should have the right to be who they want to be, enjoy their childhood, continue their education, and reach their full potential. As she stood, her mother suddenly stood up next to her and said, "I am embarrassed to admit that it took my young daughter having the courage to speak and stand up for her rights, for me to stand and speak up for her rights. I can no longer be silent." Then something unexpected happened. More mothers started to stand. And more. And they spoke. Eventually, the entire village had made a pledge to stop child-arranged marriages. All of this, started by one young girl courageous enough to stand up and speak

out for what she thought was right. Wow. Talk about being courageously you. As he told me this story, tears of joy started streaming down my face.

I wish I could dedicate an entire book to the amazing projects these girls have done (SUBLIMINAL MESSAGING TO DISNEY—THE NEXT ONE!). My hope in sharing these "Choose to Matter" projects is that you will be inspired to do the same. And that you realize there is no hidden talent necessary for these leadership projects to be successful. No formal training. These girls succeeded because they:

☑ 1) FOUND A CAUSE THEY WERE PASSIONATE ABOUT,
☑ 2) BROKE IT DOWN INTO SMALLER, REALISTIC GOALS,
☑ 3) BUILT THEIR DREAM TEAM, AND
☑ 4) CHOSE TO MATTER.

Speaking of building your dream team—this step greatly influences your likelihood for success. We have found at our leadership academies that the students who thoughtfully bring together their "team of supporters" are the ones who complete their projects. Gather people around you who want to see you succeed, are invested in helping you succeed, and can help make the connections for you to succeed. Maybe it's a friend's parent who is an expert in the area you are interested, or a past teacher who shares your same passion, or a friend/sibling who consistently reminds you that *you can* when you are doubting if you will. You need people on your team who will get you back on track when you have faltered. And people who will help you find a brand-new track when needed, as well. People who will hold you accountable. Or maybe even someone to tell you that you are not crazy, just courageous (as was the role of my U.S. Women's National Team teammates for many years). Plus, building your team is a wonderful skill set for LIFE. As we have discussed in this book, find friends who will push you to dream the impossible. Surround yourself with people who will help you chase that impossible. And then hug those who help you accomplish the impossible. Keep them close. And buy them many donuts.

And of course, as step four states a little earlier, eventually, you have to CHOOSE TO MATTER. You have to act. You have to raise your hand. You can think about it, you can feel it. But eventually we all must act.

Amy Liss, our incredible JFSLA staffer with cerebral palsy, gives a talk each year at our Leadership Academy. At the end of her speech, she actually gives each girl a spoon to take home. She says,

"I am giving you a spoon because knives are for cutting, forks are for stabbing, and a spoon is for serving."

So, here is your Amy Liss Spoon.

GO SERVE.
GO CHOOSE TO MATTER.

CHAPTER 15

THE F-WORD

> "Would you like me to give you a formula
> for success? It's quite simple, really.
> Double your rate of failure. You're thinking
> of failure as the enemy of success. But
> it isn't at all. You can be discouraged by
> failure—or you can learn from it. So go
> ahead and make mistakes. Make all you
> can. Because, remember, that's where you'll
> find success. On the far side of failure."
>
> —Thomas J. Watson

Here is something we don't share enough. Those same JFSLAers who did the awesome projects that you read about in Chapter 14? Well, those JFSLAers failed many times before getting it right. Failure with your leadership project is a rite of passage.

Yes, *that* F-word. FAILURE. Say it out loud. FAIL. Scream it. Hug it. Sing it . . .

> *Fail fail bo bail*
> *Banana fanna fo fail*
> *Fee fi mo mail*
> *FAIL!!!*

What they learned by doing their projects is that failure is not defeat. It simply means you need to adjust. And most importantly, failure is not something to be feared. Often it leads to a new path—a better path.

Instead of thinking of failure as the enemy to success, start accepting it as success's best friend. Because, without question, the common denominator of successful leaders is that they all see failure as a gift that keeps on giving. Sue Enquist says,

"For people who perform over time, they see failure as a beacon of what you need to do next."

I fully appreciate and understand why so many teenagers and young adults (and not-so-young adults) are stressed out by the prospect of *what's next.* What college can I get into? What am I going to do postcollege? Post-grad school? What am I going to do with my life? Or how about when the thought *half of my friends already have a job and I have nothing* starts to creep in, like it did for me postcollege? I remember graduating from Stanford, sitting out on my apartment patio one day soon after graduation, and spiraling into a complete panic that I HAD NOTHING CONCRETE JOBWISE. I was playing on the U.S. team at the time, but that brought little security financially and mentally, so I went into *the-world-is-crashing-down-on-me* mode. "I need to get a real job!!! WHAT. AM. I. DOING. WITH. MY. LIFE!?! Should I go back to school?!!! Did I choose the right major?!!! Is medicine (my major) even something I want to do?!!"

Or maybe you are having the common thoughts of *I am not doing enough. I need to pad my resume. I need to be at this function or this event or on this committee to get ahead. Ahhh*, it is exhausting just watching young women and men navigate it all.

ALL STRESS IS NOT CREATED EQUAL

Life can become a wicked maze of stress. And in the back of your mind, through it all, sits that burning question: "And what if I fail? What if I simply *cannot do it?*"

But maybe we are looking at stress and the *possibility* of failure through the wrong lens. We all cannot live in a stress-free world, of course. Taking on new challenges brings stress. Taking a test brings stress. A new job brings stress. And actually, a bit of stress can be a good thing. Because there are two kinds of stress (all stress is not created equal :)): **good stress and bad stress.** Good stress can actually propel you to do more, be more, even create more. Good stress motivates you to get a task done, take on a new challenge. Good stress is not harmful to the body, and in fact is healthy when channeled properly, because it can help make you sharper, more focused, more present. And most importantly, it is not long term. You are not being dragged down by a constant feeling of fright or anxiety. It is more associated with the excitement that you have indeed succeeded in a task, or the adrenaline of taking on a new adventure.

Bad stress, on the other hand, can be debilitating and unhealthy. Bad stress can cause you to never even take on a task for fear of that F-word. Or maybe it is grief or a bad boss or a job that demands too much or bills that won't stop. Whatever the cause, bad stress over the long term can wear your body down, physically and mentally.

When your body constantly perceives a threat, it isn't able to recover.

No one wants that dreaded feeling of being overwhelmed by tasks that seem insurmountable. Start by recognizing that stress is going to exist; that is life. The key is minimizing the bad stress or pushing it onto the good stress side of the scale. And yes, you can do that. I think that is the first step in getting a grip on stress. Realize that, again, YOU have the power to change things. *Yep, you.*

Here is how Jessica Mendoza did just that. When Jessica accepted ESPN's *Sunday Night Baseball* role as the program's first female commentator, she recalled the excitement of that moment:

JESSICA: "This was a dream beyond a dream. I had grown up watching *Sunday Night Baseball*. And also, it was about doing something that hadn't been done. I believe you need to challenge the way things have been done and, if you feel like you can be good at it, go do it."

The stress came when Jessica started to process that thought:

"Suddenly I realized I had a responsibility. This is about more than just me. If I mess up, if something goes wrong, I'm closing a door for more than just myself. There's a whole gender that's a part of this."

Knowing Jess, I knew this had to bring a ton of pressure. Because Jess is a person who would gladly hand you her heart if yours stopped beating. She would offer up her lung if you needed more oxygen. For Jess, her friends, her colleagues, and her teammates always come first. Jess is all about helping and empowering others. So, naturally, my next question was: "How does that not become overwhelming?"

"It did. I wasn't sleeping. I wasn't really eating. I was a mess. I was stressed, truly stressed. I wasn't happy. And a big part of it was, I had put so much pressure on myself I couldn't see through it. I had to figure it out. I could not be everything to everybody. I had been saying yes to everything. My phone is ringing. Everyone wants to talk to me. So I just started saying no. I had to get to a point where I said, I need to do my job and I need to be a mom and wife. And beyond that, until I can see clearly again, I'm just going to say no and be OK with that."

When Jessica let go of needing to be all things to all people, the joy came back. That's an important reminder for us women, because we have this tendency all too often. And if you find you are indeed having a hard time saying no, here is the strategy I deploy, borrowed from famous cartoonist Bob Mankoff: **"No, Thursday's out. How about never—is never good for you?"**

As Robin Roberts says, "NO is a complete sentence." You don't have to provide any other explanation. *NO* is enough.

EXCEPT WHEN YOU DON'T, BECAUSE SOMETIMES YOU WON'T

It is easy to get in the funk of thinking, *well, I can't change jobs, I can't find new friends, I can't manage my schedule, I can't . . .* Do not let yourself go there. And if there, get out, like Jess.

A teammate's mom from my Soccerette* days (go Green Machine!) used to give us a reminder when our perception was a little off or we were seeing things in a negative light. She would say, "GIRLS, PUT ON YOUR

*Yes this was really the name of our team.

GLASSES and LOOOOOOOOOOK!" I'd laugh, as I knew she meant look elsewhere . . . look again . . . look through another lens and find the positive. Similar to what we talked about in Chapter 2 in terms of changing negative thoughts to those that are positive, know that you can control that. Take a breath. Look for your glasses, put them on, and find perspective. There are often two sides to every situation.

When you see your problem as insurmountable and when you think you're the only one dealing with tough stuff, remember this piece of advice from Robin Roberts: "Everyone's got something." In fact, Robin's mom told her that if everyone wrote down her problem and put it in a bowl, and you looked in that bowl, chances are you'd take your problem right back. The truth is, you have no idea what everyone else is dealing with. It's often a lot uglier than what's on your plate.

Worried about what's next after high school or college? Use the time to learn from others. Ask for advice. Seek mentors. Be curious about the possibilities out there. Think outside the norm. Remember, you control what goes into that precious head of yours, so train your brain to focus on how you can grow. Teach the butterflies to fly in formation. Learn to accept challenges as gifts in life. Just ask anyone you admire. They will tell you the key to a healthy attitude is having the mind-set to improve and accepting the fact that setbacks bring growth.

As Dr. Seuss reminds us in the greatest book ever (errr, besides this one, *of course*), *Oh, the Places You'll Go!*:

> WHEREVER YOU FLY, YOU'LL BE BEST OF THE BEST.
> WHEREVER YOU GO, YOU WILL TOP ALL THE REST.
> EXCEPT WHEN YOU DON'T.
> BECAUSE, SOMETIMES, YOU WON'T.

Yes, sometimes you won't. And then what do you do? Enter Julie Johnston.

JULIE JOHNSTON, the starting center back and young star on the U.S. Soccer Women's National Team, was not even on the team seven months prior to the 2015 Women's World Cup.

"If you had asked me seven months prior to the World Cup if I would even be on the team, I would have said probably not."

She told me about how getting cut from the roster before the World Cup was the best thing that happened to her:

"It was an eye-opening experience about what I actually wanted. How much I really did want it. I realized that's what I wanted more than anything. . . . I wanted to make that World Cup team."

Johnston then goes from not making the roster to soon after becoming a starter and eventual star of the World Cup–winning team. So what changed, you are wondering?

"Everything. The way I ate, the way I trained, the amount I trained. I found people that were willing to push me and I told them these are my goals. I need you to get me here. I don't need any excuses, I won't make any more excuses. I am done making excuses."

And when Julie put in the work, confidence followed.

"Mentally I became more confident because I was more fit. I became more confident when I felt more prepared. The mental part flew in when I started believing I changed everything for a purpose. When I set goals. Now I was just thinking about what else I can give to this team."

Johnston spoke of surrounding herself with people who were willing to push her and help her achieve her goals. People who could lift her up, help her believe in times of doubt.

And this we know. There will be times of doubt. There will also be times when life is going really well. And then, out of nowhere, tragedy strikes. How do you deal with that? How do you summon the courage to carry on?

Sheryl Sandberg shares her story of a tragedy that struck in May of 2015. Sheryl and her husband, Dave Goldberg, were on vacation in Mexico when Dave suddenly passed away. He was forty-seven years old. Sheryl explains how this unexpected tragedy, this jarring grief, affected her in every possible area, including her confidence:

> SHERYL: "When I lost Dave suddenly, it hit my confidence in everything. Not just in the personal realm but in the professional realm as well. I was so upset and so distraught and so devastated, I thought, how could I do anything? And how could I do anything at work?"

Sheryl's admission hit me hard. Here is someone so capable and so powerful, and an unbelievable tragedy shook her confidence. The first time Sheryl spoke publicly about losing Dave was one year after his death at the University of California at Berkeley commencement.

> "I was swallowed up in the deep fog of grief . . . an emptiness that fills your heart, your lungs, constricts your ability to think or even to breathe. . . . But I also learned that when life sucks you under, you can kick against the bottom, break the surface, and breathe again. . . . I'm sharing this with you in the hopes that today, as you take the next step in your life, you can learn the lessons that I only learned in death. Lessons about hope, strength, and the light within us that will not be extinguished."

By sharing, we pass on hope. By sharing, we deliver perspective. We learned that Sheryl Sandberg, *the seventh most powerful woman in the world*, is human as well. And raw. And real. *And resilient.*

COMMUNITY

FAIL FORWARD

Life Lesson #741: Find people, groups, companies, and teams that embrace challenges and failure. And if you don't know if they embrace failure, *ask* people in the group. They will know. (If yes, make them part of your life.)

Sue Enquist could write manuals on this, and in fact, she is.* She has said this was the secret sauce to their success at UCLA over the years—that there were a lot of good teams out there, but none were better than UCLA at failing. Here is Sue on making failure part of UCLA softball's culture:

SUE: "We would literally say, where are the places we're gonna fail? And then how do you want to be loved in your failure? Because there are two kinds. *Love me up because I feel crappy* or *Don't touch me because I'll blow your face off*. So we have to get to know how we want to be loved in failure. And then you have to have your routine. Everyone had her own routine of recovery after a failure:

- I'm gonna find my focal point. Every field has a focal point Yours is different from mine. For me, it's the second base bag. I focus on the bag and remind myself that I work harder than any batter in the country. It's a point you can look at when failure takes over. A point of strength.
- I'm gonna take two deep breaths because we know that slows down the heart rate.
- I'm gonna have one trigger word. So I clear my head going forward.

"And that was our mental routine.

1. Focal point
2. Breathe
3. Trigger word."

*Sue launched a Web site: ONEsoftball.com

COMMUNITY

Routines like these help your team start to feel comfortable in failure. And, equally important, comfortable with each other.

Failing is never necessarily fun (come on, kids, LET'S GO FAIL!), but when I look back at the failures in my life, I realize I am a much better human being for having failed. Especially because my outlook when I fail has been to FAIL FORWARD. Extract the lesson. Learn from it. Move forward. From our losses at World Cups and the Olympics (which still hurt like heck) to failing at work to failing as a mom and wife and friend at times. It happens. Of course it does. Why did it happen? How can I get better next time around? What details did I miss? Perfection, although many will portray it as noble, is the stuff of fairy tales. Nor is it much fun. And Sheryl Sandberg adds,

> "I think we are always learning and growing. If we are doing things perfectly then we are not trying anything hard."

Lose the idea of perfect. I want to be around people who embrace adventure . . . who seek the road less traveled . . . who fall and fail, but at least live knowing they tried. Cue "The Man in the Arena," from Theodore Roosevelt's famous speech:

It is not the critic who counts; not the man who points out how the strong man stumbles, or where the doer of deeds could have done them better. The credit belongs to the man who is actually in the arena, whose face is marred by dust and sweat and blood; who strives valiantly; who errs, who comes short again and again, because there is no effort without error and shortcoming; but who does actually strive to do the deeds; who knows great enthusiasms, the great devotions; who spends himself in a worthy cause; who at the best knows in the end the triumph of high achievement, and who at the worst, if he fails, at least fails while daring greatly, so that his place shall never be with those cold and timid souls who neither know victory nor defeat.

I learned a wonderful way to accept mistakes and failure through a friend, Betsy Crouch, who founded ImprovHQ with Zoe Galvez. ImprovHQ does fun, interactive improv exercises that foster collaboration and teamwork. They do activities at our leadership academies (and for a lot of top companies in the country), and one of the things they teach from the beginning is that when you make a mistake, you raise both hands in the air and let out a quick and loud **WOOOOOO**, then immediately move on. There is something incredibly powerful, liberating, and *joyful* when more than a hundred girls are together in a room intermittently yelling WOOOOOOO with both arms in the air, giggling out loud, whenever they make a mistake. And just like that, ImprovHQ has created a culture that says, "Failure happens; acknowledge it, learn from it, move on." They have now created a safe space where these young women understand that is part of the process. And to not only acknowledge failure, but to celebrate it as well. The wonderful by-product that occurs organically is that our staff and campers start doing WOOOOOO on the soccer field as well. So literally in the middle of an exercise, the campers are lifting their arms in the air when they miss a pass or a make a bad touch, hollering **WOOOOOOO**. Ha. A beautiful thing. Thank you, Betsy, Zoe, and ImprovHQ.

GO BUILD ANOTHER LEVEL

Another fabulous lesson I learned regarding stress and failure is to understand what you can and cannot control. Sometimes we waste so much energy worrying about things *out of our control*. This lesson came from the one and only Colleen Hacker, aka FLASH. I called her

Flash because she was like a flashlight who shines light when most needed. And since I am still admittedly a fan of toilet humor (yes, I just said that out loud), this lesson is near and dear to my heart. Colleen told our U.S. team one day: control the things you can control and let go of those you cannot control. She discussed how worrying about things out of your control is like going to the bathroom. When you go to the bathroom and you go No. 2 (yes, poo poo, for those not versed in the wonderful language of toiletology), you  do not stop and look at it sitting there in the toilet bowl. You don't bend down and examine it (or at least you *do not admit* if you do). Noooooooo. YOU POO AND THEN YOU FLUSH IT. (Colleen actually had a little toilet in her hand that made this beautiful flushing sound.) Yes, YOU FLUSH IT. When you make a mistake in the middle of a game, don't stop and analyze it. Don't examine the content. **Just flush it**. And move on. Flush it. Move on.

Well, as you can imagine, the JUST FLUSH IT slogan became wildly popular among our incredibly mature audience, and to this day, we still use it. In fact, a decade later, if I said to an old teammate who was stressing about something out of her control, "JUST FLUSH IT," she would laugh and say, "Yes, you're right." No more questions asked. It was our guiding principle, and a damn good one at that. Thank you, Flash.

And for things we *can control*, Colleen also had a creative way of getting us to think about handling failure in those moments. "Park it," she would say. To which we would look at her cross-eyed. She then would tell us: there is a time to Flush It and a time to Park It. We don't always want to forget about it and move on, as people often say. We don't want to forget mistakes or errors that can help us. . . . We want to learn from them and build on them. It is *when* you think about them and *when* you mull them over that the good stuff happens. Colleen would say, just like when you go shopping. You drive, park your car, remember where you parked it, and then go about the business of why you drove there and parked there to begin with: TO GO SHOPPING. You don't park and then check to make sure your car is still there over and over and over and over again, or you'd be a poor and inefficient shopper. No, you park it, shop, and then go back to the car AFTER you've completed the main task . . . shopping. It's the same with sports and life.

Make a mistake (not your first or last of the day, game, etc.). Park it. Know it, but don't keep checking on it, dwelling on it, revisiting it during the game (or whatever your task may be) . . .

And then AFTER you've finished the main task, *then* you can go back to where you "parked it" and learn from it, use it, benefit from it . . . for next time. So when someone makes a mistake or is upset about something they can't do anything about right now, PARK IT and come back to it at the appropriate time.

Thanks to Colleen's sage advice, we spent the entire 1996 Olympics telling players to PARK IT. Make a mistake? PARK IT. Trip over the ball? PARK IT. Well, it is the Olympic final, as in the GOLD-MEDAL match of the 1996 Olympics. Colleen is an assistant coach on the team, so she is on the field with us. We are warming up before the game, and a player catches Colleen's eye. Well, this player is clearly frustrated and mad. She does a direct beeline to Colleen, stomping over to her, and starts unloading to Colleen about all the things that are bothering her right then. As in, right before the Olympic final is about to start. And as Colleen describes the exchange:

COLLEEN: "So I let her unload . . . get it out . . . let it go. But she was still so upset, so I just relaxed my shoulders, put on the longest, most real smile I could produce, and said, 'You know what I'm going to tell you, don't you?'

"The player (to this day I don't know who it is) answers, 'Yeah, you are going to tell me to PARK IT. Park it, park it, park it' (said with exasperation, anger, and complete frustration). 'Well, guess what?! MY PARKING LOT IS FULL.'

Colleen (calmly and quite deftly, I might add) immediately responds, "Well, then, GO BUILD ANOTHER LEVEL." To which both the player and Colleen laugh so hard that it breaks the anger. The player continues to laugh, jogs off, and plays the game, and we win the Olympics. Ha. That is one of my favorite stories still to this day. PARK IT. And when your parking lot is full, go build another level. Of course.

THE JUNGLE GYM

Finally, if I can leave you with one last thought on failure and success: don't be afraid to zig and zag.

Life is not linear.

Sheryl Sandberg shares a wonderful analogy in regards to life and success not being linear in *Lean In*. She talks about a phrase she learned from Pattie Sellers of *Fortune* magazine (who launched the "Most Powerful Women in the World" list). Pattie spoke of how people often think of success as a ladder you climb, but that life and success better resemble a jungle gym.

> SHERYL: "Ladders are limiting—people can move up or down, on or off. Jungle gyms offer more creative exploration. There is only one way to get to the top of a ladder, but there are many ways to get to the top of a jungle gym."

Plus, as Sheryl points out, who wants to keep staring at the butt of the person above you? Jungle gyms allow for better views for everyone, from all over. When I first heard this analogy, I smiled out loud. Yes, you may come to a dead end or to monkey bars that seem too difficult to navigate, or even to a hot slide that burns your bum on the way down, but you keep climbing and you keep growing. And this I know:

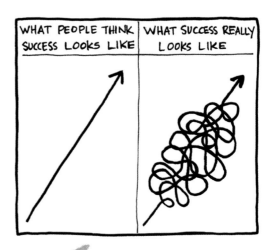

WHAT PEOPLE THINK SUCCESS LOOKS LIKE	WHAT SUCCESS REALLY LOOKS LIKE

Plus, life becomes so much more fun when you accept that obstacles and failure are just part of the scenery.

So put on your glasses, climb on that jungle gym, soak in that scenery, and

LOOOOOOOOOOK.

EXERCISE:

This is one of my favorite exercises.
Rarely do we stop and think about this question:

**IF YOU KNEW YOU COULD NOT FAIL,
WHAT WOULD YOU DO?**

Let go of all barriers, all inhibitions, all fears, all
obstacles. Whatever you want to do, you can do.
What would it be?!

JULIE: Jess, if you knew you
couldn't fail, what would you do?
JESSICA [without hesitation]:
I'd like to run our country.
JULIE: There you go. President?
JESSICA: Yeah.
JULIE: Can you aim higher, please?
[Both laugh.]

(And so that it is on the official
record, I then said, "Well, I guess I will
have to be your chief of staff." And
Jessica said, "YES. OF COURSE.")

BOOK IT!

CHAPTER 16

TURN
AND PULL

"A mentor is someone who allows you to
see the hope inside yourself."

—Oprah

As we close out this section on community, I cannot
leave without touching on something I feel could help
resolve so many issues in this world (OK, maybe that
is a bit dramatic . . . or maybe not). If we all did just
three words, I am convinced this world would be a
better place. **TURN AND PULL.** Yes, turn and pull. It is
that simple. Those three words need to be part of your
vernacular—whatever your language, culture, color,
gender, occupation, obsession, astrological sign, or age.
Three words that can impact so much. **Turn and pull**
others along with you. Help others succeed. Share your
wisdom. Be a mentor. You may know the quotation by
Muriel Strode:

"Do not follow where the path may lead.
Go instead where there is no path and
leave a trail."

COMMUNITY

You may also have noticed that Muriel Strode doesn't just say she will choose to find a new path. She says she'll find a new path *and leave a trail*. Ding. This is the most important part. How often do you see something you really want to explore in life and have no idea how to get there? I think the greatest gift we can give those coming behind us is to leave a trail . . . to build a pipeline . . . to show them what is possible . . . to turn and pull.

DING.

As Oprah mentions, a mentor helps someone grow. Yet I find that, often, lost in all the mentorship discussion is the fact that *we all* can play a role in turning and pulling. I am not just talking about the president or CEO of a business. I am not just talking about the class president or captain. I am not talking about only the teacher or boss or oldest person on a team. I am talking *all of us*. I have this conversation with my eight-year-old son and my ten-year-old daughter.

It requires no formal training, no special degree, and thankfully no personalized T & P certificate on your wall that reads . . .

CONGRATULATIONS!

YOU, YES YOU,
are a Turner & Puller.

Signed by

_____

(person whom you pulled or who saw you pull or was told
by a friend of a friend that you pulled)

As Sue Enquist points out,

> "Mentoring isn't about having all the answers. It's about saying I've been there. That's the first step to mentoring. It's not you need to do this dude. And then *blahblahblah*. You just need to start with, 'I've been there, I've got you.'"

I've got you. And you've got this. That is right. Turning and pulling means simply empowering others. And in my opinion, empowering others is the greatest form of leadership.

So when my daughter, Izzy, asks a girl sitting on her own to join her at recess, she has now given this girl an opportunity to play and smile with others. That simple act can be so profound. And I make sure to tell her that.

It's like when Fahima Noori speaks of her T & P teacher in Kabul:

> FAHIMA: "Lila Jan always encouraged me and always gave me energy by telling me, 'Fahima, do not give up and do not accept life as a failure.' For example, I never attended weddings or events in general, not because I would be sad, but because of other people, because of the children. Whenever I would go to a wedding with my family, people would ask my mom what happened to me. My mom was basically forced to tell them. And also, children would get scared of looking at my face. For that reason I always preferred to stay home. So, when my teacher found out that I didn't attend weddings or events and I always stayed home, she got mad at me. She told me, 'You are a strong woman and you should defeat these difficulties. You cannot just stay home because of other people.'"

After this, Fahima started attending events in public. And her confidence blossomed. Fahima started to understand that she too could turn and pull. Her form of T & P-ing came with sharing her story—having the courage to not just go out into public, but now to share it with the world.

Fahima's teacher, as one turner and puller, made a huge difference in the life of Fahima. And now Fahima is "paying it forward" by turning and pulling herself. What if we all did that? What if when someone pulls you along, you do your own version of "pay it forward"? YOU *PULL* it forward. Your thank-you is the assurance that you will reach out and help someone as well.

Or how about those T & P-ers like Amy Liss? When I asked her what she wishes for in life—instead of wishing for independence or the ability to walk or material things—she says:

> "My wish is keep motivating others and making them happy . . . and hoping that everyone I meet feels my love or hopefully how genuine I am. Actually, I wish that not everybody could have the experiences I have had through all of this, but that they could have a minute to feel the ounce of joy that I *feel* when things like this happen to me. I wish that everybody has the opportunity to feel a dose of joy."

I challenge you to spread just as much daily joy as Amy Liss. PULL it forward.

Also important to note, don't be afraid to ask for help. Don't hesitate to ask to be pulled. For example, with our JFSLA "Choose to Matter" projects, one of the keys we have talked about is building your team around you. Building your team means asking for help. It also means asking people to support your dream. That can be a scary, uber-intimidating thing. Just saying a dream out loud is hard enough. Now you want me to ask people to help me accomplish that dream!?!*

Yep, I do. With these two things in mind. . . .

1) *You are not asking others to do the work for you.* Grrrr. There is nothing more annoying than someone saying,

*This Foudy woman IS crazy.

"Hey, I have this *incredible* idea, and YOU are going to do it all for me." (My eight-year-old son is already excellent at this, by the way.) You are simply asking for guidance and wisdom from someone who hopefully has not just lived it, but loved it as well. And that is an important differentiator when building your team. There are those who have lived it, and then there are those who have lived it AND loved it. Seek the latter.

2) *You have done your homework.* You are much more likely to get people to join your team when you can show them that you care SO MUCH about the issue, you have already spent time digging in.

There you go. Your toolbox is full. Now it is time to take that step forward to turn and pull, to *Choose to Matter*. As Sue Enquist's mom, Mama E, used to tell her:

"Just keep flapping those wings and eventually you will fly."

And I always find it helps to give myself little reminders. A little nudge.

SOOOOOOO . . .

EXERCISE:

Write a note to yourself.

DEAR _____ , . . .
              (your name)

Write to yourself about your "Choose to Matter" project and where you want to be in five months. Include something to help you get there if you are behind. . . . Maybe it's motivating words, a quotation, a funny phrase; anything that is basically a kick in the booty to remind you to **GET GOING**.

Put it in an envelope with your name and home address on the front. Seal it. Put a stamp on it. Give it to your parents. Tell them you would like it mailed to you in five months. (They should actually drop it in a mailbox.) Tell them not to forget. Set a reminder on your phone for months time so they don't forget.

Even though I know it will be tempting to do just this, do not do just this:

DEAR ME, I AM AWESOME. LOVE, ME

Write that (of course) and add to it. Write about your happy place. Write about why you care so much about doing your project. Why you want to turn and pull. Write about what inspires you and how you will get out of your comfort zone if you have not already. Remind yourself to breathe . . . enjoy the moment . . . get out of your junk . . . put on your glasses. Whatever it is. But take the time and write it. I promise you, in five months' time, you will love, love, love getting a letter to yourself from yourself in the mail. Who gets handwritten letters anymore, BTW?! **YOU DO.**

DON'T JUST
THINK IT, INK IT

SECTION 5

LIFE

An audible **AHHHHH**. Drumroll, please. Ladies and gentleman, now to our last empowerRING, called LIFE.

Let's get REAAAAADDDDDY to *ruuuuuuummmmmmmbbbbllllle*. Buckle in. Yes, it's time to take all that you have learned in the other rings and bring that to the big party called LIFE. And not to be a buzzkill here (foreshadowing), but this is the hardest ring of all of them. You have to act. You have to **DO**. You have to apply all that you have learned and actually LIVE IT. (GASP!) And equally horrifying, friends and people in your life, when
they see the fabulously, courageously new you, will say to you, "*Who are you?* I don't even know you anymore." And with *that* in mind, we at the JFSLA have always felt that the best way we can prepare you for this last ring is to give you our final nuggets and reminders on, well—shhhtuff we wish we had known earlier. And to remind you to not beat yourself up, because it's not easy. But it is the hard that makes it great. Frankly, so much of the battle is *just knowing* it is going to be hard and knowing you will be ready to face whatever comes your way. You will get through it. Yes, YOU will find a way. So here you go. Here are our best little nuggets of advice to make the great dance of life spin gloriously on and on and on.

DID SOMEONE SAY DANCING AGAIN?

CHAPTER **17**

OWN YOUR AWESOME

"You don't have to be great to start, but you have to start to be great."

—Joe Sabah

Get on the dance floor. No wallflowers allowed. In other words, get in the mix. Sometimes that is not easy, I know. And research has shown that it is especially not easy for women. The confidence gap between men and women is real. In Sheryl Sandberg's book *Lean In*, she talks about women being plagued by self-doubt and how we women constantly underestimate ourselves. And it should not come as a surprise, but this is critical: **Success correlates just as closely with confidence as it does with competence.** Let me repeat that. Success correlates just as closely with confidence as it does with competence. Ask any woman and she will tell you she has indeed had those moments (and for some, maybe even large chunks of their lives) of self-doubt. In our **#socktalk**, Sheryl added,

"There is also a real gap in how we attribute success. When men are successful, they attribute the success to their own skills. When women are successful, we attribute the success to help from others, working hard, and getting lucky. Why that matters is it eventually leads to a confidence gap. When you attribute success to your own skills, you know you have your own skills there the next time around, but if you attribute success to help from others, you are not sure if they will show up the next time."

Of particular concern to Sheryl Sandberg is that when women are faced with a new task or asked to take a new job, their response often is, "I've never done anything like that before" or "I still have a lot to learn in my current role." In *Lean In*, Sheryl speaks of her six and half years at Google, where she hired a team of four thousand employees. (I actually had to reread that line three times as I thought my eyes were failing me. Yes, it was four thousand.) Here was just one observation about the differences between men and women in the workplace:

"When we announced the opening of a new office or the launch of a new project, the men were banging down my door to explain why they should lead the charge. Men were also more likely to chase a growth opportunity even before a new opening was announced. They were impatient about their own development and believed they were capable of doing more."

She went on to say that women had to be persuaded to take on a new task. They didn't think they were ready. And nowadays, few managers have the time to actually *convince* people to take a job. So, of course, it often becomes *his* job.

When I read this chapter, I immediately cringed. I had that moment early in my TV career when I did this exact thing. I was out to dinner with a group of ESPN colleagues one night when one of my bosses mentioned to me that he thought I should consider adding hosting shows to my list of abilities. That he thought I could do it. I remember thinking, and regrettably saying out loud, "HUH?! I have no experience doing that. Really? I am not sure I have the skill set for that." All the things Sheryl Sandberg mentions above. Just typing it now makes my heart drop to the floor, because *of course* it would have been wonderful to learn that skill set, and the best way to learn is by in fact *doing*. How I wish I'd had the courage to get out of my comfort zone at that moment. I know that, if I had that night back, I would say, "Awesome. Thank you. YES. I would love to learn, and think I can do it as well. Let's do this!" But alas, I cannot change that night, I can only learn and move forward. And tell you not to do what I did. :)

BE THE IDIOT
WHO SAYS YES

My ESPN memory above reminds me of a story the great Mary Carillo once told me. Carillo is a giant in the TV business from her work with covering the NBC Olympics to HBO's *Real Sports* to her coverage of tennis. I think she is one of the most talented personalities we have on television. And she's incredibly diverse with all that she does. Well, one day I was picking her brain about why and how she covered what she covered in television. I was asking her how she was able to break away from just covering tennis (she was a former professional tennis player). She said, "Because *I'm an idiot* and I just kept saying YES." And then she broke into her glorious, roaring laughter. "They would ask me if I wanted to host ice skating at the Olympics and *this idiot* would say YES. You want to host late night and *this idiot* would say YES." She went through about five different scenarios with her perfect inflection of *this idiot* followed by her contagious laugh. Her point, of course, was . . . **BE THE IDIOT WHO SAYS YES.** By the end of the conversation I had sworn to not just be an idiot, but an idiot who says YES going forward.

Of course we don't always know how to do the next job yet. But neither does the person sitting next to you. Never underestimate your ability to learn and grow.

Jessica Mendoza shared a story about when she was the idiot who said yes.

JESSICA: "I had an awesome coordinating producer at ESPN, Phil Orlins, who said, 'You know, Jess, if you really want to be seen as an analyst we need to put you in the booth.' And I was like, 'When? When are we doing this?' He said, 'August 24.'"

JULIE: "Wait, stop right there. When he said, 'We're gonna put you in the booth,' you didn't go, 'What? I don't have the skill set for that.'"

JESSICA: "All of that was happening in my head, of course. But when he said that, there was no way I was saying no. I was so scared when he said that. I was like, *In the booth?! Up there?!* [*She's pointing up to the commentator's booth.*] 'Yeah, totally. Let's do that.' Oh my gosh, if you could see internally what was happening. It was crazy."

There was no way I was saying no. Yeah, totally. Let's do that.

Cue the church bells ringing. Now picture me dancing through the streets to the ringing bells. This is so damn awesome. And to remind you, Jessica was the first woman at ESPN to ever call a Major League Baseball game. (No pressure there.)

So, my question is: How do we get THERE? And consistently there. And by there, I mean: *Yeah, totally. Let's do that.*

Sheryl Sandberg shares a story in *Lean In* about her brother, David, who went to Harvard with her. They were both in the same class together (European Intellectual History, for those wondering). Sheryl tells of the time they went to take the final exam:

SHERYL: "My roommate, Carrie, also took the class, which was a huge help since she was a comparative literature major. Carrie went to all of the lectures and read all ten of the assigned

257

books—in the original languages. . . . I went to almost all of the lectures and read all of the books—in English. David went to two lectures, read one book, and then marched himself up to our room to get tutored for the final exam. We all sat together for the test, scribbling furiously for three hours in our little blue books. When we walked out, we asked one another how it went. I was upset. I had forgotten to connect the Freudian id to Schopenhauer's conception of the will. Carrie, too, was concerned and confessed that she hadn't adequately explained Kant's distinction between the sublime and the beautiful. We turned to my brother. How did he feel about the test? 'I got the flat one,' he announced. 'The flat one?' we asked. 'Yeah,' he said, 'the flat A.'

He was right. He did get the flat one. Actually, we all got flat A's on the exam. My brother was not overconfident. Carrie and I were overly insecure."

Sheryl goes on to talk about how she will "never possess her brother's effortless confidence, but [she] could challenge the notion that [she] was constantly headed for failure." That she would learn to "undistort the distortion." I love that, because it says YOU have the ability to train your brain. Which, of course, you do. **OWN YOUR AWESOME**. Learn to recognize when those moments of distortion are about to occur, and then consciously focus on not allowing them to happen. Just as we discussed earlier in the book, you control what thoughts go in that pretty head of yours. Control the message. Undistort the distortion. Especially because we gals are really good (*frightfully good*) at underselling ourselves. As Sheryl points out, "If you ask men why they did a good job, they'll say, 'I'm awesome. Obviously. Why are you even asking?'"

There are lots of reasons why girls and young women have a hard time owning their awesome (books full of reasons, in fact). But at the top of that list is the common cultural occurrence: boys and girls, but especially girls, are told from a young age to be polite and humble and not interrupt. And the problem is, girls have a hard time letting that go. Of course we strive to be humble and respectful in life. I am not asking you to wear a T-shirt that says, I OWN MY AWESOME (I am demanding it), but we do need to make sure we *stand up and speak out.*

Complicating the *owning* is that our brains are wired a bit differently than guys' brains are, as Sue Enquist notes:

"I also think we need to teach girls that it's OK to be uncomfortable. Let us explain why. The reason you're uncomfortable to say 'I killed it today' is because your brain is a bird's nest with lots of thoughts and connectors. And you're uncomfortable because by saying 'I killed it today'—what will other people think? Are they gonna say I'm cocky? That's because your brain often works differently than a guy's brain. Guys' brains are like autobahns. There's nobody on the road. It's one line A to B. Think, feel, GO! Well, we gals have more connectors. Don't feel badly. We just need to practice it. We are going to make it a new habit."

And making it a habit means you must work at it. Or gather people around you who, like Robin Roberts, insist that you work at it. :)

ROBIN: "I don't like the word survivor. I mean, I respect it, but no, **I don't want to survive. I want to thrive.** I really do, and there's nothing that frustrates me more. The other day, a young intern came to me. She was interning in another department in ABC. So I'm talking to her, and she was telling me things that she wanted to do, and she goes 'whisper whisper whisper.' I'm like, 'Excuse me. *You're gonna have to speak, you're gonna have to talk up.*' I was like, 'Come on, *lean in.*'

"And I said, 'You got it going on, you have so much talent, now grab it.' And she goes, 'Well, I am a little shy.' And I said, 'There's nothing wrong with being shy. But you've got to speak up, and you've got to USE THAT VOICE.'"

The ability to own your awesome is there, it is inside you. You just have to summon the courage to let it free. Like when Fahima Noori decided that she would no longer hide in the shadows due to her external physical scars.

FAHIMA: "I think I'm very brave, and I consider that one of my talents (owning it, I love it). It was very difficult for a young woman like me to come out into society. I left all that behind when I went out in public. I came to understand that external beauty is temporary and will not last long. But our talent and internal beauty can last as long as we are alive. Also, I think we can use our talent more than we use our beauty. I want to one day help those women and children who suffered and tolerated the most injustice. That is my biggest dream."

That's it right there. The wonderful benefit of owning your awesome is just that . . . you are now free to dream. If it could only be as easy as that: *Attention, Wal-Mart shoppers!* You are now free to dream.
The great news is that, well, it kinda is. You decide. Own your dream. Let it free.

And finally, allow others to help you undistort. One evening, pre-kids and pre–Leadership Academy, just after I had retired from soccer after the 2004 Olympics, I sat with my husband, Ian, over dinner. We were discussing the formation of the Leadership Academy and how the curriculum should look and feel. I mentioned that I was not sure if I had the necessary training to do the leadership component and that maybe we were aiming too high with this idea, this dream. Or that maybe we should bring in outside experts to run that part of the academy. I was verbalizing my doubts. He looked at me sideways and said, "You not only *can* do the leadership component, you *should* do it. This is about passing on what you have learned, what wisdom you have gained. You can always keep learning from others, yes, but YOU have every credential to do this right. You have the passion and the experience to help kids blossom. So stop hesitating, and go do it."

I am pretty sure I made a self-deprecating joke instead of just saying, *Hell, yes, I can.*
Thankfully, Ian was there to help me own my awesome. And with that, the Leadership Academy was born.

Obviously, you can't tell a person *BE CONFIDENT* and just like that (I am snapping my fingers), she suddenly becomes confident. No, it is not that easy, of course. But you can train your brain to **BE THE IDIOT WHO SAYS YES.** You can train your brain to get on the dance floor. Be in the mix. Be present. *Sit at the table*, as Sheryl Sandberg says. *Proximity is power*, as Robin Roberts points out. However you say it, raise your hand and own your awesome.

Because when you do, as Jessica Mendoza so beautifully shares, this is what it can lead to:

"I've learned now in life that the things I was scared of *the most* have been *the best things* I've ever accomplished. The things where I am scared—can't sleep, want to throw up, freaked out—I now say *let's do it* because I know what's on the other side."

EXERCISE:

Your goal this week is to get on the darn dance floor.
To be the idiot who says yes. It could be saying yes to
something you previously have said no to because you
thought you lacked the skill set. Or it could be finding
your teacher or boss and throwing out that idea you have
always wanted to tell her/him. It could be finally sitting in
the front of the room when you have always been in the
back. It could be raising your hand in class or at work.
Whatever it is, make it a goal to do it once this week.
And the next. And the next. And so on. Start small, but
get there. Challenge a friend to do it as well and hold
each other accountable. Make it a fun competition. Keep
score. The loser each month has to buy the winner a box
of chocolates. Or cook her dinner. Or do her laundry.
Or wash her car. Or wear a T-shirt all week that says **BE
THE IDIOT WHO SAYS YES.**

And while we are at it. . . .

AN OWNING MY AWESOME
MAD LIB

I, _____ , will start taking credit for
(your name)

my achievements.

I, _____ , will no longer say I got lucky.
(your name)

I will remind myself it had everything to do with the fact

that I worked _____ dang hard.
(positive adverb)

_____ will continue to tell myself just
(first-person singular pronoun)

how _____ I am, especially when I
(synonym of "strong")

have those moments of doubt.

_____ will also gather my dream team
(first-person singular pronoun)

around me for added _____ support.
(positive adjective)

I am a _____ .
(female version of "king")

And I OWN MY AWESOME.

Signed, _____
(name of that awesome queen)

(Thank you and bear hug to Jessica Bennett for the Mad Lib idea from her book Feminist Fight Club!)

CHAPTER 18

BE INTERESTED >
BE INTERESTING

"Esse quam videri."

—in Latin

"To be, rather than to seem."

—in English

I am so bloody tired of it. There, I said it. I don't care if I sound old. I don't care if I sound grumpy. I don't care. I am sick of everyone with their dang selfie sticks, ruining beautiful scenic photos by getting their mugs in the way. I was lucky enough to spend a month last summer in Paris for ESPN, and our main set was right near the iconic Eiffel Tower. Well, if I had a dime for every person in Paris spoiling their Eiffel Tower picture with a silly selfie double chin, I would be a rich, rich woman. Numerous times I literally had to stop myself from screaming (my occasional restraint should be noted and commended), "GET OUT OF THE PHOTO. YOU WILL THANK ME ONE DAY."

Why do we have to be in every photo? I could tolerate it if it were every once in a while. Or if more photos looked like this *pure inspiration*:

Of course we all post pictures of ourselves and we have some selfies in our timeline. I am not asking us to remove ourselves from all photos. But it seems we have to be in almost every dang photo. I see posts on Instagram, Snapchat, Facebook, and Vine, and practically every picture or video features *that* person. Really? Why are we are so worried about looking/seeming interesting? *Look at me. Look at HOW MUCH FUN I AM HAVING, everyone. See, I am here, just in case you didn't believe me, and to prove it, I have the Eiffel Tower sticking out of my ear. I. AM. AWESOME.*

That loud ringing in your ears is me screaming.✱

Let's press reset, please. Let's begin with the premise that if we want to be *more interesting*, we can start with being *more interested*. Be interested . . . in things, in others, in growth, in learning, in nature, in life outside of yourself. I have started a game I play on social media where I check the accounts of friends or people I don't know, or people I'm wondering if I want to make room for in my life. I look at what they post. And how often they post nonsense. It tells me a lot about what those people value, what they care about. I think it is pretty clear that we need to shift the paradigm. We need to change the conversation. We need more people who are #selfieless. More people who celebrate the uncommon. Be the person who thinks differently for your age. And by differently, I mean that I watch a lot of teenagers

✱Taking a breath, gathering myself, exhaling. OK, I feel better now.

strive and struggle for recognition, for popularity. I watch as young adults seek success in the form of materialism and relevance. I see how tempting it is to think internally rather than externally. Yet, the brave souls operate on a different paradigm. Be the person who does not strive to be noticed, but to take notice. Be the brave soul whom people will want to follow because she thinks beyond herself. Be that young woman who is not afraid to be smart, competitive, compassionate, grounded, ambitious, and equally important, *interested*. The difference shows me substance in a world that often promotes anything but. It shows me a person of significance, not just success.

Sophie Healy-Thow is a perfect example of the power of being *interested*. As you read earlier, Sophie and her two classmates and friends, Ciara Judge and Emer Hickey, were told by experts that their science project would not work. Could not be done. But Sophie, Ciara, and Emer pressed on.

> SOPHIE: "We went home and we decided that we were just going to start and see where it led us, and if it led us anywhere at all."

Stunned, I asked her, *Where does that come from?* That persistence to say, "OK, thanks, Mr. Expert-who-has-been-in-the-field-longer-than-I-have-been-alive, we are just going to keep going"?

Sophie laughed and said,

> "I think we have this way of just questioning everything. Like, everything around us. If I don't question, I don't get answers. And if I don't get answers, I then keep on asking until I get the answer. It is why I so love young children with open minds. . . . We can't fly? Why can't we fly? Hmmm, how can I make us fly?"

BE CURIOUS. PERIOD.

To me, being curious is the game changer in life.
Sheryl Sandberg shared with me how she was innately
curious from a young age:

> **SHERYL:** "I always wanted to try new things and feel
> challenged. I wanted to study hard and learn. I was the geeky girl
> in high school, and that's not an easy thing to be in Miami Public
> School. As I got older, I picked the friends to surround myself who
> valued learning and who wanted to challenge themselves as well."

But being curious is not always that easy. Nor is finding
your passion. People often talk about finding your
passion and chasing your passion, but it can take years
or even a *lifetime* to discover what that passion is. Or
maybe you have many passions (or none). I completely
agree with best-selling author and (s)hero Elizabeth
Gilbert when she says, "Instead of that anxiety . . .
about chasing a passion that you're not even feeling, do
something that's a lot easier, a lot simpler: just follow
your curiosity. . . . If you can let go of passion and
follow your curiosity, your curiosity just might lead you
to your passion."

And while you are being curious, channel it to healthy
areas. Meaning, don't just be curious about the crap.
How do you define crap, you ask? Well, I think this adage
often attributed to Eleanor Roosevelt does it quite well:
**"Great minds discuss ideas; average minds discuss
events; small minds discuss people."**

One day as a young teenager, I was visiting my dear
friend Kerri McClellan (later a cofounder of our
Leadership Academy) at her house, and her dad, Ron,
was talking to us about this very topic. He said, "If
you can only do one thing each day, do this: make sure
you read the front page of a newspaper and the op-ed
(opinion) section. Know the current events of our world

and be able to discuss how to make them better." I never forgot this.

And now I would add, be able to discuss them while staying true to yourself. Worry less about impressing, and you will impress. Worry less about external beauty, and you will find internal calm. Worry less about sounding smart, and instead do the work to be smart. This was something I learned from my television work. So much (too much) of what we do on TV is about two things: impressing and external beauty. When I finally stopped worrying about both, I found calm. I found confidence. I trusted my instincts.

How did I get there? Trial and error. Mostly, by doing. By putting in the work and realizing, eventually, that I just needed to be me. That I was much better when I was just me. And honestly, by getting to the point of not caring about what others thought anymore. Well, that is not entirely true. Of course we care what others think of us. But suddenly I didn't wish to be liked—I only cared to be respected. It is one of the most liberating feelings ever. An added bonus: when we stop caring about how others might judge us, we get in touch with what we actually care about. We find *our* passions, not what people tell us to be passionate about. Here's how Sue Enquist puts it:

"Everybody strives to be *interesting* because they don't have their own story. They don't have their own engine of peace. The peace that I don't have to talk about myself. If I really see it inside, and I like what I see, then I don't have to be what I call 'a screamer.'"

GO DO YOU.
LIMA BEANS AND ALL.

To be, rather than to seem. You gotta feel good about *who you are*. About your own engine of peace. Go do you. Jessica Mendoza told me . . .

"My leadership style is just being real. Yes, I am silly and goofy, but also putting it out there about how vulnerable I am. The insecurities. The doubts. *I'm human.* I'm literally just like you. You can probably sing better and dance better.

"I definitely think the more real we are, in any kind of leadership role, people gravitate toward that. They want to see a reflection of themselves in the person that is in front of them."

I also believe that so much of having the confidence to be the idiot who says yes is letting others in. By that, I mean allowing ourselves to be vulnerable. Like when Robin Roberts found out she had breast cancer.

ROBIN: "For me, it was a question of how much of it do I share? It's so personal."

Robin decided that she needed to share her story. So she sat with Diane Sawyer on *Good Morning America*:

"The first time I shared publicly about my breast cancer, in fact, it's pretty close to where we are right now. And I'm grasping Diane's hand. I looked at the camera, and I said I have breast cancer.

"Well, I slept like a baby that night for the first time, because I let people in. I shared something in hopes that it would help others. And I was the one that was really helped in turn."

Remember, being vulnerable is not a point of weakness. Vulnerable is strong. Vulnerable is real. I think only the bravest can let people in. And the wonderful result is that it gives us the courage to try new things, because we are no longer worried about appearing to be perfect. As Tatyana McFadden says:

"And that's the hardest thing. It is not, it is not easy. OK, maybe I'm gonna try this. Maybe it's a little bit out of my comfort zone, but you *have to dip your toes in* first to see if you're gonna like it. And I think that's where you can really find your own passion, by trying out different things. And be willing to do that."

As I was typing this chapter, I suddenly started smiling, because I thought of one of my favorite stories by Dr. Seuss, *The Sneetches*. If you haven't read it, do so now. Yes, that is a command. It will take you five minutes max. And that's five minutes of your life you will one day thank Aunt Julie for. It is so clever. It is about being OK with being YOU and also embracing differences (done in a way that only the brilliant Dr. Seuss can do). Because eventually, as Rita Mae Brown notes, "The reward for conformity is that everyone likes you except yourself."

Do you remember Camilla Cream in David Shannon's book, *A Bad Case of Stripes*? Well, Camilla loves lima beans, but her friends think her love of lima beans is strange. To fit in, Camilla gives up eating lima beans entirely. And instead of fitting in, she wakes up the next day with her skin covered in rainbow stripes. Each day the pattern on her skin transforms into more ridiculous colors and shapes. When someone tries to give her pills to help, she actually turns into the shape of a giant pill. She tries all these different cures for her bad case of stripes, and it isn't until one wise woman prescribes lima beans that Camilla finally turns back into her true self again. (All together now: . . . *AHHHH!*) #BeUncommon

And here is the real beauty in all of this. Pun intended. When we learn to love the skin we're in, external beauty blossoms around us. I really believe that. I believe with everything inside me that the gift of inner beauty is external gratitude: you are able to see *beauty* everywhere and appreciate that beauty because your head is now out of the sand (and hopefully out of the picture. Ha).

On that note, here is a story we shared with our JFSLAers:

The scene: A Washington, D.C., Metro station on a cold January morning in 2007. A man with a violin played six Bach pieces for about one hour. During that time, over one thousand people walked through the station, most of them on their way to work. After three minutes a middle aged man noticed there was a musician playing. He slowed his pace and stopped for a few seconds and then hurried to stay on his schedule.

Four minutes later: the violinist received his first dollar from a woman who threw the money in the musician's hat and, without stopping, continued to walk.

At six minutes: A young man leaned against the wall to listen to him, then looked at his watch and started to walk again.

Ten minutes later: a three-year-old boy stopped, but his mother tugged him along hurriedly. The kid stopped to look at the violinist again, but the mother kept him moving and the child was forced to walk, turning his head during the entire time he continued to walk.

45 minutes: The musician played continuously. Only six people stopped and listened for a short while. About twenty people gave money to the musician while they continued to walk through the station at their normal pace. The man collected a total of $32.

At one hour: he finished playing and silence took over. No one noticed. No one applauded, nor was there any recognition.

No one knew this, but the violinist was Joshua Bell, one of the greatest musicians in the world. An internationally acclaimed virtuoso. He played one of the most intricate pieces ever written, with a violin worth $3.5 million. Three days before, Joshua Bell had sold out a theater in Boston where the seats averaged $100 each.

This is a true story. Joshua Bell, playing incognito in the Metro station, was organized by the *Washington Post* as part of a social experiment about perception, taste, and people's priorities. This incredible story was adapted from a feature written by Gene Weingarten called "Pearls Before Breakfast: Can one of the nation's great musicians cut through the fog of a D.C. rush hour? Let's find out."

Weingarten's story won a Pulitzer Prize in the feature writing category. It clearly touched a nerve in people. And the video they shot of Joshua Bell playing in the Metro station is fascinating to watch as person after person walks briskly by without noticing Bell.

Reading this story hopefully makes you stop and think (do we do that anymore?).

What does it mean that we can't take a moment to stop and listen to one of the best musicians in the world, who also happens to be playing some of the finest music ever written on one of the most magnificent instruments ever made? How many other things of beauty in our life are we missing? Is life too hectic for us to take a breath, to take a moment? Is our definition of beauty wrong? Is our focus wrong?

LET OUR WORLD
DOMINATION BEGIN

So what started as a silly game for me—checking people's degrees of nonsense on social media—has now grown into a wish/plan for world domination (a bad habit of mine). Instead of succumbing to the nonsense, let's push back. Let's *bring back sense. Let's be mindful about using social media for good.* Like when Fahima Noori—the Afghani teenager who was almost killed by a Taliban rocket fired into her house—had the courage to tell her story.

FAHIMA: "I started sharing my story with people on social media and on Facebook. And on a Web site that aims to help people who are not doing well and are depressed. So I'm hoping when people hear my story it gives them energy and appreciation for what they have, despite the challenges and hardships. Hopefully it encourages them to follow their dreams."

Let's post about positivity and ideas. Let's share how you have been inspired. What awesome book or article did you read that you want to pass on? Let's post a picture of the Eiffel Tower without it coming out of your ear. #EarlessEiffel

Share a quote that motivated you. A tree that looks beautiful with the sunlight filtering through its leaves. Show the inside of a wave while you are barreling though the tube on your surfboard. Share your favorite sunset without you in it. Share your hopes and fears. Share your vulnerability. Life is not perfect. Nor are we. And that is okay. Share your dreams. Because whatever inspires you may just inspire me. Let's take an oath to pass on inspiration. And authenticity.

inspire.

be inspired.

No more nonsense. Keep. It. Real. Make buttons if you need to. Refuse to share *another* article about what dress she wore, or what shoes she had on, or how many boyfriends she has had. Remind your friend, as she turns the camera for a selfie, to turn that camera around and instead document what actually inspires her. Let our global takeover begin. And one *interested* person at a time, one kind act at a time, one inspirational story at a time, one #EarlessEiffel pic at a time, we can start to change the conversation. We can shift from NONSENSE to INSPIRATION. Together we can start the

#CHOOSETOMATTER REVOLUTION.

EXERCISE:

Your exercise is simple: share your inspiration. Today and always. #CHOOSETOMATTER

. . . which reminds me of advice Sheryl Sandberg shared. . . .
GET IN THE HABIT OF WRITING DOWN THREE THINGS THAT MADE YOU HAPPY TODAY BEFORE YOU GO TO BED. KEEP A NOTEBOOK NEXT TO YOUR BED. THAT WAY YOU GO TO SLEEP WITH POSITIVE THOUGHTS AND INSPIRATION.

. . . which reminds me of our family "Blue Book" (it is a blue journal with blank pages . . . hence the very creative name) in our kitchen. Since the kids could speak, they would often say or do funny things (as all kids do). I would write these moments down in the Blue Book (remember, memory is not one of my talents). Now that the kids are older, we often read them old entries from the Blue Book. They laugh hysterically and say, "I did that?" or "I said that?" Now, whenever they think they say something funny, they end it with, "Put it in the Blue Book, Mom." The Blue Book is a family favorite and forever growing. It really is one of the things I cherish most in our house.

Of course, you don't need children to have a Blue Book. Just start a Blue Book to have a place where you write inspirational, funny quotes and stories. A place where you can scribble your curiosities, think on paper . . . and not just think it, but ink it. And then promise me you will not name it the Blue Book, but something very creative . . . like the Red Book.

CHAPTER 19

TO BE OR
NOT TO BE . . .
A RAT

"If you win the rat race, you are still a rat."

—Anna Quindlen

RAT RACE

YOU?

STILL A <u>RAT</u>

Have you ever had that dream where you are running on the treadmill and you cannot get off? You try to press STOP, and the conveyor belt still spins along. You try to pull the emergency plug, and it still powers on. You even try to jump off, and you are stuck like glue. *AHHHH*.

I think these dreams started back in the days when I was playing and had that nagging sense that "I am not fit enough." And then when I retired from playing, the dreams came less often, but they still came. Sometimes it would be that my body froze every time I tried to move off. Or I just couldn't reach the stop button. Or as much as I wanted to slow down the conveyor belt, it would speed up.

We've all seen a hamster wheel. The hamster or rat runs around and around and around. Going nowhere, but working so dang hard. Yes, the rat race. You get stuck in the crazy pace of life, and instead of moving forward, you spin in what feels like an endless circle. Well, I was the dang rat. And not just in my dreams. I was stuck in the rat race and I . . . could . . . not . . . get . . . off. Spinning faster and faster.

I realized it a few years out of college when I had to make the life decision of whether to go to medical school or not. I had already asked the Stanford University School of Medicine if I could defer my enrollment, not just once, but twice. So, two years removed from my original acceptance date, I had to decide if this was indeed my life path. I couldn't push it back any further. I was fascinated by science and biology and how the body worked, but I still wasn't convinced that I loved the idea of being a doctor. And I certainly didn't LOVE the idea of spending the next twelve years of my life studying to be a doctor when I was uncertain that being a doctor was even my passion. It was at that exact moment that I stepped off the treadmill.

Hallelujah. Cue my best worst celebratory jig.

Who knows, maybe in the end I would have been a happy, successful doctor. But I am fairly certain I wouldn't have *loved* being a doctor. And for that reason, I am forever grateful for having the courage to step off. Especially since, at that time, I had been accepted to an excellent medical school that many would have given a left leg to attend. So there was that. Plus, I had put the last five years of my studies and energy toward this pre-med goal while a Stanford undergrad. And as any pre-med student knows, that is a lot of darn energy. Oh, and then, of course, my parents, family members, teachers, and friends all thought this was my chosen path. They were ecstatic for me, and I didn't want to let them down. So yes, I knew there would be some backlash if I didn't go. But still, I knew it didn't feel right. After much reflection, I was able to summon the courage to step off the treadmill due to a few key moments.

1)   My parents telling me it was OK. And not just that it was OK, but that they understood my hesitation and appreciated the self-reflection. My mom was a nurse and had a front-row seat to the lives of doctors. She understood just how hard it can be.
2)   My husband, Ian, also telling me it was okay. And not just supporting my decision, but consistently supporting my soul searching (and for over twenty years now . . . yes, he deserves a medal).
3)   I asked around two bazillion doctors over the course of two years about how they enjoyed what they were doing (the answers were not encouraging, by the way).
4)   And then, thanks to my anchors being firmly in place, I followed my gut.

KNOW YOUR ANCHORS

The concept of "anchors" is something Sue Enquist taught me recently. I never knew how to identify them. Nor how to put a finger on *why* I felt so comfortable following my gut. But when she told me, I had an aha moment. Here is how she explains our anchors in life:

SUE: "Anchors come first. Meaning, *who I am* comes first to what I do. Get your anchors that you'll always have. So the girl that doesn't have the reading skill and has to read 'special books' will always be in Sue Enquist. But the celebration that I have in just getting a little bit better every day is my anchor that keeps me comfortable. I can go to the next thing, because I have these anchors that will be good everywhere.

"If you understand your anchors, whenever they become clear to you, you take those everywhere, because *who you are* can allow success everywhere. *What you do* can't. It can only get you in the door. So I can be a great athlete, attach my worth to that, and that's gonna get me in every door. Now what? Now you're in the door—and there are standards there. They think they're getting this as a person, and if you haven't identified those anchors of who you are? You're gonna fail."

I suddenly realized why my decision to step away from medical school felt like a no-brainer in the end. I knew my anchors. And what I discovered is that my medical school decision seemed to follow a pattern I have utilized during the most critical moments of my life. Gather my dream team around me, seek their wisdom and advice, ask lots of questions, be knowledgeable on the subject, and follow my gut, anchors in hand.

Never underestimate the power of that gut. Never underestimate the emotion of what lies deep within you . . . what is anchored in your soul. Because the rat race and daily grind of life can be seductive. And, I would even argue, necessary. You need that ambition to keep climbing and growing and moving forward. But when you find that you are no longer progressing, only spinning . . . when you find that you are no longer driven, only burdened . . . then what do you do? And know this: you will have that moment in your life. Maybe you are in it now. Maybe it is years down the road. Whenever it is, know also that you control the outcome. You can always get off the treadmill. You can leave the rat race. There is no easy formula or recipe to know when the timing is right. But this helps. I asked

Sue Enquist why she stepped away from coaching at her peak. Especially since she told me she felt she'd just hit her full coaching potential in the last five years at UCLA. (BTW, she had already won nine of her eleven championships by then.)

> "There's peace that comes with total clarity. It's my anchors. It's my upbringing—move forward. What's next? Well, I want to be a pro surfer. I want to be a respiratory therapist. I want to do all these things, keep moving. Because I never was raised to identify who I am with what I do. If I attached who I was to my success, how could I ever leave? I would never leave.

> "So it was very easy to step off the treadmill, because that championship coach is not who Sue Enquist is. That's not who I am. I'm not a championship coach. I'm a lifelong learner that was surrounded by great influencers, that captured a place in time, and had a blast doing it. **Who I am comes first to what I do.**"

CHECK IN ON YOUR SOUL

Only you can decide if the timing is right to step out of the race. Part of that is checking in on your soul. My soul is wired to empower others. That is so much of who I am. I didn't just want to help patients as a doctor; I wanted to empower the world. Looking back, stepping away from the U.S. Women's National Team was the easiest thing I did, because I knew those teammates were stuck with me forever as friends. Those anchors weren't leaving. And I wanted to do more, try more, learn more. Like Sue mentioned above, being a world champion was not who I was. I am sure proud of those moments, of course, but I could not wait to jump into the real world.

I know people often say, "Trust your gut." But how do you know if your gut is right? Perhaps it's easy for an optimist to trust, but how do you really know? Well, you may never know with certainty, but you can pay attention to signs. Pay attention to those anchors. Pay attention to the ease with which a decision was made. And equally important, look at what you already have, just in case it gets lost in the noise. The last thing you want to do is get out of the perceived rat race and then discover that your life wasn't so bad after all. This true story * was shared to me and our Leadership Academy gals by another one of our amazing core JFSLA staff members (and former teammate as well—see, they are stuck with me forever), Jaime Pagliarulo.

[There was] an African farmer who heard tales about other settlers who had made millions by discovering diamond mines. These tales so excited the farmer that he could hardly wait to sell his farm and search for diamonds himself. So he sold his farm and spent the rest of his life wandering the vast African continent searching unsuccessfully for the gleaming gems which brought such high prices on the markets of the world. Finally, in a fit of despondency, broke and desperate . . . he threw himself into a river and drowned.

Meanwhile, the man who had bought his farm one day found a large and unusual stone in a stream which cut through the property. The stone turned out to be a great diamond of enormous value, and he then discovered that the farm was covered with them. It was to become one of the world's richest diamond mines. The first farmer had owned literally acres of diamonds, but had sold them for practically nothing in order to look for them elsewhere. If he had only taken the time to study and prepare himself, to learn what diamonds look like in their rough state, and had first thoroughly explored the land he owned, he would have found the millions he sought right on his own property.

The reason this story has resonated with so many people is the idea that each of us, at this very moment, could be standing in the middle of our very own acres of diamonds. But the lure of greener pastures is so

*"Acres of Diamonds" by Earl Nightingale.

great, you may not have taken the time to explore and cultivate your own land.

And also realize that sometimes it may take a little patience for that cultivation to come to life. Or to establish those anchors for *who you are.*

PLANTING SEEDS

The "Acres of Diamonds" story reminded me of when my kids planted their first seed. They were very young, only maybe two and four years old. Well, they wanted to see a flower, as in RIGHT AT THAT MOMENT. We put the seed in the dirt and they immediately turned to me with a puzzled look. "Mom, where is the flower? Why is there no flower? WHY NOT NOW?" I remember smiling and answering, "Well, it takes time. You have to nurture it, give it water, be patient, feed it, give it light. Be patient some more. Pay attention to it, but do not hover. Keep it happy, but let it endure the changes in weather." Of course, at the moment and at that age, that concept is a hard one to understand. But when I was telling them this, it brought me back to why I love the garden. Plants are so much like life: You must HAVE FAITH that what you are doing will bring a flower. You have to believe that you are getting there. You have to watch over that plant but also believe it will endure the storm. Sometimes slowly, sometimes not as fast as we want, but you have to believe in the unseen . . . believe that a flower is indeed coming to life even when no one else can see the bloom . . . YET.

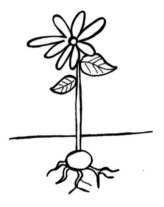

And while we are planting seeds, let's plant one more.

You know the phrase "YOU CAN HAVE IT ALL." Ohhh, it seems so sexy and enticing and alluring. And we hear it everywhere. So you think to yourself, why, yes, yes, I can have it all. And then, as Jessica Mendoza described when she spoke of trying to be all things to all people, we try to do everything. One of the best nuggets of advice I received came from Shelly Lazarus, the former chairman and CEO of advertising giant Ogilvy & Mather. Shelly was giving the commencement address at Smith College, and she said,

> "It's never about having it all. It's only about having what you want. The 'having it all' notion is an external measure. . . . It's society's judgment of what you must aim for. I have come to know that when you let others define your success, you always lose."

It is about having what you want. If you find yourself stuck somewhere on your path, or spinning on a hamster wheel, spend some time thinking about how you can make your soul leap again. Anna Quindlen says it so well in *A Short Guide to a Happy Life*:

> When you leave college, there are thousands of people out there with the same degree you have; when you get a job, there will be thousands of people doing what you want to do for a living. But you are the only person alive who has sole custody of your life. Your particular life. Your entire life. Not just your life at a desk, or your life on the bus, or in the car, or at the computer. Not just the life of your mind, but the life of your heart. Not just your bank account, but your soul. People don't talk about the soul very much anymore. It's so much easier to write a resume than to craft a spirit.

And while you are crafting that spirit, keep this simple advice from Sue close:

> "Who you are is not what you do."

Find who you are first. And the doing will gleefully follow.

CHAPTER 20

BECAUSE
YOU CAN

"Here's to the crazy ones. The round pegs in the square holes. The ones who see things differently. You can quote them, disagree with them, glorify or vilify them. About the only thing you can't do is ignore them. Because they change things. They push the human race forward. And while some may see them as the crazy ones, we see genius. Because the people who are crazy enough to think they can change the world are the ones who do."

—Apple

I have gone back and forth on what I want this final chapter to be. Because you have all that you need. You have what it takes. Now is the time to DO. So I've decided that I will leave you with one last thought: a simple reminder from these amazing women that leadership is *many things*. . . .

LEADERSHIP IS being authentic . . . leadership is what you make of it.

—Mia Hamm

LEADERSHIP IS helping others lean in.

—Sheryl Sandberg

LEADERSHIP IS being your best self and having the courage to take that stage.

—Tatyana McFadden

LEADERSHIP IS not about the people around you . . . it's about you and what you can do.

—Sophie Healy-Thow

LEADERSHIP IS standing out from the group and finding what it is about you that's different.

—Jessica Mendoza

LEADERSHIP IS honesty and being there for others in every situation.

—Fahima Noori

LEADERSHIP IS being who you are and making that environment the best you can.

—Alex Morgan

LEADERSHIP IS bringing out the absolute best in others.

—Robin Roberts

LEADERSHIP IS finding a way to make a positive impact in others' lives.

—Amy Liss

LEADERSHIP IS chasing excellence.

—Sue Enquist

LEADERSHIP IS personal, not positional . . . leadership is YOU.
—Julie Foudy

LEADERSHIP IS _____

_____

_____

_____

— YOUR NAME

YOU can Choose to Matter every day. The question is, will you?

So go on. Start now if you haven't already. Pull the I CHOOSE tab. Go lead. Laugh. Fail. Repeat. Go be fabulously, courageously YOU. The world needs you.

It is not a question of if you can lead, but when.

#CHOOSETOMATTER.

BECAUSE YOU CAN.

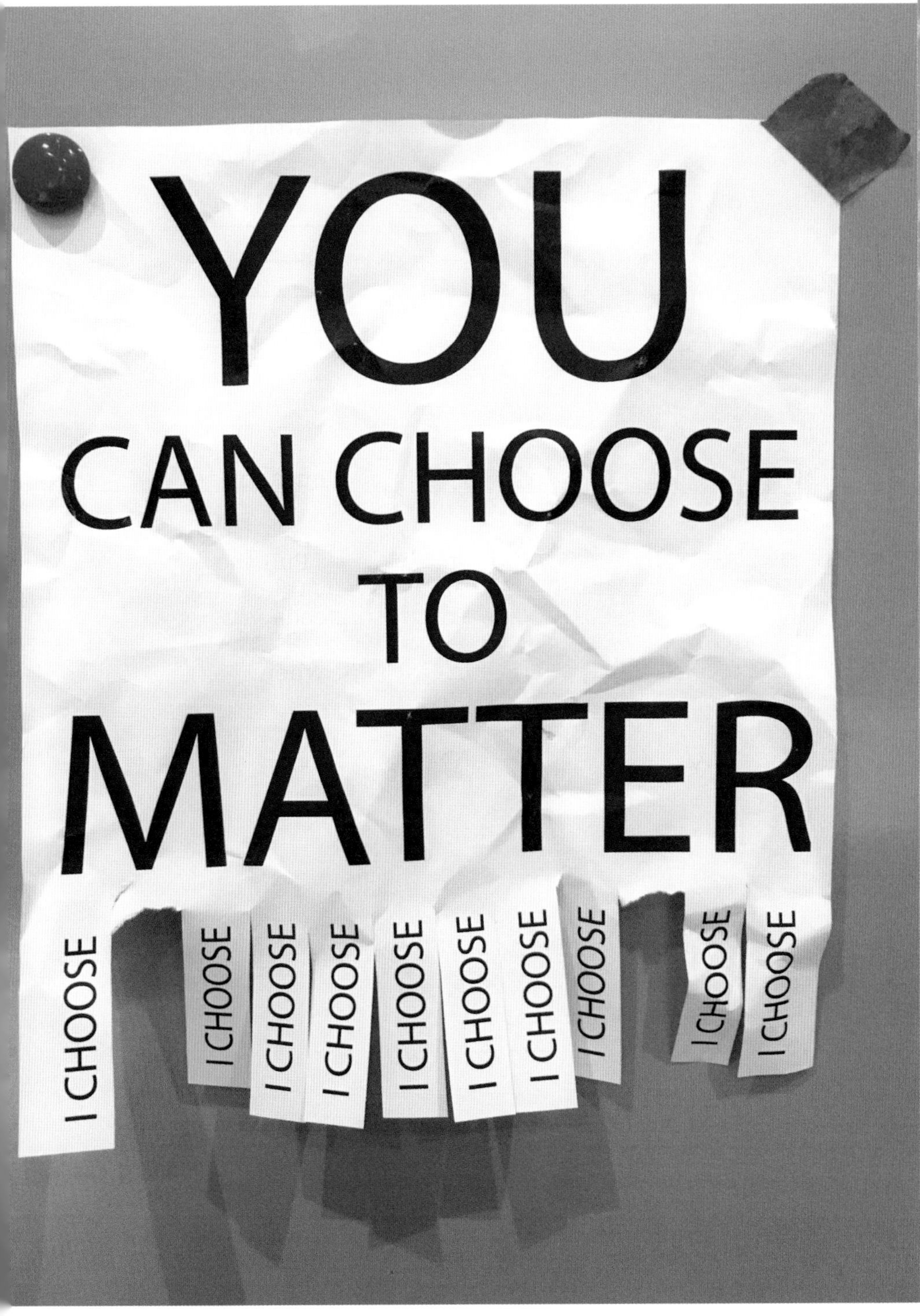
YOU
CAN CHOOSE
TO
MATTER
I CHOOSE
I CHOOSE
I CHOOSE
I CHOOSE
I CHOOSE
I CHOOSE
I CHOOSE
I CHOOSE
I CHOOSE
I CHOOSE

BIOS:

If Sue could start her bio any way she wants, it would say this: The "Enquist Innovation Group" just completed the largest indoor family sports and competitive greatness facility. The first-of-its-kind-high-performance sports tent spans four states (California, Arizona, Nevada, and Oregon). This community of greatness will teach free play techniques to children, while adults will be in class fourteen hours a day to learn how to un-parent. The feedback from the children has been outstanding thus far. Parent feedback has been mixed; half the parents suffered serious withdrawal when they were barred from hopping on their helicopters during class.

Sue Enquist is a legend in collegiate softball. For twenty-seven years she coached her alma mater UCLA and became the most successful softball coach in Division I history with a record of 887-175-1 (an .835 winning percentage). She is the first person in NCAA Softball history to win a championship as a head coach and as a player.

As a coach, she won eleven national championships, which is more than anyone in the history of college softball, and is UCLA Softball's first all-American, national champion, and Hall of Famer. During her tenure at UCLA, she coached sixty-five all-Americans and twelve Olympians.

Sue is a member of six hall of fames as a player or coach, including the National Softball Hall of Fame, Women's Sports Foundation International Hall of Fame, and the UCLA Athletics Hall of Fame. She is also the recipient of multiple National Coach of the Year honors.

After she retired as UCLA's softball coach, Enquist went on to do incredible work off the field. She founded *ChampionsFestival.com*, which sets up leadership events for parents, players, and coaches. Her most recent project is ONE Softball (*ONEsoftball.com*), an educational digital platform, that provides best in class education directly to softball families.

Sue grew up in and still resides in San Clemente, California, and is a former professional surfer.

Sue's fun fact: I was the first girl to play on the San Clemente High School's baseball team. I played girls softball and boys baseball in the same season.

And most important, her go-to karaoke song: "September" by Earth, Wind & Fire.

MIA HAMM

If Mia could start her bio any way she wants, it would say this: When Mia isn't teaching quantum physics to the next generation of astrophysicists, she is hard at work in her gastronomy lab making dinner for those same students when they travel into space.

Mia Hamm is the most well-known and influential female soccer player in the history of the sport. During her seventeen years of playing for the United States Women's National Team, Mia won two World Cup titles and two Olympic gold medals.

Named the greatest female athlete of the past forty years by ESPN, Mia was the youngest player ever to appear in a match for the U.S. National Team when she made her debut at age fifteen.

During her illustrious career playing for the national team, Mia shattered an array of American records, most notably those for international goals (158) and assists (144). She was a five-time U.S. Soccer Player of the Year and a two-time FIFA World Player of the Year (yes, as in best in the *world*). She also won four NCAA National Championships during all four years that she played at the University of North Carolina.

In the years since her dominant run as a player, Mia has continued to serve as an inspiration to young girls. She has stayed engaged in the soccer community and served as an advocate for Title IX and gender equality across sports. She is part owner of the new MLS Los Angeles Football Club, becoming the first female owner in a men's professional soccer league.

Mia also founded the Mia Hamm Foundation, which is dedicated to bone marrow research, in honor of her brother, Garrett, who passed away from aplastic anemia, a rare blood disease.

Today Mia resides in Southern California with her husband Nomar Garciaparra, a former Major League Baseball all-star with several teams, including the Red Sox and Dodgers. They have twin daughters, Ava and Grace, and a son, Garrett.

Mia's fun fact: I was fluent in Italian until the age of 4.

And most important, her go-to karaoke song: "Friends in Low Places" by Garth Brooks.

SOPHIE HEALY-THOW

If Sophie could start her bio any way she wants, it would say this: This loving mermaid swims through the deepest depths of the ocean making friends with new species of fish. She lounges on the shores of a different white beach every day singing to the passersby.

Sophie Healy-Thow is an eighteen-year-old Irish student who is passionate about food security, ending poverty, sustainable development, and women's rights. She is a Board Trustee for ActionAid UK, a leading international charity working on behalf of poor women and children throughout the world. Sophie is also a One Campaign Youth ambassador in Ireland, an advocacy organization made up of more than seven million people worldwide working to end extreme poverty and battling preventable diseases, particularly in Africa.

Sophie, along with two teammates, Ciara Judge and Emer Hickey, won top prize at the Google Science Fair in 2014 for conducting research that found that rhizobium bacteria increased the germination rate of cereal crops. The team found that using diazotroph increased the germination rate of plants by 50 percent and the dry mass yield by up to 70 percent compared to water. The results suggested that this discovery could be used to produce more crops and be vital in the fight against hunger.

The teenage scientist is on a global mission to create awareness of food security and—in particular—educate young people and children about it. She was selected as a Zero Hunger Global youth leader and was a panellist at the UN Mobilizing Generation Zero Hunger gathering at the UNGA Sustainable Development Summit in New York September 2015. Healy-Thow has also presented a TEDx talk entitled "Food Security: Everybody's Business" at the Science Gallery, at Trinity College, in Dublin, Ireland.

In 2014 Sophie was even named one of *Time* magazine's most influential teens.

Sophie is a regular speaker and contributor on the topic of food security at events around the globe. She is a youth ambassador for the ISPCC [Irish Society for the Prevention of Cruelty to Children] Shield Award Anti-Bullying Campaign, a movement in schools across Ireland. She advises on promotional material, judging the "Schools Anti-Bullying Competition," and promoting the campaign through interviews in the media and attendance at various events.

Sophie's fun fact: I can put my foot around my head! I'm also very good at finding your doppelgänger in a household utensil or in an animal.

And most important, her go-to karaoke song: "We're All in This Together," from *High School Musical*.

AMY LISS

If Amy could start her bio any way she wants, it would say this: Amy started life small and mighty as a premature twin and grew to be a small and mighty adult. At four feet eight and almost seventy pounds, Amy and her three-hundred-pound power wheelchair are moving forward in life. With an "attitude of gratitude" and a positive spirit, Amy works daily to make others feel valued and appreciated.

Born with severe cerebral palsy and needing help with all daily living skills, Amy lives each day with an *attitude of gratitude*—it's her motto in life. Her passion is volunteering and making people smile. Amy works as the relationship coordinator at Easterseals DuPage & Fox Valley in Villa Park, Illinois. She loves mentoring families, encouraging clients in therapy, and educating others about the mission and services Easterseals provides.

Amy receives physical and occupational therapy there weekly and also volunteers at Easterseals twenty-five hours a week. For the last sixteen years, Amy has also had the opportunity to help teach children the importance of acceptance and inclusion by volunteering weekly at Hillcrest Elementary School in Downers Grove, Illinois. She loves listening to students read, helping with spelling tests, and answering questions about living with a disability.

Outside of work, she has had the opportunity to spread her personal message across the country speaking to businesses, college athletes, and schools on service, gratitude, and giving back despite limitations. Amy lives with her parents in Downers Grove and is a lifelong Chicago Cubs fan. The 2016 Cubs season was a magical ride. She is still recovering from the awesomeness of *her* Cubs winning the World Series after a 108-year drought.

Amy has a twin sister, Kelly, and a younger sister, Lindsay, who have each made her an aunt. Being an aunt to Owen and Eve is Amy's greatest joy. She is a staff member at the Julie Foudy Sports Leadership Academy, where she has learned to believe in the power of self.

Amy's fun fact: Meet me once, tell me your birthday, and I'll remember it for life and send you a card.

And most important, her go-to karaoke song: "Lean on Me" (because I literally lean and like others to lean on me) by Bill Withers.

TATYANA MCFADDEN

If Tatyana could start her bio any way she wants, it would say this: When Tatyana isn't grand slamming the Abbott World Major Marathon series or sitting on top of the podium in every single track event, she leads a pretty normal life. She'll be found walking her puppy, Bentley, continually around her neighborhood, training with her teammates in the vast flatness of the Illinois landscape, and making sure everyone is welcome to join her for dinner off the grill; she's a grill and apple crisp master.

Winning seventeen Paralympic medals, sixteen World medals, and sixteen major marathons is no easy feat, especially when you are facing the adversity that Tatyana McFadden has had to battle. Tatyana was born with spina bifida, a hole in her spine, and spent the first six years of her life in a Russian orphanage. Being paralyzed from the waist down, having no wheelchair access, and learning how to walk on her hands would lead **McFadden** down a path that she could have never envisioned— though she's not done yet.

Tatyana made her first appearance in the 2004 Athens Paralympic Games at just age fifteen, where she brought home two medals. She continued on to the 2008 Paralympics in Beijing, where she added four more medals, and then the 2012 London Games, where she collected another four medals, three of them gold. McFadden also tasted success outside the Summer Games. At the 2014 Sochi, Russia, Paralympic *Winter* Games she garnered a silver in cross-country skiing. Two years later she was back at the summer 2016 Rio de Janeiro Games hauling in her most medals at one event to date: four golds and two silvers.

Tatyana wanted to challenge herself even more a few years back, so she entered the professional wheelchair marathon circuit in 2009, winning the Chicago Marathon. In 2013 she was the first man or woman, able-bodied or disabled, to win the Grand Slam (Boston, London, Chicago, and New York marathons in the same year). She has repeated this remarkable Grand Slam achievement three more times since—in 2014, 2015, and 2016. (That's four years in a row if anyone's counting.)

Tatyana's sister, Hannah, is a Paralympic track and field athlete as well. They competed together in the London and Rio games.

In 2016, Tatyana published a children's book based on her life, *Tatyana McFadden: Ya Sama! Moments from My Life.*

Tatyana's fun fact: My teammate, who met me for the first time while I was in a coffee shop eating sugar cubes, nicknamed me THE HORSE because I like sugar and can race like a racehorse. :)

And most important, her go-to karaoke song: Anything Beyoncé. I even listen to her on the rollers while working out.

JESSICA MENDOZA

If Jessica could start her bio any way she wants, it would say this: Well, I run the world. So there's that. Biggest objective is getting people to really like each other again. Find something positive about every person you meet or come across. Pretty simple really.

Jessica is currently an analyst with the ESPN Sunday Night Baseball team, a position she started in 2015 (which proved to be historic for Mendoza, and media as a whole). That year she became the first female analyst for a nationally televised Major League Baseball postseason game on October 6. Earlier that year she also broke ground by becoming the first female analyst for a Men's College World Series telecast.

Mendoza is a two-time Olympian and was a member of the U.S. Women's National Team from 2001 through 2010. Her softball team won the 2004 Olympic gold medal at the Summer Games in Athens and a silver medal at the 2008 Summer Olympics in Beijing.

She is both a three-time World Champion (2002, 2006, 2010)

and World Cup Champion (2006, 2007, 2010). In addition, Mendoza was a four-time, first team all-American as an outfielder at Stanford University, where she finished her collegiate career setting school records—still intact—for highest batting average (.475) and hits (94), plus most stolen bases (31), runs scored (71), and career home runs (50).

One of the most notable softball players in the last decade, Mendoza's used her on-field experience to seamlessly make the transition to television sports analyst. In addition to her role as an analyst and a reporter for Major League Baseball, the Men's College World Series, and the NCAA Women's College World Series, Mendoza is also a contributor to the espnW network.

Jessica is originally from Camarillo, California, and still resides in Southern California with her two sons and husband, Adam.

Jessica's fun fact: I am a *kleptofoodiac* (real term). I think that all meals should be shared; regardless of how well I know you, I may or may not steal a French fry, or scallop, or brownie from your plate when you're not looking. Or when you are looking right at me. I'm that good.

And most important, her go-to karaoke song: I will sing anything. And I am restaurant-clearing awful (reason No. 538,415 that Julie loves Jessica Mendoza). But it doesn't hold me back. "I Will Survive" by Gloria Gaynor is a must, or I can knock your socks off with any Snoop Dogg, circa 1993.

ALEX MORGAN

If Alex could start her bio any way she wants, it would say this: A cat, dog, dolphin, and killer whale lover, you'll never know who will greet you at the door of Alex's home.

Over the last several years, Alex has become a role model to thousands of young girls across the United States. The U.S. Women's National Soccer Team star forward, 2015 World Cup

Champion, and Olympic gold medalist grew up in Diamond Bar, California.

She attended the University of California, Berkeley. While in college, she represented the United States in numerous international tournaments. In 2008, she scored the winning goal in the final game of the FIFA U-20 Women's World Cup to help the national team win the U-20 World Championship.

Morgan also won two national titles in women's professional soccer with the Western New York Flash in 2011 and the Portland Thorns in 2013. Alex has been named a U.S. Soccer Player of the Year and a FIFA World Player of the Year finalist. She now plays with the Orlando Pride and is married to professional soccer player Servando Carrasco.

Alex is the face of the U.S. Women's National Team with a massive social media following across all platforms and the marketing world. She was named to Forbes' prestigious 30 Under 30 list in 2016. And in 2015, Morgan, along with Canada's Christine Sinclair and Australia's Steph Catley, became the first female players to make the cover of FIFA video games. Alex also appeared alongside Lionel Messi on the covers of FIFA 16 video games sold in the United States. In addition, Alex has written a series of books called The Kicks, which has been made into a TV series on Amazon Prime.

Alex's fun fact: I can catch in my mouth any gummy bear or jelly bean thrown in the air.

And most important, her go-to karaoke song: "Waterfalls" by TLC.

FAHIMA NOORI

If Fahima could start her bio any way she wants, it would say this: My grandfather named me discerning/mature when I was really young among his grandchildren, because I carried myself like elder people. I am happy to report I am a wise soul in a young body!

Fahima Noori is an eighteen-year-old from Farah Province in Afghanistan. She has five sisters and one brother. When Fahima was only a year old, the Taliban fired a rocket into her house. Fahima's father had worked with the Afghani government before the country came under Taliban control, so the family was considered a target of the Taliban. One-year-old Fahima had been sleeping when the curtain above her caught on fire after the rocket exploded. She was badly burned along much of the right side of her body and face, losing three fingers, and vision in her right eye.

But Fahima survived. Her entire family fled into the mountains of Afghanistan to escape, and then moved to Iran so the children could go back to school. Eventually, years later, the family moved back to Farah Province, but Fahima was left with the scars from the Taliban rocket.

Despite the wounds, Fahima has always been an excellent student. She recently graduated from high school and was studying in Kabul, the country's capital. Then, in the summer of 2016, Fahima received great news: she was accepted into Central Piedmont Community College in Charlotte, North Carolina, to study nursing for three years. She is now in the United States going to college.

Fahima dreams of one day being a plastic surgeon so she can help people with physical deformities who, like herself, could not afford treatment. She has also now made it her mission to share her inspiring story of hope, love, and beauty so that others can overcome challenges as well.

Fahima's fun fact: My talent is my ability to draw. Sometimes when I draw pictures people compliment me a lot. But I'm not sure if the compliment is sarcastic or for real. :)

And most important, her go-to karaoke song:
A song from Afghanistan called "Eshgh Love." (The song is about loving the moment and not worrying too much about the future and things.)

ROBIN ROBERTS

If Robin could start her bio any way she wants, it would say this:
Robin Roberts is the coanchor of Good Morning America, *president*
of Rock'n Robin Productions, and most impressively, the former Junior
Bowling champion of Mississippi.

Ha. Yes, she really is the Junior Bowling champion of Mississippi.
And since becoming coanchor at *Good Morning America* (GMA),
the daily news/entertainment program has won four Emmy Awards
for Outstanding Morning Program under her leadership.

In 2016, Robin was inducted into the Sports Broadcasting Hall
of Fame. In 2014, she received the Walter Cronkite Award for
Excellence in Journalism, was inducted into the Broadcasting &
Cable Hall of Fame, and named one of *Glamour's* Women of the
Year. That same year Robin launched her production company,
Rock'n Robin Productions, which creates original broadcast and
digital programming for ABC and other networks.

When not traveling around the world covering breaking news
events, Robin is at GMA's studio in New York City's Times Square
conducting interviews with a diverse group of news makers,
including former President Barack Obama, Facebook founder Mark
Zuckerberg, former First Lady Michelle Obama, and NBA superstar
LeBron James of the Cleveland Cavaliers.

Robin was diagnosed with breast cancer in June 2007. Five years
later she faced another health battle when she was diagnosed with
MDS or myelodysplastic syndrome, a disease of the blood and bone
marrow once known as preleukemia. Her courageous, public battle
has been recognized with many awards and honors, as her reports
inspired hundreds of potential bone marrow donors to register.
Robin was recognized with the Arthur Ashe Courage Award at the
ESPY's in July 2013 for the courage she displayed throughout her
life and career.

In 1983, Robin graduated cum laude from Southeastern Louisiana
University with a Bachelor of Arts degree in communications. She

was a standout performer on the women's basketball team, ending her career as one of the school's all-time leading scorers (1,446 points) and rebounders (1,034). Nearly thirty years later, in 2012, Robin was inducted into the Women's Basketball Hall of Fame. (Amazingly, she still has not been inducted into the Mississippi Bowling Hall of Fame.)

Robin's fun fact: I lived in Turkey for a few years when I was a little girl. I told my parents I could speak Turkish and said, "Gobble, gobble, gobble." I don't think they were amused.

And most important, her go-to karaoke song: Diana Ross's version of "Ain't No Mountain High Enough."

SHERYL SANDBERG

If Sheryl could start her bio any way she wants, it would say this: By day Sheryl runs Facebook's business operations; by night she practices reading to her kids in funny voices.

Sheryl Sandberg is chief operating officer at Facebook, overseeing its business operations. Prior to Facebook, Sheryl was vice president of global online sales and operations at Google, chief of staff for the U.S. Treasury Department during the Clinton administration, a management consultant with McKinsey & Company, and an economist with the World Bank.

Sheryl is a best-selling author with her second book, *Option B*, released in April of 2017. Her first book, *Lean In*, was an immediate best seller. She is the founder of LeanIn.Org, a global community committed to empowering all women and helping them achieve their ambitions. She serves on the boards of Facebook, The Walt Disney Company, SurveyMonkey, Women for Women International, and ONE (Bono's organization to fight extreme poverty).

For the fifth consecutive year, Sheryl has been named the most powerful woman in technology on the *Forbes'* 100 Most Powerful Women list, placing No. 7 on the list overall.

Sheryl is a member of the fundraising council of the Second Harvest Food Bank, and cochairs StandUp for Kids and the campaign to end childhood hunger in California's Santa Clara and San Mateo counties.

She graduated summa cum laude from Harvard University with a degree in economics and received an MBA with highest distinction from the Harvard Business School.

Sheryl lives in Menlo Park, California, with her son and daughter.

Sheryl's fun fact: I taught aerobics in college.

And most important, her go-to karaoke song: "Shut Up and Dance" by Walk the Moon.

HOW I LOVE THIS... AND WHAT I WOULD GIVE TO SEE A PICTURE

ACKNOWLEDGMENTS:

Even though I am told it is a book, I am convinced I just delivered another child. What a wonderful and intense process. So many people helped make this dream a reality.

I start of course with my incredible parents, SLIM JIM and FRUITY JUDY, who taught me from an early age that I could do and be anything I wanted. They never told me tackle football was a bad idea. Nor did they ever say to me (about anything), "Well that seems *unladylike*, darling." And for that, I especially thank them. I grew up in a genderless world. They also showed me daily that if you treat everyone with kindness and respect, the world is just a better place.

A gigantic hug to my husband, IAN, for always believing in me as I dream up projects like: "Wouldn't it be fun to write a book?!!" And he then supports the dream to make sure it becomes a reality. From the leadership academy to writing this book to all the crazy spaghetti I throw at the wall, he gives me the confidence to know I can do it all.

My deepest gratitude to our Julie Foudy Sports Leadership Academy (JFSLA) family members, who helped build out the material of this book over the last ten-plus years. From our fellow cofounders—TODD SMITH, KERRI MCCLELLAN, and EDSON MCCLELLAN—to our incredibly loyal and passionate JFSLA STAFF who made so much of this book come to life every summer at our Leadership Academies. I am in constant awe of this amazing group. Thank you!

A huge thank you as well to LAURA GENTILE and ALISON OVERHOLT, my two Wonder Women at espnW who believed in this book from day one. I sent them an e-mail back in December of 2014, explaining my idea. They both responded within five

minutes with a resounding "YES! We are in, in, in."
They suggested Disney partner with us. And like that,
Choose to Matter was born . . . simply by dreaming
out loud and having women support that dream. Bless
you, Laura and Alison.

And to JOHN SKIPPER, our leader at ESPN, who
also championed the book through the entire process
and continues to support the many great women at
ESPN. Thank you John for your continued support.

An enormous thank you to my *dream team*, which came
together to help me create the book from the beginning:

*   My editors LAURA HOPPER and WENDY
LEFKON at Disney Publishing. In this book-
writing process, I have come to realize that I need
deadlines in my life. I just sometimes have a hard
time remembering when deadlines are. (Please
don't judge.) Laura and Wendy are the best new
teammates who have come into my life; they calmly
guided me through it all . . . with lots of laughter
and perspective along the way. Similar to my soccer
teammates, Laura and Wendy are now stuck with me
for life.

*   THERESE STEINER, who was my right-hand
woman keeping this ship on course (no easy task, as I
tend to zig and then zag . . . oh, and miss deadlines).
Therese always gets me to think beyond what others
think is possible, and for that I will always thank you,
Therese. We all need those friends in our lives.

*   DEANNE WILLIAMSON, my dear friend (and
incredible artist), who I asked, "Can you help me
bring this book to life?" She gladly agreed and her
artwork and design have literally done just that—
brought life and a wonderful energy to this book. It
has been so much fun to watch Deanne take words
and concepts on paper and make them come alive as
images. I bow in admiration.

✳ **LYNN OLSZOWY**, my producer at espnW, who helped me film the interviews and, equally important, brainstorm ideas and writing concepts. She has become a great friend and a soundboard. Whenever I am in doubt, Lynn steers me back to what matters and why it matters.

✳ To **WINNIE HO** and **MARGIE PENG**, my Disney designers, who fabulously laid out the book so that it feels fun, bold, and authentic. My biggest concern was a lot of black text, and when they sent me the first draft of the layout design, I let out an audible *Ahhhh*, as I knew the book was in great hands with DeAnne, Winnie, and Margie.

✳ And last but not least, my dream team teenager, **JANA PHILLIPS**. Jana is my neighbor who is a senior in high school and is a voracious reader. When I told Jana I was writing this book, she offered, "Hey, if you need any help reading through it all, let me know." She may have come to regret that offer as she became my go-to focus group, and I constantly peppered her with questions and thoughts. Her teenage perspective, edits, and wisdom beyond her years were an absolute gift. Thank you, Jana. I cannot wait to see what publishing company you are running in ten years.

And a hearty shout-out to ALL THE JFSLA STUDENTS over the last decade who inspire me daily with their stories and Choose to Matter projects. They show the world what owning your awesome looks like: how strong, engaged, interested, passionate young women can lead in so many thoughtful ways. And they inspire others to choose to matter as well.

And, of course, my eternal gratitude to ALL MY TEAMMATES on the U.S. team, at Stanford University, and with the mighty Soccerettes for showing me that leadership exists in many different, wonderful forms. And for showing me the power of bringing people together for a common goal, a shared vision. And for always reminding me that the older we get, the better we are.

And to DR. COLLEEN "Flash" HACKER for consistently shining light on all of us. For making me think differently, to sweat the small stuff, train my brain, make my butterflies fly in formation, and, thankfully, *flush it* when necessary. *Ahhh*, I miss laughing with you and the gals on a daily basis. Thanks Flash for inspiring so much in this book.

Thanks as well to my agents at the Montag Group: SANDY MONTAG, SUE LIPTON, and JILL DRIBAN. You all worked tirelessly to ensure this book did indeed come to life. I owe you many large drinks with umbrellas in them. Thank you, thank you.

And finally, much thanks to the ten women I interviewed for this book: ROBIN, MIA, ALEX, FAHIMA, SHERYL, SOPHIE, TATYANA, AMY, JESSICA, and SUE. They graciously offered their time and wisdom so that others could benefit from hearing their stories. I just love that others get to be inspired by these rock stars.

I have come to believe that so much of life is building your dream team around you. I am lucky indeed as my dream team grows. And so grateful to all the wonderful friends and family members who constantly remind me that life is about so much more than job titles or fancy shoes. It is about significance. And good chocolate chip pancakes. Seek to help others, spread joy, and spray laughter. Only good can come from that. So pass it on.

BECAUSE YOU CAN.